(A TALE of TWO WORLDS)

Also by Michel Faber

Under the Skin
The Hundred and Ninety-Nine Steps
The Courage Consort
The Crimson Petal and the White
The Fire Gospel
The Book of Strange New Things

MICHEL FABER

(A TALE OF TWO WORLDS)

 A NOVEL

HANOVER
SQUARE
PRESS

**HANOVER
SQUARE
PRESS™**

ISBN-13: 978-1-335-91674-7
ISBN-13: 978-1-335-50014-4 (Barnes & Noble Exclusive Edition)

D (A Tale of Two Worlds)

First published in 2020 in Great Britain by Transworld Publishers. This edition published in 2020.

This edition published by arrangement with Harlequin Books S.A.

Hanover Square Press
22 Adelaide St. West, 40th Floor
Toronto, Ontario M5H 4E3, Canada
HanoverSqPress.com
BookClubbish.com

Printed in U.S.A.

WITH LOVE AND THANKS
TO LOUISA

(A TALE of TWO WORLDS)

First
(slightly shorter and significantly less hazardous)

Half,

Set in THIS World

To Begin With

The first ray of light each morning always made her feel the sun was in the wrong place, or she was in the wrong place, or both. She would wake in her big soft bed, under a duvet decorated with smiling blonde princesses, and the cold English light would already be busy filling up the room, looking weird.

She told her friend Mariette about this, and Mariette said, "It must be because you're missing the light back home."

"Home?" said Dhikilo.

"Where you're from."

"I suppose so," said Dhikilo.

But she didn't suppose so, really. She had no memories of where she was from, and she'd never been back there. It didn't even exist.

Mariette, Dhikilo's best friend, came from France. Dhikilo hadn't been there, either, but it existed for sure. People went there all the time. It was just across the Channel. On clear days, peering out over the cliffs at Cawber, she could even see it. It was a subtle haze between the silvery grey of the water and the blue of the sky.

The continent of Europe was very near. Ferries sailed back and forth from the white cliffs of Dover to a vaguely visible port called Calais, passing Cawber on the way through. Under the sea, there was a tunnel for cars, lorries and other vehicles, connecting England to the world beyond. During the summer, it brought busloads of tourists to visit Cawber. The buses would park next to the avenue called The Promenade, and whole families of French people would walk along the cliffside, speaking their language, eating English snacks. Germans and Japanese and Spaniards and Italians and Americans, too. All these people came from proper countries, countries that got mentioned in newspapers and had politicians who shook other politicians' hands while photographers took pictures.

Fiona, one of Dhikilo's other pals, came from Scotland, which was also a country, even though you didn't have to cross the sea to get there. It was cool to come from Scotland. Everybody had heard of it, yet it was far away with magnificent ancient mountains and big modern cities and it was on TV quite often. A good combination.

The place Dhikilo came from was never on TV and nobody had heard of it. Sometimes people would say they'd heard of it, but after a while she would realize that they really meant another country whose name sounded similar but wasn't it.

"I'm not from Somalia," she would say. "I'm from Somaliland."

People would look at her disbelievingly, as if she'd just told them that she came from Franceland or Australialand. As if she was just being silly. Or they would ask: "What's the difference?"

And she couldn't answer, because she didn't really know.

A Leaflet with Advice

Some names were a problem to have and others weren't. Names like Gail and Sarah and Mariette and Lucy and Susan and even Siobhan were OK, but "Dhikilo" was too unusual and needed tweaking. Her friends called her Dicky. A few of the other girls called her Dick and she wasn't sure if they meant it to be insulting.

Dhikilo sometimes had trouble figuring out if the other girls were being friendly to her or not. Not long after starting at secondary school, she'd been given a leaflet with advice about how to cope with bullying. She hadn't yet got around to reading it when an older girl called Kim squirted glue in her hair on purpose. Dhikilo had a book in her hands at the time, a big heavy one about history, and she hit the older girl on the forehead with it so hard that Kim fell over backwards and knocked over several of her chums. It was a very bad thing to do and it could have caused brain damage (as her Guidance teacher explained later), and when Dhikilo got home she read the leaflet about bullying and had to admit that the suggestions in it didn't include knocking your tormentors flat.

Anyway, nobody bullied Dhikilo after that. Unless you counted being called "Dick" and not having as many friends as the average girl at school. She'd done the maths on this. The most popular girls had thirteen to fourteen pals they hung out with, and the least popular girls had zero, while seven was the median (she'd learned that word in Maths class). Dhikilo had three. Arithmetically speaking, that put her in the bottom percentile of befriendedness.

But that was OK. Three was plenty to be getting on with. People were so strange and sometimes you got tired just thinking about them.

Laascaanood

The last place Dhikilo lived before being relocated to the south coast of England was a town called Laascaanood, which sounded like a drink on a Middle Eastern restaurant menu that you think you might try but then you get worried you won't like it and order a Pepsi instead.

There was a big dramatic story attached to her and Laascaanood, but it was all quite confused and hazy because she'd been less than a year old at the time and there were various adults involved who were all unavailable now.

Basically, there was a war on and her parents had split up and she was being carried around by her father, but there was fighting between Somaliland and Puntland, and her father decided she would be better off not going where he was going. So he gave her away and before she knew it she was in Cawber-on-Sands.

When other girls talked about their early life, there were usually loads of details and the story went on and on until it grew big enough to fill a book. Her own story was awfully short, she had to admit, and there were quite a few holes in it. She should maybe have kept her eyes open and paid more attention at the time.

But she was only a baby then, and babies slept a lot and usually had their eyes closed. Each day, as Dhikilo walked home from school along The Promenade, she would see the young mothers trundling their prams, and the babies would be asleep even when the seagulls were screeching and the wind was fierce. They were charging their energy, postponing the day when they had to sit up and deal with stuff.

When Dhikilo was eleven, just a couple of years ago, her mum told her that her mother was dead. That is, Ruth, her English mum, gave her the news that her original mum had died. Dhikilo had trouble thinking of the right thing to say.

"How old was she?" she asked.

"Thirty-one," said her English mum. "It says here." She was holding a piece of official paper with the news printed on it.

"That's not very old," said Dhikilo, after a long pause. "Was she sick?"

Ruth stared at the piece of paper and frowned. "It doesn't say."

"What about Dad?"

Ruth looked at her indulgently. "You mean your Somaliland dad?"

"Yes," said Dhikilo.

Her English mum smiled, her face all complicated with knowledge about grown-ups that couldn't be explained. "Still the Mystery Man, I'm afraid." That was how she often referred to Dhikilo's original father: the Mystery Man. Nobody seemed to know what had become of him after he'd tossed Dhikilo through the air into the arms of a nurse.

By contrast, Dhikilo's English dad was not a Mystery Man at all. He was in the next room reading a book about a retired politician, with a mug of tea balanced on the arm of the sofa, and his name was Malcolm—Malcolm Bentley. Which made his adopted daughter Dhikilo Bentley. Or sometimes, if she was in the mood to write a nice long line at the top of her school jotter, Dhikilo Saxardiid Samawada Bentley.

WHAT WORDS MEANT

For a while after getting the news about her mother, Dhikilo tried to learn more about her. At first it seemed that Malcolm and Ruth didn't know anything, and then after a while it seemed there might be some official stuff that Dhikilo could find out, maybe, but not until she was eighteen.

"Why eighteen?" she asked.

"Because that's how the law works," said Malcolm gently. "They've thought very carefully about these sorts of situations."

"Who's 'they'?" asked Dhikilo.

"The people whose job it is to figure out the best and kindest way to help children with…questions," said Malcolm. "And they decided there are things that are easier for a child like you to understand if you're a little bit older."

"But when I'm eighteen I won't be a child any more," said Dhikilo.

"Yes, exactly," said Malcolm, as if she was seeing his point instead of disagreeing.

★ ★ ★

Next, Dhikilo had tried to learn more about the country of Somaliland, in case it helped her understand anything about her parents. Her Geography teacher was no use, and there was nothing in the school library. She got the impression that no matter how hard you looked, there wasn't much to be found, especially if you were a young girl in Cawber-on-Sands who spoke only English (and a little French).

There was a bookshop on the High Street, which had thousands of books but none specifically about Somaliland. On their Travel shelf they had one guidebook for tourists who fancied going to lesser-known places in Africa that were beautiful, uncomfortable and maybe dangerous, and in the middle of that book there was a chapter about Somaliland. Dhikilo read it in the shop. It didn't take long.

Somaliland was big—almost as big as Britain—but had far fewer people living in it. It wasn't exactly desert, but it was desert-ish. It had a lot of cute goats and black-faced sheep who sometimes died of hunger when there wasn't enough rain to let crops grow. It had bats and pythons and squirrels and giant guinea-piggy things called hyraxes. The skies in the photos were very blue and empty. The women wore headscarves. There weren't many shops and you were supposed to buy stuff with a special kind of money that only existed in Somaliland and wasn't worth anything anywhere else. The rest of the world still hadn't decided whether to accept Somaliland as a real country or not. It might happen one day maybe, but not soon.

Somalilanders were very keen for tourists to come, but this wasn't as simple as just going there in a tour bus and walking around eating ice cream. The war that had made Dhikilo's father do what he did was officially over, but every now and then people started fighting again regardless. You weren't supposed to venture outside the main cities of Hargeisa and

Burburu. If you wanted to go to Laascaanood, the government insisted that you be accompanied by special soldiers who would make sure nothing had happened to you. You were also supposed to buy a few bundles of chat leaf to give to guards at checkpoints so that they would let you through. Dhikilo turned the page hoping there would be a helpful picture of a chat leaf, but the next page was already a different country. She put the book back on the shelf.

At home, Dhikilo tried researching Somaliland on the internet. The internet had a million pages on just about every subject in the universe, but amazingly little from Dhikilo's country of origin. There was a website where Somalilanders argued with each other, in a mixture of their own language and English, about stuff you could only understand if you were in their gang, and another one where they discussed football.

The most interesting websites were the ones explaining what words meant. They couldn't agree on the spellings, or whether the words were Somali or just generally Arabic, but there were some beautiful meanings. "Saxansaxo," for example, meant the smell and the coolness carried on the wind from a place where it's raining to a place where it isn't. How could one little word mean something so marvellous? It made you realize that language wasn't just a code to communicate with: it was magic.

Anyway, the word "magacaa" sounded like it should mean "magic" but it actually meant "what's your name?" The word for "dog" was "eey" and the word for "eye" was "isha," although it seemed you needed a completely different word if you had two eyes instead of just one. Dhikilo got the impression that learning Somali would be quite hard unless you had parents to teach it to you when you were a baby. However, there were some easy words like "bataato wedjis" and "furuut," which meant "potato wedges" and "fruit."

People's names had meanings, too, although there was dis-agreement about what the meanings were, or maybe there were just lots of meanings. One person wrote that whenever his family had to move someplace else, his father would load all their possessions onto the back of a camel, taking care to balance the weight evenly. There must be an equal number of dhikilos hanging off each side of the camel, he said. Sadly there wasn't a picture, so Dhikilo could only guess what a dhikilo might be. She liked the idea of hanging off the side of a camel, though, especially if there was another one of her hanging off the other side.

There were loads of different words for camel, none of which sounded anything like "camel," and "Khamiis" meant Thursday.

The word for father was "aabo." Mother was "hooyo."

The word for "daughter" was harder to figure out. At first she thought it was "inanta," which sounded rather grand. But then other websites said that "inanta" was just the word for "girl" and that "daughter" was actually "gabadh." But then other websites said that "gabadh" meant "slave-girl." Or "chestnut." Finally, the most trustworthy-seeming people she could find said that when a father in Somaliland speaks to his daughter, he calls her "aabo," the same name as himself. That was a bit strange. But sometimes strange things are true.

Just in case she would ever need them, Dhikilo wrote "aabo" and "hooyo" on the back cover of her school jotter, the one for History.

The Second-Best
School in Cawber

awber School for Girls was the second-best school in Cawber and was officially classified by government inspectors as "Improving." It had been "Excellent" once upon a time and "Poor" for a while and much better again recently. The whole town was a bit like that. Back in the nineteenth century it used to be a seaside resort where people from London would come for their holidays. Then it was bombed in the Second World War and never really got over it. The funfairs and ballrooms closed down, and the houses got shabby and crumbly. But Cawber had the sea and the cliffs and some handsome architecture and a high-speed train to the capital, so lots of rich people were moving there lately. And immigrants. People from all over the world, making a fresh start in a town that was improving.

Only one person from Somaliland, though.

She could still remember the man in the school-uniform shop commenting on her colour. He was trying to be nice, saying how the pale green of the school blouse went very well with her "black skin." Her skin wasn't black, though, it was brown. Brown like cinnamon toast, or hazelnuts. And the other people in Cawber weren't really white, they were the colour of uncooked pork sausages, except for the Indians and Pakistanis, who were more like fudge.

Dhikilo liked food.

In fact, Dhikilo *loved* food. Not just eating it, but making it. She cooked as often as Ruth would allow her, and she made different things each time, which meant that sometimes it didn't work out and Ruth would sigh as if to say, "Good parents are tolerant when their children try foolish things and fail," and the leftovers would go into a plastic container at the back of the fridge and grow mould.

But on other occasions, she would make a delicious meal— maybe a lamb stew with ginger and basil, and cubes of potato all yellowy-orange from the tomato—and Malcolm's eyes would widen with pleasure when he ate his first mouthful and he'd say, "Well, *this* makes a lovely change, doesn't it?" and Ruth would look at him strangely and Dhikilo would be proud of making the flavours all work together.

Frying onions was just about the best fun ever. If you fried them slow and used plenty of oil they would go soft and golden and caramelly, and if you fried them fast they would go crispy and brown with burnt black curly bits that were actually the tastiest part. And if you had a mushroom you could make fried onions and mushroom on toast, which was as delicious as anything you'd get in a restaurant.

"You should be a chef when you grow up," Ruth told her, while carefully picking out any bits of onion that were even slightly burnt, or while eating a totally different thing from the thing Dhikilo had prepared. Maybe she was just doing her grown-up best to give a clueless kid happy fantasies of something that was never really going to happen, like being an astronaut.

But Dhikilo truly did fancy being a chef when she grew up. Or maybe a waitress. If you were a waitress, you could see the happy expressions on the customers' faces as they got their meals, whereas if you were a chef you'd be stuck inside the kitchen. Maybe she could be a new kind of chef who also brought the food out. She could have a different apron that was specially for that part, a clean colourful apron that didn't have kitchen stains all over it, maybe in yellow or gold with swirly embroidery.

It could work, she was sure. The restaurant just needed to let her try it. Or maybe she'd even be the owner of the restaurant and not have to ask anyone's permission.

Don't limit your dreams, that's what the school Careers Adviser said. *Within reason*.

So, Let Me Try
to Help You

I've told you about some of the people who appear in this book, including two of Dhikilo's three friends. The third friend was Molly, whose mother was a teacher at the school, and whose mother's godfather was also a teacher at the school when Dhikilo first arrived there, although he'd since retired. He was a professor and his name was Charles Dodderfield.

I understand that you are not very far into this story yet, and there have already been a lot of names, some of them quite difficult to remember. Also, relationships can be confusing. Dhikilo's friend's mother's godfather, for instance: you almost need a diagram to figure that out! (And what exactly *is* a godfather anyway?)

So, let me try to help you. Professor Dodderfield is important. Very important. We won't meet him for a while, so maybe I should've waited longer before mentioning him, but on the other hand, he will be dead by the time we first encounter him so it's probably best to flag him up now.

You can relax about Kim the bully. She is irrelevant to the

rest of this story. She will grow up to be one of those women who stand around at the Duty-Free perfume shop at Gatwick Airport asking if she can squirt passers-by with special fragrances and she will not be nasty any more, just a bit dull.

You can also forget about Molly's mother, because the only significant thing about her is that she used to work with Professor Dodderfield, who, as I said, is definitely important.

Ruth and Malcolm Bentley are moderately significant because they are Dhikilo's English mum and dad, and if it wasn't for them, she wouldn't have anywhere to live. They are good people and care about Dhikilo a lot, even though they're too shy to hug or kiss her much. Ruth and Malcolm don't even hug each other, and once when Malcolm's father came to visit, Malcolm shook the old man's hand and patted him awkwardly on the sleeve of his coat, even though they hadn't seen each other for ages. But Malcolm knows a lot about politics, he makes excellent breakfasts (his poached eggs are always soft but never slimy), he replaces light bulbs when they pop, and the bathroom always has warm dry towels hanging in it. Ruth irons Dhikilo's school uniform, and makes sure that the duvet with the princesses on it is always clean. You would probably like her if you got to know her, but getting to know a very shy person like Ruth would take you a long time and we don't have a long time in this story.

Dhikilo's friends Mariette, Fiona and Molly are nice enough people but if you forget their names it's OK, because they won't be going on the adventure that you and Dhikilo will be going on.

At Dhikilo's school, there are various teachers who will float into the story for a moment or two but then float straight out again, so don't worry about them.

As for Dhikilo Saxardiid Samawada Bentley, she's the heroine, obviously, but you don't have to remember every bit of her name if it's too much of a strain; just don't call her "Dick" and preferably not even "Dicky."

Respect never hurts.

To Begin With, Again

The previous beginning was just the *preamble*: this is the real start.

It was a Monday morning after a perfectly standard Sunday, and Dhikilo woke up to the usual wrongness of the light and the usual sense that the duvet was a little thicker than she truly needed. She got up and had a shower. She put on her school uniform and went down to breakfast.

Her mum and dad were there as normal. Malcolm brought her a plate with a poached egg and some bacon on it. There was toast in a metal rack on the kitchen table. Ruth was drinking coffee and reading the local newspaper, which came out once a week. She liked to read bits of it aloud to Malcolm as he was fussing around.

"Not much going on this week," she said, flipping through the pages.

"What's the healine?" asked Malcolm.

Ruth flipped back to the front page and held it up:

GOOBYE CARS, HELLO SKATEBOARS

"The council has ecie to emolish the Leisure Centre car park to make way for a skateboaring rink," Ruth recited.

"Goo iea," said Malcolm, putting a glass of fresh milk in front of Dhikilo. "I'm all for it."

Dhikilo paused, with a bit of toast raised halfway to her mouth.

"Demolish?" she ventured.

"Emolish," her mum confirmed. "What I on't unerstan is, where will all those cars go instea?"

"People shouln't be riving cars to a leisure centre," said Malcolm. "It efeats the purpose."

Dhikilo looked at Malcolm's face and then at Ruth's and back again. Everything about the way they were talking was 100 per cent normal and relaxed, and pronounced just as it should be, apart from the missing Ds.

Ruth continued reading from the article. "It says here that some Cawber resients have raise concerns that a skateboar rink will lower the tone of the whole area an attract hooligans an juvenile eliquents."

Malcolm sat down with his cup of tea. "Better to have them skateboaring, surely, than taking rugs. There's a rather spleni skateboar rink at the South Bank in Lonon; you pass it on your way to the National Film Theatre. It's quite a tourist attraction. Something out of the orinary."

Dhikilo took a big swig of milk. She wasn't imagining this and it wasn't going away. A most peculiar change had come over her mum and dad since she'd gone to bed last night.

"Erm... Have *I* seen that skateboard park in London, Dad?" she asked, carefully enunciating the Ds, as if to feed her parents a helpful reminder of where to insert them.

"I on't think so," said Malcolm. "Tell you what: next time I go to the South Bank, I'll take you along. If it oesn't interfere with school, of course."

"Woul you like some more breakfast, arling?" asked Ruth. "Something else to rink?"

"No thanks, Mum."

"i you finish that homework you ha yesteray?"

"Almost."

Ruth put on the vague frown she always wore when she was about to say something sternly parental. "You've really got to learn not to be istracte by…erm…istractions." But then she reached out and stroked Dhikilo on the shoulder, half tenderly and half as if she was brushing off some dust, which was her way of saying, "You're a good kid. Have a nice day at school and work hard."

Dhikilo always walked to school, unless it was snowing. Sometimes even when it was snowing. One and a half miles there, and one and a half miles back. It was quite a long way and most girls took the bus. But it was good to give the body some exercise before the brain got stuffed with information. And anyway, walking was one of her hobbies. Most of the other girls in the school had hobbies like sport and shopping and gadgets and boyfriends. Dhikilo liked to *ambulate*.

On the morning when the letter D disappeared from her parents' conversation, Dhikilo set off for school on foot as usual. And soon discovered that things were not as usual at all.

A street sign said:

STRANLOPER AVENUE

which was strange because it had always been called STRANDLOPER. Dhikilo walked right up to the sign, squatted down to have a careful look. The D just wasn't there.

It hadn't been painted out, or scratched off. There wasn't even room for a D in the spacing of the letters.

So...did that mean that council workers had been running around during the night, replacing the street signs? She didn't think council workers would do things like that. At least, not unless they got paid a lot extra for working when they should be in bed asleep.

She straightened up, and a bird launched itself from a branch overhead, sending some loose leaves scattering down. They landed gently on the window of a parked car. The car was a fancy one, well used and a little rusty, but expensive: a Mercees-Benz, according to its badge. Dhikilo walked on, checking the names of the cars. She didn't know much about cars—Malcolm disapproved of pollution and liked to tell people that his family used public transport or the legs God gave them (although Ruth did fetch home the supermarket shopping in her little hatchback, which had a roof-rack for bicycles). Anyway, Dhikilo recognized some of the names of the Japanese vehicles and they were fine. She was pretty sure, however, that "Aewoo" had not been the name of a car yesterday, and there was definitely something wrong with "Lan Rover." She was surprised to discover that there was a car called a Bentley.

A tottery old lady whose name Dhikilo didn't know, but who she often met at this time of morning walking her Dalmatian, called out to her as they passed on opposite sides of the street.

"Nice ay so far!" warbled the old lady, and the dog waved its tail.

Dhikilo almost called back, "What sort of dog is that?" just to check whether the old lady would say "Almatian," but she stopped herself. Everyone knew what a Dalmatian was, so it would sound like a really dopey question.

About halfway to school, she stopped off, as she often did,

at the convenience store opposite the Chinese restaurant. Her dad's breakfasts were nutritious and filling, and the school canteen had plenty of healthy lunch options, but it was always good to have a packet of crisps on hand for that hungry patch after the first lesson.

On her way to the counter to pay, Dhikilo noticed the newspapers laid out with their headlines showing.

MIGRANT FLOO MUST STOP, PM VOWS

said the *Aily Mail.*

EPORT THE FREELOAERS

said the *Aily Express.*

FOREIGN OCTORS BLOCKE BY NEW IRECTIVE

said the *Guarian.*

PIGEON MESS A ISGRACE, SAY LOCAL MUMS

said the latest edition of the *Cawber-on-Sans Heral*, fresh out this morning.

Dhikilo bought her crisps and walked the rest of the way to school. Mariette and Fiona were hanging round near the gate waiting for her. They liked to walk in together. It was more pleasant that way, and also it meant that Miss Yeats, whose job it was to stand by the entrance checking the length of skirts, would have less chance of spotting that Fiona's was too short again.

"Hi, Icky!"

Dhikilo jerked back as if someone had flicked her nose.

But Mariette and Fiona looked as friendly as ever.

"What's wrong?" said Mariette.

"Please don't call me Icky," said Dhikilo.

"You were always fine with it before," said Fiona, confused.

"Has anything ba happene?" said Mariette.

"My name is Dhikilo," said Dhikilo.

"Hikilo, sure," said Mariette, and smiled. *"Accor!"*

Dhikilo blinked. "I'm sorry?" she said.

"It's French for 'OK.'"

The three of them walked through the gate together, just like always, except it wasn't like always.

"On't think I in't notice, young lay!" said Miss Yeats.

EEPER UNERSTANING

It was a long, long day without the D.

With twenty-six letters in the alphabet you'd think that losing one of them wouldn't be so bad, but it was very bad indeed (or *very ba inee*, as everyone around her would put it). Dhikilo had to sit at a esk and pay attention to what was written on a boar, she had to put up her han when she knew the answer ("Yes, Hikilo?"), she was cautioned by Mr Dawkins (who was now Mr Awkins) that a science experiment was angerous, she was supposed to tell the ifference between poetry and oggerel, and she was expected to evelop a eeper unerstaning of natural isasters. She handed in a piece of writing to Miss Forster, and Miss Forster shook her head and said, "Honestly, Hikilo, your *spelling…!*" and proceeded to cross out every D with her red felt-tip pen, until Dhikilo's little essay looked as if it had been used for cutting up strawberries on. Even the name in the top right corner got corrected: Hikilo Saxarii Samawaa Bentley.

"That's not my name, Miss," said Dhikilo, trying hard to keep her voice quiet and calm.

"I think you'll fin that it is," said Miss Forster with a tight smile, and several of the other girls in the class tittered.

★ ★ ★

At lunchtime, half the things on the canteen menu were not right. Dhikilo had no desire to eat brea or nooles or umplings or puing.

"What are *you* having?" she asked Mariette.

"I'm trying to eat more healthily," said Mariette. "So I think I'll have the sala."

Dhikilo looked her right in the eyes. "You know that 'salad' should have a D in it, don't you?"

Mariette turned away and gazed through the transparent shields on the canteen. "I think this one has tomatoes, lettuce, olives an…erm…cucumber in it. Or maybe I'll have the shepher's pie? That has onions an carrots. Carrots are super healthy."

Dhikilo stood back while her friend ordered her food. One of the dinner ladies, Pat, who was now an inner lay, smiled at Dhikilo over Mariette's shoulder. Pat knew exactly what each of the pupils liked or disliked, and she always made some recommendation or comment about the menu to Dhikilo.

"You might 'ave to starve toay, ear," she joked.

"Sorry?" said Dhikilo.

"We've got nuffing you aore, an loas of fings you ain't too keen on."

Mariette carried her plate of pie away from the counter, and it was Dhikilo's turn to choose.

ON'T FORGET YOUR FIVE A AY, said the little sign above the steaming display. Dhikilo chose a chicken rumstick, peas and potato weges.

She looked around the canteen for Mariette. Mariette had seated herself at a table with a couple of other girls and there wasn't a spare chair. It was the busiest part of the lunch break. The dining area was chock full of girls eating shepher's pie and rumsticks and toa in the hole and puing and custar. They were chatting excitedly about homework they'd forgotten to o, fashion moels, holiays, pop stars, boyfriens. This was the way things were now. Nobody had a problem with the vanishment of the D. She, Dhikilo Bentley, was the only one.

Maybe she should just get used to it? She couldn't force the world to change back to the way it was yesterday. And Miss Forster's tight smile and tone of voice had hinted that if she tried, she would regret it.

After lunch there was Music. Yay! Music was Dhikilo's favourite subject. Her favourite subject used to be History, but that was in her first year when Professor Dodderfield was still at the school. Since he'd left, Music had gone up to the top spot.

Cawber School for Girls had a terrific music room with three keyboards and a big drum kit and a bouzouki and a clarinet and a magnificent wall-mounted rack of recorders of various sizes. Dhikilo could get a nice noise out of most instruments she was given; it just seemed to come naturally. You put your fingers into a comfortable spot and then moved them around like a happy spider dancing.

Also, she loved to sing, and the class had been working all week on the Hallelujah Chorus by Handel. It was supposed to be sung by men as well as women because it had some deep bass parts in it, but Mr Berger took responsibility for those and Mariette managed to do the tenor bits without cracking up and the rest of the girls were altos and sopranos. Dhikilo sang some high Hallelujahs and also played a keyboard that could sound like a cathedral organ if you pressed the Cathedral Organ button. The first few sessions had been full of mistakes and laughing, and then they got the hang of it and it was really starting to sound rather majestic.

"Hello, girls! This afternoon we will begin on 'Sloop John B,' a traitional folk song as arrange by The Beach Boys," said Mr Berger.

Dhikilo sat blinking while the other girls picked up the sheet music. "What about the Hallelujah Chorus?" she said.

"It's too ifficult to sing," said Mr Berger.

"But weren't we all having fun?" said Dhikilo. The other girls' eyes were downcast, studying the new notes.

"It was in the wrong key," said Mr Berger, and his voice, normally smooth and low, had a sharp edge to it, warning her not to get herself into trouble.

Dhikilo spent the next forty-five minutes trying to sing "Sloop John B" and deciding it was the worst song she had ever heard.

Onkeys, Only a Fiver

'm not going to tell you much about the weeks that fol-lowed, because Dhikilo found them increasingly frus-trating and upsetting, and there's no point making you frustrated and upset, too.

In short: the D didn't come back; the D stayed gone.

But it was worse than that.

For a while, Dhikilo thought she must simply get used to all the words with D in them not having D in them any more. That was annoying, but being annoyed didn't change anything, so she decided ("ecie"?—no, that was ridiculous!) that if the whole world had made up its mind to be stupid, she would just have to put up with it.

Unfortunately, stupidity, like rust and weeds and lies and mould, tends to spread. And as the days passed, the disap-pearance of the D began to have some creepy consequences.

There was an old cobbled street in Cawber where the most characterful little shops huddled together. One of them sold musical instruments and Dhikilo always stopped to gaze through the window, especially at the drums. But after the D disappeared, the drums did, too. The shop put an extra saxophone in the empty space but it wasn't the same. She hoped that the drums had been sold rather than locked away or discarded.

Outside the Mermai, the oldest pub in Cawber, there was a sign that said:

> **UE TO THE CONFUSION BETWEEN ARTS AN ARTS, IT WILL NO LONGER BE POSSIBLE TO PLAY ARTS HERE**

On the corner of Stranloper Avenue there was a dentist's surgery—now a entist's surgery—which had always had a flower garden out front, to make people feel less frightened of going in and having stuff done to their teeth. Just before the D went missing, the garden was gorgeous yellow with dozens of daffodils—or "affoils" as Dhikilo supposed they must now be called. But after a few days, the daffodils all vanished. Maybe selfish flower-thieves had stolen them? No. Next day, the denuded garden itself was gone, replaced by a rectangle of grey pebbles. And by the end of the week, the sign advertising the entist had been taken down, too, and a different sign said, PRIVATE PROPERTY: KEEP OUT.

Further down the street was the Health Centre, an ugly concrete building with a glass front door that slid open and shut by itself when people walked through. There were always people walking through, usually very old ladies being helped by their very old husbands or the other way round. On the day that the KEEP OUT sign went up at the entist's surgery, the Health Centre seemed quieter than usual. Dhikilo ventured nearer to the big door, hoping she wouldn't make it slide open, because the people inside might think she was just fooling around, wasting electricity. She needn't have worried. the door was sealed shut and would remain that way for ever. UE TO LACK OF OCTORS, THIS CENTRE IS NOW CLOSE, said a sign. FOR UR. GENT MEICAL ATTENTION, PLEASE RING THESE NUMBERS.

And then there was this:

One of Dhikilo's favourite things about living in Cawber was that every summer, in the park opposite the railway station, there was a Donkey Derby organized by the Cawber Lions Club. She always went. Once, when she was little, Malcolm paid for her to ride on one of the donkeys and she'd loved sitting on the back of an animal. But you were supposed to race other children and she disappointed Malcolm by not wanting to do that. The last couple of years, she'd just enjoyed stroking the donkeys' flanks and looking into their patient inhuman eyes and watching their amazing horsey heads swinging to and fro. Also she enjoyed seeing the farmers' sons in their green overalls and big boots following the donkeys around, picking up their poo with shovels and buckets.

This year there'd been banners in the streets advertising the Donkey Derby and she'd marked the date in her diary so that she wouldn't forget. After the D disappeared, the banners advertised the Onkey Erby instead, but Dhikilo was determined not to let that spoil her fun, and on the big day she rushed to the railway station straight after breakfast.

The park was already crowded with people. There were lots of food stalls, and an ice-cream van, and a Test-Your-Strength pole, and stalls where you could win prizes by throwing things at other things, and a merry-go-round, and an inflatable bouncy castle. Dhikilo hurried straight to where the donkey enclosure had always been. There was no enclosure and no donkeys. Instead, there was a shop selling a strange-looking plastic toy.

"Get yer onkeys 'ere!" hollered a fat man in a bright yellow polo shirt. "Only a fiver! Get yer onkeys!"

He demonstrated the toy for some children who ventured near. It was a kind of plastic gun that was shaped like a trumpet. The man pointed it up into the air and pulled the trigger. It made a honk and fired a piece of pink fluff towards the sky. The fluff expanded into a ball and began to float slowly back towards the ground. The children squealed with delight and their father pulled his wallet from his trouser pocket.

Dhikilo went to the tent where the old folk from the Lions Club hung out.

"What happened to the donkeys?" she asked.

"What are they, poppet?" asked the kindly old lady with the spectacles on a silver chain.

"The donkeys," said Dhikilo exasperatedly. "You know: they're like small horses."

"I think you may mean ponies?" offered an old man. "There's a pony club in Chalkton, I believe. Not too far."

"I mean donkeys!" said Dhikilo, almost crying. "The same donkeys who were here last year. The donkeys who are always here! What have you done with the donkeys?"

The Lions Club folk looked pained and concerned.

"On't shout, pet," the old lady said. "You'll scare the little chilren. Where's your mother an father?"

So Dhikilo walked home, and even though the weather was warm, she was feeling shivery and strange. She passed the old Catholic church, which was now covered in scaffolding because workmen were ismantling the ome to replace it with something more moern. And when she got back to her house, Ruth was oing some garening, pulling the aisies out by their roots, while Malcolm was inside watching television, listening to a politician saying that iversity was all very well, but not if it got in the way of forging a strong, safe nation.

HEL IN OUR HEARTS

When too many things in your life change all at once, you get very attached to the things that haven't changed. That's certainly the way it was for Dhikilo.

Most mornings, on her way to school, she still saw the tottery old lady taking her Dalmatian for a walk. Dhikilo waved to her as usual and the old lady would wave back, but she didn't look happy and she didn't call out "Nice day so far!" any more, or even "Nice ay so far!"

And one day, a couple of weeks after the disappearance of the D, her Dalmatian was absent; the old lady walked alone.

"Is your dog all right?" called Dhikilo.

The old lady jerked as if someone had thrown a stone at her. "Sorry?" she said.

"Is your dog all right?" said Dhikilo. "Your nice Dalmatian."

The old lady's eyes glimmered and her mouth went stiff. "I on't have a og," she said. "I've never ha a og." And she walked away as fast as an old lady with stiff legs can walk.

In the days after that, Dhikilo noticed that it wasn't only the Dalmatian who had disappeared. All the dogs were gone.

Cawber-on-Sands had always been a fine town for dogs because of The Promenade, which allowed people to show off how splendid and well-behaved their animals were, and allowed the dogs to smell the bums of lots of other dogs, and also there were plenty of bins for the poo. At weekends, Dhikilo loved to sit on one of the benches along The Promenade and watch the dogs and their owners go by. It was like watching a really excellent nature documentary, except you could sit in the fresh air instead of having to view it inside on a screen.

The weekend came—even though everyone called it the weeken—and Dhikilo went out in the sunshine to sit on a bench. The young mothers wheeled their prams as usual. A group of Germans walked past in one direction and a group of Japanese walked past in the other. Small children on scooters, disabled people whizzing along in their motorized wheelchairs, elderly couples holding hands. But no dogs. Not a single one.

She looked round for the poo bins. They were all gone, too. In their place were signs saying things like:

WATCH YOUR SPEE
and
LOAING & UNLOAING ONLY
and
KEEP CAWBER TIY

She sat back down on the bench and watched the passers-by for a while longer. It was impossible that all the dogs were gone! English people loved their dogs! They surely wouldn't give them up and pretend nothing had happened! Any minute now, some big beefy man with many tattoos would stride along The Promenade with his Jack Russell, or the silver-haired lady in the fancy mobility buggy would drive past with her silver-haired poodles panting to keep up.

But no. Various big beefy tattooed men strode past, swinging their empty arms. And eventually the silver-haired lady trundled past, too, and the sides of her buggy still had the metal loops to which her poodles' leashes were always tied. But always was not now.

Dhikilo stood up to go home. Her bench, like many of the benches along The Promenade, was a memorial to a dead person who used to live in the town. Dhikilo always felt happy at the idea that, year after year, strangers would relax on these benches and be reminded of how much someone had been loved by their family. She looked down at the little bronze plaque on her bench, and it said:

> *To our belove a an granpa*
> *Early misse every ay*
> *Hel in our hearts for ever*
> *From your aughter an granaughter*

NOT KNOWING

Despite being in the bottom percentile of befriended-ness, Dhikilo used to love school. After the disappearance of the D, she didn't like it so much any more. However, she tried her best to do the work and not get into trouble, and some lessons were almost fun. Miss Meek was still a good Art teacher even though all the drawing materials had been mysteriously removed and there was no longer any red paint in the paints cupboard. In its place there was extra blue and white, and Miss Meek got the whole class sitting outside on the grass to paint the sky, which was deeply relaxing.

"How i you like that, Hikilo?" asked Miss Meek when they were all filing back inside.

"It was deeply relaxing," said Dhikilo.

"*Eeply*, ear," corrected Miss Meek, with a gentle wink, as if the challenge of living without the D didn't need to be unpleasant as long as everyone kept their good humour.

Mathematics with Mr Gragrin was still sort of OK, too, and Geography with Mr Onalson was tolerable, because even though he had a boring droney voice, he was very keen on wildlife, and took the whole class to the woods to install bird-boxes in the trees, which was a nice outing in the fresh air, even though he spoiled it a bit by referring to birs feeing in the woos.

History and English were horrible, though, and seemed to get worse every day. That was a shame, especially in the case of History, which was taught by Mr Unstable, who was bad news even before he lost his D. It made Dhikilo regret all the more that Professor Dodderfield had retired.

Speaking of whom…! One Monday afternoon, when it was almost time to go home, Molly said to Dhikilo, "O you remember Professor Oerfiel?"

"Professor… Oerfiel?" echoed Dhikilo, not understanding for a moment. Then: "Oh! Professor Dodderfield! Of course I do."

The Professor was not the sort of person you could easily forget. He was wildly eccentric and bushy-bearded and acted out incidents from history in different voices like a one-man pantomime. Also, he was blind and had a guide dog. The dog was a chocolate-brown Labrador whom the Professor called Nelly but required the girls to address as Mrs Robinson. Mrs Robinson was the only dog allowed in the school, and Dhikilo always felt a thrill of surprise whenever she walked round a corner and almost tripped over a big brown beast lapping water from a bowl.

Most teachers retire in their sixties but the Professor kept going until he was in his nineties, as ancient as some of the history he taught. Some of the girls found him slightly scary—his eyeballs were milky from whatever had blinded him, and he didn't bother to cover them up with dark glasses. But he was the best History teacher *ever*. And he knew all about Somaliland! Even the Geography teacher didn't know much about Somaliland—he got it muddled up with Somalia.

"Most of us are from nations that are old and tired," the Professor had announced to the whole class, waving his arms around so that his oversized tweed jacket flapped like a cloak. "Dhikilo here is from a nation that's still being born! Keep abreast of the news, ladies, and any day now you'll see its little head poking out!"

Several of the girls had gasped or giggled. The Professor was always saying things which a particularly sensitive parent might object to. The girls therefore lived in fear of him being removed from the school for saying too many outrageous things. Each year, fresh classfuls of youngsters fell under his spell and hoped he would hang on a little longer, even though he was twice as old and twice as mad as any of the other teachers.

"Invaders and interlopers, the lot of us!" he was fond of declaring. "Do we have any Iron Age originals among us today? Hmm? Any Regni? Any Jutes? Anyone who arrived here before the great Age of Migrations in the fourth century? Or are we all scavengers? Foxes sniffing the rubbish bins at twilight?" Extending his palms towards his open-mouthed audience, the Professor would then grin broadly. "All right. Let this old fox teach you some *real* history."

It had been Professor Dodderfield, too, who comforted Dhikilo when she was upset about her mother. He had a little office where he and his dog would hang out between classes; Dhikilo visited him there to explain why she hadn't handed in her essay on the Egyptians. She didn't bother to hide her tears because she figured he couldn't see them anyway. But he must have heard or smelled or sensed them, because he said, "Don't cry, it distracts the dog."

"I can't help it," she replied.

"Then cry," he sighed. "But explain the historical context."

"My mother is dead," Dhikilo told him.

"What, Ruth Bentley? That's terrible! I taught her when

she was as young as you are now! Barely more brain than a hamster, but still…dead! Not right at all."

"I'm talking about my *real* mother," said Dhikilo. "In Somaliland." She wiped her wet cheeks with the heel of her hand. "She was thirty-one."

"That's not very old," said the Professor. "Was she sick?"

"I don't know," said Dhikilo. "I don't know anything about her."

"Well, that's a hard thing. Not knowing. And a hard thing for her, too. Not having known you, when she would undoubtedly have wanted to know you. Sadness is definitely called for. In her case, not so much, because she can't feel bad if she's dead. But in your case, I would recommend crying quite a bit more. Certainly for the next twelve minutes. Then hold off for the duration of Double English, then it will be time to go home. Don't cry while walking, you might bump into something or get run over. Cry until dinnertime, hold off during dinner, do your homework if you have any, then cry until ten-thirty p.m. if need be, then get a good night's sleep. Don't be sad on an unslept brain, it stops the memories settling where they should."

"I don't have any memories of my mum."

"Yes you do, you just don't remember them," said the Professor.

Two years on, Dhikilo still didn't remember anything about her mother, but she remembered Professor Dodderfield as vividly as if she'd seen him yesterday.

"He's ie," said Molly.

"Died?"

"That's what I sai."

Dhikilo blinked. "How awful," she said.

Molly didn't seem at all upset. "He must've been a hunre years ol."

"It's still awful," said Dhikilo.

"My mum's going to the funeral."

"I'll go, too," said Dhikilo. "When is it? And where?"

"I on't know. It's in the newspaper."

"What's going to happen to Mrs Robinson?"

"Who's Mrs Robinson?"

"The dog. The Professor's dog. Don't you remember her?"

Molly's eyes went unfocused and dull. "I on't remember any og."

"Don't *say* that, Molly!" exclaimed Dhikilo. "You can't mean it. Mrs Robinson. We weren't allowed to call her Nelly. She was his guide dog. She was dark brown."

Molly stared Dhikilo straight in the face. "Guie ogs are pale yellow."

"Molly!"

Molly flinched, then looked as if she might start crying. "Please, Icky," she said softly. "I want to be your frien."

"You *are* my friend," said Dhikilo crossly. "Even if you can't say the word all of a sudden."

A tear jumped onto Molly's cheek. "You on't unerstan," she said. "I want to *stay* your frien." She touched Dhikilo gently on the forearm, then ran away.

A Note from a Parent

Malcolm and Ruth weren't enthusiastic when Dhikilo told them she wanted to go to a funeral.

"It's not as though you were family," said Ruth.

Dhikilo opened her mouth to say something about herself and "family," but decided against it. "Molly's mum isn't family, either, and she's going."

"But they were colleagues."

"Well, we were… I was his…what's the word?"

"Pupil," said Malcolm.

"Student. I saw him every day for a year. And when I was upset, he was very good to me, he was."

"Well," said Ruth, "I hope *we've* always been very goo to you, too."

Dhikilo looked down into her mashed potato. "The school says it's OK, but I need permission from you." She was well aware that many other girls did whatever they wanted, even bad things, without bothering to ask their parents' permission.

"I on't know," said Malcolm uneasily. "A chil, on her own, at a funeral… Maybe I coul cancel my meeting…"

"I'll be inside a church," said Dhikilo. "And Molly's mum will be there."

That seemed to clinch it. A mother on the spot.

Later that night, after Dhikilo had gone to bed and was almost asleep, her bedroom door opened a crack and her mum—Ruth—was standing in the doorway.

"Sweetie?"

"Yes, Mum?"

"i I ever tell you he was my teacher, too? The Professor? Many years ago."

"No, but he told me."

"I wasn't very clever at History, I'm afrai. I suppose he tol you that?"

"Not exactly," said Dhikilo, searching for the right words. "He said…he said you had a brain."

"Well, that was…chivalrous of him."

Dhikilo turned over on the pillow to face the silhouette in the doorway.

"What does that mean?" she asked. It wasn't very often that a word she didn't know came out of Ruth's mouth. And learning new words was another of Dhikilo's favourite things.

Ruth hugged herself and sounded wistful. "It's when someone's a gentleman, an is amazingly respectful an treats a person as if she's more special than she really is."

"Oh," said Dhikilo.

"Chivalrous," repeated Ruth. "Goonight, sweetie."

"Goodnight, Mum," said Dhikilo, getting settled on the pillow again.

In the last moments before drifting off, she was picturing a strange new creature, a Shivalrus—half man, half walrus. It wore a saggy tweed suit and stood on all fours and had a kindly face.

An Unacceptably Odd Burial

Saint Ursula's, the church which hosted the Professor's funeral ceremony, was very beautiful and very ancient and very small, with a graveyard that wasn't much bigger than the school canteen. The gravestones were all mossy and leaning sideways, and the writing on the granite was worn away by hundreds of years of wind and weather. No new bodies had gone into this ground since 1847 and Dhikilo wondered if the church was going to make an exception for the Professor because he was so old and extraordinary. But no.

When she walked in, she was given a leaflet about the funeral by a dignified lady with a what-are-you-doing-here-this-is-not-your-place face. It was a look Dhikilo got all the time from people who didn't know her and most people didn't know her so she was used to it. She nodded thank you.

There were about twenty other mourners here, the youngest of whom was Molly's mum. There were some other middle-aged ladies and quite a few decrepit-looking gentlemen with wet noses and skin like bark. Dhikilo had thought the Professor was extremely popular with the Cawber School for Girls pupils but maybe, on reflection, he was just popular with her. Or maybe the other girls didn't want to miss Art with Miss Meek and PSE (Personal & Social Evelopment) with Mrs Geering.

Dhikilo sat down in one of the pews and looked around. Her mum and dad were not churchgoers and only took her along at Christmas "for the carols" (not to Saint Ursula's, though—to a bigger, brighter church on the High Street). Saint Ursula's was spooky and candlelit. There were paintings on the walls that depicted terrible things being done to holy individuals who didn't seem particularly fussed about being shot with arrows, whipped, stabbed with spears and so on. That was the creepy part about churches. But they were kind of magical, too.

Dhikilo examined the leaflet, which was actually just one piece of paper folded in half. It contained the words of two hymns to be sung, a tiny photograph of the Professor's face and the dates of his birth and death. Also the location of the graveyard where he would actually be buried afterwards, which was quite some distance outside the town centre. A helpful map was provided. The Professor's final resting place would be between Cawber Academy (the boys' school) and the sad retail park where the bed showroom and the sporting goods superstore were. The Professor's body would presumably travel there in the black limousine that was parked outside the church, but Dhikilo was pretty sure the Number 42 bus went the same way.

The vicar shuffled up to the pulpit and began to talk about the Professor. Well, actually, not really. He mentioned the Professor's name—"Charles Oerfiel"—and spoke for a few seconds about what an excellent and well-respected teacher the Professor had been, and then he devoted the rest of his speech to Go Almighty and Heaven. Then everybody sang "The Lor Is My Shepher," except for Dhikilo, who put the

Ds in. Pretty soon it was all over and the vicar was thanking people for coming.

Four tall old men in black overcoats carried the coffin out to the hearse. Then they got into the car with the vicar, scrunching themselves up rather than taking their top hats off, which was odd, and the hearse drove off.

It was drizzling as Dhikilo hurried to the bus stop, and the sky was grey with rain that was all set to come down. Sometimes when she and Mariette and Fiona and Molly were playing—or whatever you were supposed to call what you did with your friends when you were too old to describe it as "playing"— Dhikilo would pretend she could change the weather. If they all wanted it to stay fine and the weather threatened to spoil everything, Dhikilo would raise her hand to the drizzle and say, "Sun!" and, more than half the time, the drizzle would go away and the sun would come back out.

She raised her head and said, "Sun!" now. The drizzle intensified into proper rain. The bus pulled up, its windscreen wipers beating hard.

By the time she arrived at the cemetery, it was pouring. Nobody else got off the bus and there were no cars parked near the cemetery entrance. Dhikilo had assumed that the other people from the church service would come, too, but it seemed she was the only one who'd bothered. When she hurried across the grounds towards the right spot, she found that the four pallbearers and the vicar were already at the graveside and the coffin was already in the hole.

Dhikilo actually had a small umbrella in her shoulder bag, but she felt it wouldn't be right to use it, because the four old men didn't have umbrellas. They stood as still as statues, their waterlogged hats tipped slightly forward, dripping from the brims.

"Ashes to ashes," the sodden vicar was saying. "Ust to ust."

Dhikilo walked nearer, but not right up close. The vicar wasn't being very friendly—too wet and miserable, maybe— and the four men in black frightened her a little. This funeral was all wrong, somehow. When you planted a dead person in the ground, there should be lots of people singing and dancing and eating nice food and telling stories while the sun beamed down. Maybe that was a daft idea, but that's how she felt.

"...for now an evermore," said the vicar, making a special gesture like a dance move.

Having finished his own contribution to the ceremony, he looked at the men in black, inviting them to speak if they had anything to say.

"Marmalade," said one, in a dull, distant monotone.

"Soft grain bread," said another, in exactly the same voice.

"Coconut macaroons," said the third.

"Maybe a couple of bananas, if they're ripe," said the fourth.

The vicar blinked in befuddlement. "Paron?" he said.

"I have brought my own bag, thank you," said one of the men in black.

After that the weather got ridiculous, as though the sky was emptying huge buckets of water from a flood in Heaven. The vicar ran off as soon as he could. The pallbearers continued to stand utterly still, their hands hanging by their sides, their heads bowed, four streams of water pouring from their hats.

Then, above the noise of the rain, Dhikilo heard a dog barking. The men lurched into movement, shambling single-file along a path between the gravestones, towards the great iron gate where the cemetery joined on to the public park where nobody ever went except the boys from Cawber Academy when they wanted to smoke. At the gate, hardly visible through the rain, a large dog was slowly pacing round and round.

It's Mrs Robinson! thought Dhikilo.

The dog barked again, and the four men walked faster, in fact almost trotted out of the graveyard gate, and disappeared into the park.

Dhikilo stared open-mouthed for a moment or two, then ran after them. The rain had made the ground boggy and she went up to her ankles in mud, almost slipping, but she didn't care; she was soaked to the skin anyhow. Even so, the quagmire slowed her down, and by the time she got into the park, the dog was nowhere in sight. She heard some car-horn beeps coming from the streets behind the park, which might mean that Mrs Robinson was dashing across the road in a dangerous manner, or might simply mean that cars were having trouble seeing each other in the downpour.

The four men, too, were nowhere to be seen, despite the fact that they were old and surely in no state to run. Dhikilo peered in all directions, breathing hard as the rain continued to plummet down. There was nothing to pursue. She would just have to go home.

Her first steps towards the street felt so unpleasant that she had to stop walking—there was mud squelching inside her shoes; she could see it oozing out when she pressed her heel on the ground. So she leaned against one of the park's litter bins and, standing on one leg, took off a shoe. She wanted to wipe the mud out of it, but the only wipy thing she had was some paper tissues in her pocket and those had turned to clots of mush. She lifted the lid of the bin, hoping there might be something more useful in there.

Inside she found four black overcoats, four pairs of trousers, four sets of shirts, ties, underwear, socks and shoes, and four hats.

Sniffing Out the Truth

ack at home, Dhikilo rinsed out her shoes in the bath-
tub. They seemed to contain more mud than the volume of her feet, which was inconveniently amazing
and made the bath look as though a gang of moles had had
a fight in it. She knew that Ruth would want her to clean
up the mess but she had urgent things to do. Like putting on
fresh dry clothes and phoning Molly's mum.

"Do you know the Professor's address?" she asked.

"Yes," said Molly's mum.

"Can I have it?"

"Well, I'm not sure about that," said Molly's mum. "I mean,
he's not with us any more, so I can't see what…erm…"

Dhikilo looked through the window. The sun had come
out. She considered making up a story about wanting to send
a condolence card to the Professor's relatives, who might be
checking his mail. But she didn't like to lie. Lying was wrong
and also it was a lot of bother and when other people did it
she just felt sorry for them, getting themselves so tangled up.
Anyway, she wasn't sure how to pronounce "condolence."

"Can I have it?" she said again. "Please?"

So Molly's mum told her the address.

Twenty minutes later, Dhikilo turned the corner from Oughty
Yar into Gas Hill Garens. They were funny names for streets,
in her opinion, but maybe they'd lost a D or two.

The houses—or actually flats—were a long row of old buildings which were not quite historical enough to be protected by the government, so the people living in them had replaced the original nineteenth-century windows and doors with new ones, added modern security fencing and so on.

The only building in the whole row which looked as though it hadn't had anything done to it since it was first built was Number 58 and that was the number Dhikilo had written down on her scrap of paper. In fact, not only did the house look unmodernized, it looked uninhabited. It was three storeys high and every window in it was shrouded with curtains. Large shards of plaster had fallen off the exterior walls, exposing the brickwork underneath, quite a few of the ledges and arches and other decorative features were crumbling away, and the windows were all cracked in their handsome wooden frames, though none was actually broken. The tiny front garden was entirely dead and smelled of cat pee.

Dhikilo stood at the massive oak door and knocked. The wood was solid and thickly varnished and made almost no noise. Knocking harder only hurt her knuckles. There was no bell. Two small drill-holes, clogged up with dust, could still be seen in the wood as evidence that there'd once been a doorknocker which had come off, or been removed.

"Hello!" called Dhikilo. "Is anybody there? Hello-o!"

She bent down and squinted through the big rusty keyhole. Immediately she yelped and jumped back, almost falling over backwards into the street. Behind the keyhole she'd seen an eye—definitely an eye—but not a human eye! Violet in colour, with a cat-like pupil, glowing as if it had a light bulb inside it.

"H–hello?" said Dhikilo again, leaning her ear close to the door.

"What do you want?" came the reply. "Why have you come here?" The voice sounded female, and not British, although you weren't supposed to say that at Dhikilo's school. "We're all British, aren't we? Even you," her classmates would say. Well, the voice behind the door was very noticeably from somewhere far away. There was a weird hissing noise attached to it, as if the uttering of each word released a jet of steam.

"I knew Professor Dodderfield," Dhikilo called out uncertainly.

"No, you did not," came the voice again.

"Yes, I did," said Dhikilo. "I liked him. I think he liked me." The last part felt a bit wrong to say, as if she was claiming knowledge that wasn't hers, just to win an argument. She recalled how the Professor would exclaim, in his History classes, "Facts! Stick to the facts! That gets rid of 99 per cent of everything anyone's ever said or written, which cuts your homework down to a nice manageable size, doesn't it? Sniff out the truth!"

Dhikilo waited for further communication from the strange female on the other side of the door. There was only silence.

"Are you still there?" she called.

"Go away." The voice was like a stormy wind that rattles windows at night.

Dhikilo leaned against the door, pressing her ear against it, and spoke to the old wood with her eyes shut tight.

"I can't go away… Madam. I can't, because…" She thought fast. Because what? "Because I have some questions. About the Professor's funeral, and the old men in black, the ones who carried the coffin. I don't know the right word for them, is it pawbearers? And…and about the Professor's dog. Mrs Robinson."

Another silence followed.

"Your quessstions," said the voice at last, "cannot be anssswered. Go away."

"I'm sorry, but who are *you*, please?" said Dhikilo, trying to sound polite, although it was hard to make a question like that sound polite. There was not a sound except for the traffic on the street. Dhikilo pressed her cheek harder against the door, and began to get the strangest feeling that time was running out, as if the house was about to move away from her like a train moving away from a person on a railway platform.

"Please!" she called out. "Are you still there?"

"No," came the voice at last. "No, we are not." And that seemed to be the end of that.

Dhikilo waited for a long while before she had the courage to look again through the keyhole. When she did, it was dark. This upset her. The house really had left her stranded, it seemed. She started banging on the door with her fist.

"Hello! Hello! Hello-o!"

This racket fetched the voice back.

"I have now called the police," it said.

"I don't think you have," retorted Dhikilo. She was amazed at her rudeness. But she hadn't come this far only to be tossed back like a piece of junk mail. Anyway, the person behind the door was being very rude herself. So they were kind of equal. "I'm going to sit here until you open the door."

"All right," said the voice. "Sssit."

Dhikilo sat, feeling cross and confused. A lorry passed by in the street, making everything seem hopeless and too big. Clouds covered the sun and it began to rain. She tried her "Sun!" trick again, and again it failed. Arithmetically speaking, that meant that her success rate was dropping towards a random 50/50, indicating that she didn't have any special powers at all. If she went home now, she could clean up the bath before Ruth came back from work. Maybe she could even catch the last lesson at school. It would be either History or Geography, she couldn't remember which. Or maybe Citizenship?

At her back, there was a clunk and a creak. The door swung open, inwards.

ANTIQUE SPLENDOURS

"Oh!" cried Dhikilo, at the sight of a large Labrador standing in the hallway, its paws resting on a dark Persian carpet. A line of such carpets, overlapping and of different designs, was laid all the way down the hall, which was painted dark blue and rather gloomy.

"Mrs Robinson?" said Dhikilo. She hadn't recalled the Professor's dog being quite so big. But it was the right colour: chocolate, rather than the more common pale gold. "Mrs Robinson, remember me?" She reached out her hand to pat the animal.

The Professor's dog bared its teeth, and Dhikilo drew her hand back. Then the teeth-baring turned into a yawn, and the dog padded up the hall and disappeared around a corner. And, from somewhere around that corner, a voice rang out.

"Come in, Miss Bentley! And shut the door!"

It was the same voice, and even the same sentence, with which Professor Dodderfield had summoned her into his office at school. Dhikilo took a deep breath and entered.

As soon as she'd shut the door behind her, the hallway was as dark as the inside of a wardrobe, or so it seemed to her unaccustomed eyes. She hurried towards the light around the corner, and so made a rather sudden entrance into the room where the Professor sat with his dog.

It was a large room, with very high walls painted the same dark blue as the entrance hall and, as Dhikilo had already noticed from the street, thick curtains shrouding the windows. A fantastically ornate and dusty chandelier hung from the ceiling, with only three or four of its bulbs working, throwing a feeble yellowy light on the parlour's antique splendours, which included:

A grandfather clock, several vast glass-fronted bookcases filled with leather-bound volumes, a big wooden lectern like the pulpit in Saint Ursula's Church, more Persian rugs, Mrs Robinson (difficult to see, at first, in the gloom, but she was there, near the fireplace), a tall brass lamp that wasn't switched on, a sagging spinach-coloured sofa piled high with oak branches and twigs and bits of broken furniture that looked as if they'd been dragged out of skips, a preposterously plump purple armchair and…seated in that armchair, dressed in his usual suit, with a dressing gown on top…the Professor himself.

"If I'm not mistaken," the old man said, "it's a school day. Which means you're committing an act of truancy." With a grunt of exertion, he stretched his legs and wiggled his feet, which were loosely shod in threadbare tartan slippers that were far too large. "Sad to see a good girl go bad."

"I have permission," Dhikilo pointed out. "To attend a funeral, actually."

"Ah," said the Professor.

"*Your* funeral."

"Ah," said the Professor.

In truth, even though he wasn't dead, he didn't look very well. In his last year teaching at the school he'd looked about 58 and now he looked about 158. He had grown his beard longer and tried to sculpt it into a perfect triangle, like an upside-down V hanging off his chin, but it was thin and straggly. His moustache drooped over his lips. The hair on his head was sparser than she remembered, and stuck up at random. All the wrinkles in his flesh had deepened, particularly the bags under his eyes, which gave the impression of unimaginable exhaustion. And, although it was perhaps a trick of the dim light, his eyes no longer seemed milky, but dark as shoe-polish.

"How are you?" said Dhikilo.

"Oh, fair, fair," sighed the Professor. "I've seen better days. Tens of thousands of them, as a matter of fact." He gestured towards the sofa. "Take a seat."

"There's no room," observed Dhikilo. "It's covered in firewood."

"Ah, yes," said the Professor. "Well then, sit on the floor. Children often sit on floors, don't they? And it's good enough for Nelly."

Dhikilo knelt on the carpet, which was none too clean. She looked towards the fireplace, and noticed that it was crammed with logs and other lumps of wood, but so poorly organized that it was alight only in one small corner where some air could accidentally get in.

Mrs Robinson was nicely settled near this modest glow of warmth. She was on her belly, but with her head held high. At her side was a tiny pedestal table on which was balanced a tall glass half-full of milk, with two straws in it.

"I have some questions," said Dhikilo.

"Always a good thing," said the Professor, leaning forward as though he could see her.

"I was at your funeral today…" she began.

"Ah, that," he said, clapping his bony fingers together in a nervous gesture. "Not a good effort. All done in a hurry, no chance to think it through. And what weather!"

"You're supposed to be dead."

"Well, yes, if you're inclined to be a stickler for the rules. But it seems rather harsh."

"And also," said Dhikilo, "those men who carried the coffin. The men in black…"

"Black is customary, I believe."

"I followed them out of the graveyard…"

"Miss Bentley, Miss Bentley!" said the Professor, leaning back in his armchair so abruptly that one of his slippers fell off. "All this talk of graveyards, coffins, death and funerals! Most inappropriate in a girl of your age. You ought to be talking about…ah…whatever it is girls your age talk about. Cheerful topics. The latest fashions? Beautiful young millionaires who sing of love? I confess I am ignorant, but willing to be enlightened. Tell me, Miss Bentley, what's your impression of the world in general since I retired?"

Dhikilo was getting fed up. She'd come here for answers and the Professor was doing his best not to give them. In a minute he would send her away and she would walk home in the pouring rain.

"The D is gone," she said. "The D is gone from everything and nobody admits it. They just pretend it hasn't happened." It was only as the words were leaving her mouth that she realized the Professor's speech was normal. Well, not exactly *normal*; it was rather mad—but at least it had all the Ds in.

The Professor leapt up from his chair. Dhikilo, still squatting on the carpet, was so startled that she fell over backwards. But he wasn't about to assault her; instead, he fumbled all around his armchair for his walking stick. The dog had disappeared; Dhikilo hadn't even noticed her leave.

"Miss Bentley, forgive me," he muttered. "All this time I've kept you here without offering you a cup of tea. Or what is it that young girls drink? Not coffee, surely? I'm almost sure I have some lemonade somewhere. Does it improve with age, like wine? I confess I may have had it for quite some years…"

"*Charlsss!*"

Dhikilo froze in fright. It was the strange voice she'd heard at the door, coming out of nowhere. "Charles, you are wasssting time and wasssting what has come to usss. This girl is the one who will do what you and I cannot."

The Professor stopped rummaging about, stood up straight for a moment, then slowly lowered himself back into his arm-chair. The exertion had made his cheeks and nose very red and brought a twinkle of sweat to his wrinkled forehead.

"This girl? You really think so?" he murmured, turning towards the empty space by the hearth where his dog had been. "Hmm, yes… I suppose…"

"Your brain is ssslower than it once was, Charles," the voice from nowhere whooshed again.

The Professor folded his arms and sulked.

"There's no need to get personal." He was still addressing the hearth.

Suddenly the empty space beside the little pedestal began to shimmer. Dhikilo's view of the fireplace and the smoul-dering logs grew hazy and the air wobbled and shook. Even the glass of milk trembled and the straws in it moved around. Then the hazy parts of the air took shape and began to fill up with the outlines of a large creature.

In moments, it was all there. First, the head and neck of a woman, with a great thick mane of golden curls. Then the body, legs and paws of a very large cat—not as big and bulky as a lion, maybe the size of a cheetah, but without spots, and tawny in colour. Lastly, a tail that stuck up in the air and swayed around, with a tiny forked tongue flick-ing in and out of the tip, because it was actually a snake. The woman-face lifted its chin, blinked its violet eyes and opened its thin lips.

"Don't be afraid," it told Dhikilo. "I'm… I am… I do not know the word."

"Tame?" guessed the Professor.

"Yesss," said the creature. "Tame." But in making the sound of the word, it opened its mouth a little wider, and Dhikilo saw that its teeth were sharp as spikes.

Ectoplasmic Helpers

hikilo gratefully accepted the cup of tea handed to her by the Professor. The saucer had quite a lot of tea spilled in it, as the Professor had stumbled on the edge of one of the Persian carpets on his way back from the kitchen. But a couple of sips of hot drink really helped with the fright.

Was there anything to be frightened of, truly? Nobody was threatening to harm her. Nobody was waving a weapon. Outside the house, she could hear the sound of small children laughing quite near by. That was comforting: it helped her push away the feeling that she was trapped in a strange dream. The world outside was normal (well, sort of normal, apart from the missing Ds), so the world inside this room must be normal, too. She was simply (she told herself) sitting in an old house in an ordinary street, drinking tea, and the rain had stopped, the sun was peeking through the tiny gap in the curtains, and no doubt she would soon be out there, waiting for a bus.

Until then, she was simply visiting an old teacher of hers

called Professor Dodderfield, who had maybe gone a little bit mad in his extreme old age, but was almost certainly harmless. And it was also quite possible that the creature with the human face, body of a large feline and tail of a snake was an optical illusion. Like those times when you think you see a spooky monster in a tree but it turns out to be a plastic bag caught in the branches.

Or maybe the creature was just an ordinary young woman in fancy dress. Or even if she wasn't, she—it—was quite busy right now licking its paws and flanks with its long tongue, shaking its luxurious hair away from its face every few seconds. A creature calmly licking itself was surely nothing to be afraid of?

"Nelly is a sphinx," said the Professor, feeling his way back into his armchair. "You'll remember sphinxes from Egyptian history, I trust? That's if you were paying attention in class, of course."

Dhikilo drank some more tea. One of the children playing outside let out a shriek. It didn't sound like harmless play any more.

"She isn't unfriendly, really," the Professor went on. "She can't help the voice, it's just the way sphinxes are made. She is, in fact, rather a treasure. You'll get to know her a lot better when you travel with her."

Dhikilo lifted a soggy macaroon out of the wet saucer and pretended to be perfectly calm. "Am I going somewhere?" she said.

"Oh, I hope so, Miss Bentley, I do hope so."

"How soon?" asked Dhikilo, wondering how far she would get if she made a dash for the front door. The sphinx's claws looked terribly sharp, especially now that it had them stretched all the way out to lick the furry spaces between them.

The Professor frowned, obviously in deep thought. Absentmindedly he looked down at his wrist, which had not had a watch on it since he'd gone blind ages ago, so he grunted in annoyance, and thought some more. At last he said, "When do the shops close?"

"Sorry?" said Dhikilo, caught by surprise with her mouth full of macaroon.

"Miss Bentley: for your journey, you'll need to be much more warmly dressed than you are now."

Dhikilo was so taken aback she forgot that it's not polite to remind blind people they're blind. "How do you know how warmly dressed I am?"

"Well…" said the Professor. "Are you dressed for snowy weather? Woolly hat? Fur-lined boots? Mittens?"

"No," admitted Dhikilo. She was getting that trapped-in-a-dream feeling again, and she couldn't hear the children's voices any more, either, which was a bit worrying.

"So, when do the shops close?" repeated the Professor.

"Uh…" struggled Dhikilo, too nervous to think straight.

"Half passst five," came the unearthly voice of the sphinx. "Or sssometimes sssix." A pause. "Sssupermarkets, later."

The Professor swivelled round in his chair and laid his hand on the sphinx's hair in obvious appreciation, though the creature's face remained impassive.

"Nelly does all my shopping, you see," he explained.

"I've never seen her in town," said Dhikilo.

"She stays in the shadows."

"There aren't any shadows in Tesco's."

"She sends in her little helpers. Well, not so little. The tall, silent men. You saw them at the funeral. They all come from Nelly."

"Come from Nelly?"

"She…ah…hmm, how best to explain this? I suppose you could say she makes them. Except they're only temporary. Like…ah…human-shaped balloons. Balloons without the skins. They're made of ectoplasm."

"Ectoplasm?" Dhikilo had never heard of it. It sounded like plastic but stickier and squishier.

"It's the same stuff ghosts are made of," the Professor explained, as though ghosts were as normal and everyday as grass. "Partly solid, partly not. A highly versatile substance. Or do I mean volatile?"

The sphinx drew a deep breath, as if fed up with the old man's prattle.

"Anyway, Nelly can do six of them, if she has to. Six ectoplasmic helpers. But if she makes six, they're shorter and weaker. Two is optimal. Then they can run around fetching the baked beans and the tea and the milk and so on."

Dhikilo thought of Mrs Plummer down the street, who was blind and didn't need supernatural assistance to get her shopping done, just a friendly staff member willing to leave off stacking shelves for ten minutes.

"You could shop by yourself, if you'd rather," said Dhikilo. "The people working in the shop would help you."

The Professor did that thing with his eyebrows and neck that grown-ups do when they're thinking, *That's an excellent suggestion and would certainly solve my problem except that I've already decided it is something I'm never going to do, ever.*

"It wouldn't be…ah…advisable for me to be seen in public," he said. "Now that I'm supposed to be in my grave."

"But what about before?"

"Well, to be wholly frank with you, Miss Bentley, it wasn't so advisable then, either. You see, I've been rather…what's the word? Naughty. Yes, naughty." He grinned, not looking the least bit sorry.

"What did you do?"

"Well, I probably shouldn't have applied to work at Cawber School for Girls. It was a return to employment after I'd…ah… retired from another career quite some years previously—1870, to be precise."

He scratched his beard and looked towards the fireplace, his blind eyes glittering. The sphinx had turned back into a Labrador. Dhikilo wondered which was the real Mrs Robinson and which was the thing Mrs Robinson sometimes turned into.

"I tried for many decades," the Professor went on, "to adjust to my new life of idleness. I read a great many books, went to the theatre, developed a taste for new-fangled entertainments like the cinema. Then I went blind and had to find something else to do." He stared down at his tartan slippers, as though the answer had originally revealed itself there. Mrs Robinson let out a deep doggy sigh.

"Teaching a schoolful of girls History seemed as good a way as any," he said, "to keep me out of mischief."

Dhikilo remembered the uninhabited appearance of the building in which the Professor's flat was hidden, and Mrs Robinson's attempts to frighten her away, and the creature's reference to some mysterious thing the Professor and Mrs Robinson couldn't do which needed doing.

"Are you in trouble?" Dhikilo asked.

"Oh, yes, I should think so," said the Professor, and pointed vaguely towards the outside world. "If I dare to step outside that door, I'm a dead man."

Before Dhikilo could ask another question, the Professor clapped his gnarly hands and declared, "But enough lugubrious talk! There are important things to be achieved, and an adventure to be embarked upon, and I think Nelly is quite right to have identified *you* as the person to fulfil this mission. Of course, it will mean taking some time off school, which, strictly, is against the law, but I really think an exception should be made in the circumstances, and I speak as an ex-teacher. Also, we should not deny that there is some degree of hazard. As in, you may get yourself killed. But you've always struck me as a sensible and resourceful girl, and I'm sure

you'll do your very best to stay alive." The Professor began
to search the pockets of his coat and trousers, humphing and
huffing. "And don't skimp on the boots! Proper snow boots,
with fur lining and tough soles!"

After another few seconds of searching, he pulled out a bat-
tered old wallet, from which he extracted a wad of banknotes.

"Here," he said, offering them to Dhikilo with his bony
arm outstretched. "I cannot see the denominations. Is this
enough?"

Dhikilo took the money without looking at it. She was
frightened now, and quite keen to escape, and it seemed she
would get her opportunity if she just said yes to everything,
no matter how bonkers.

"Yes," she said. "Shall I go now, Professor?"

"Yes, yes," urged the old man, standing up from his armchair. "By all means." He located Dhikilo's trembling hand
and shook it firmly. "Splendid! Until this evening, then! Or
tomorrow morning, perhaps. You might want to have one
more night's sleep in your own bed."

"Yes," said Dhikilo, feeling extremely odd. "Thank you."
And she made for the dark hallway, hoping the front door
would simply open and let her out.

"Choossse wisely," said Mrs Robinson, in a voice that tick-
led the small hairs in the nape of Dhikilo's neck.

Back to Normal

Dhikilo walked briskly back towards the familiar part of town. Walked? Well, OK, maybe she ran.

I've just escaped, she told herself, *from great danger.*

The sky was calm and the sun had come out again. Birds twittered in the trees and there was no thunderous spooky music coming out of nowhere, like you get in a movie where dangerous things are happening.

The Professor has gone mad, Dhikilo told herself. *He was already mad before but he's much madder now and he should probably be in a special home for mad people.*

She thought of the Professor's dog turning into a sphinx. That was impossible and must have been an optical trick. Malcolm and Ruth had once taken her to a museum in London called Believe It or Not! where a man welcomed you in but he wasn't real and you could see through parts of his body and when the welcome speech was over he vanished. That's what the sphinx must have been: a hologram.

Dhikilo crossed a street and turned a corner and was back in the part of Cawber she knew well. Everything looked reassuringly normal (well, she would've preferred the Pound-land shop not to be called Pounlan, but *fairly* normal) and that made her feel better. She passed the secondhand book-shop with the plastic bins full of tatty, rain-dampened old books and the books looked exactly the same as always, and that made her feel better, too. Normal was good. She should definitely have as much normal as she could get.

The most normal thing Dhikilo could think of was to go back to school for last period. She didn't know what time it was. Malcolm and Ruth had given her a phone for her birth-day but she seldom remembered it and was always leaving it uncharged and comatose in the kitchen, and anyway, it wasn't much use to someone in the bottom percentile of befriend-edness. She looked up at the sky and decided it wasn't as late as the Professor thought.

"I'm back from the funeral," said Dhikilo to the school sec-retary when she got in.

Miss Dowd, who had a sign on her desk informing visi-tors that she was Miss Ow, looked at Dhikilo as if she didn't quite recognize her. "Oh, yes?" she said, frowning. She didn't seem to recall the arrangement, even though she was the one who'd required the permission letter from Dhikilo's parents.

"Am I in time for last lesson?" asked Dhikilo.

"It's alreay starte," said Miss Dowd. "Ages ago."

"Which lesson is it?" asked Dhikilo.

Miss Dowd looked disapproving. "On't you remember your timetable?"

"I'm having a very strange day," pleaded Dhikilo.

Miss Dowd checked. "It's History," she said.

"History is important," said Dhikilo.

"It's almost over now," said Miss Dowd.

"Can I go in anyway?"

Miss Dowd peered at Dhikilo over the edge of the desk. "You're not in uniform."

"I didn't have time to go home and change," said Dhikilo. "Because I didn't want to miss any more school than I had to, Miss. Because I love school so much, Miss." She took a deep breath, hoping that Miss Dowd would be smart enough to get the message. "Especially History," she added.

Everyone stared at her when she entered the classroom. The clock said there were only eleven minutes to go before the bell would ring. The other girls must think she was insane to have bothered to return. Their fingers were twitching in anticipation of getting hold of their phones and doing all the stuff that Dhikilo didn't do.

"Miss Bentley will forgive me," said Mr Dunstable, now known as Mr Unstable, "if I on't repeat the centuries we've covere so far."

A ripple of laughter went through the room. Mr Unstable couldn't help smiling himself, probably thinking he was awfully clever, although, in Dhikilo's opinion, a genuinely clever teacher never makes children laugh at other children.

The lesson was about the ancient Egyptians. The ancient Egyptians got quite a lot of attention in the British Education System. When you were a little kid you drew pictures of pyramids, and when you were older you learned about Dynasties and various Invasions, but it was always the Egyptians and sometimes a bit of Hitler, Napoleon or the Romans. Somaliland didn't exist. One nice thing about ancient Egypt, however, was that it included the long-lost Land of Punt, which Dhikilo was convinced was modern-day Puntland, which was right next to Somaliland, which brought the subject closer to home, even if home was actually Cawber.

"Miss Bentley," said Mr Unstable in a slightly annoyed tone. "I have mae the effort to inclue you, but it appears you are not making the effort to inclue us. So, let me ask again: what were the reasons for the ecline of the Egyptian empire?" Seeing no spark of inspiration on the face of Hikilo Bentley, he surveyed the class as a whole. "Anyboy?"

No hands went up.

"Noboy?" said Mr Unstable, sounding mightily disappointed in the youth of the modern world.

When Dhikilo got home, Ruth was angry with her.

"The bath is filthy," she said. "Absolutely filthy!"

Dhikilo couldn't deny that. Ruth had left the tub untouched and, sure enough, it still looked as though a bunch of moles had had a fight in it, except that Dhikilo now noticed that those same moles had apparently rolled around on the floor as well and flicked mud onto the walls and the mirror.

"I'm sorry, Mum," said Dhikilo. Usually calling Ruth "Mum" made things all right, but not this time.

"I on't know what to o with you," sighed Ruth. "I really on't."

"I'll clean it up now, shall I?" said Dhikilo.

"No, I'll o it," said Ruth. "You've misse school toay; I'm sure you must have some homework."

So that was that. Within a few minutes, Dhikilo was in her room staring at a Science book while the clunking and sloshing noises of an angry person cleaning a bathroom carried through the house. The words on the page danced in front of Dhikilo's eyes and stubbornly refused to enter her brain. Then it was time for dinner.

"How was the funeral anyway?" asked Ruth, not angry any more, as Dhikilo sat down at the table.

"It was…weird," said Dhikilo. She wondered if she should talk to Ruth about what had happened. Discussing it with grown-ups might help the normalness come back.

"Well, I hope it in't upset you, that's all," said Malcolm.

"It's not goo to think about sa things," said Ruth.

"An this Oerfiel chap ha a jolly goo innings," said Malcolm. "Ninety-nine! A few more weeks an he woul've got a tele-gram from the Queen an been a celebrity in the local paper!"

"He's gone to a better place," said Ruth.

Dhikilo ate some of the cauliflower cheese on her plate. She could see that talking about the Professor with Ruth and Malcolm would only make things weirder.

"Can I cook tomorrow?" she asked.

"Why?" said Ruth. "On't you like the cauliflower cheese?"

"It's delicious," said Dhikilo. "Thanks, Mum. But I could cook tomorrow's dinner. To make up for the mess I made in the bathroom."

"You on't have to make up for anything, sweetie," said Ruth, smiling wearily. "Just try not to make such a mess in future."

"Anyone for puing?" said Malcolm brightly.

After dinner, Dhikilo went back up to her room and tried again to read about Science and the words refused again, and she tried to write an essay for English, but as soon as she'd written her name at the top of the page she started to worry about what Miss Forster would do to it with her nasty red pen. Then she felt unbearably tired and sleepy, even though it wasn't very late, and she got into bed, and it was no use try-ing any more to push away the memory of Mrs Robinson's sharp teeth because when you're asleep you can't control what comes to you in your dreams.

And Dhikilo dreamed of running down a dark dead-end street, pursued by a sphinx.

Because

The next day was a Saturday and all was forgiven. Malcolm made avocao toast for breakfast, and Ruth suggested that they might all go to Over later in the ay. Dhikilo didn't fancy going to Dover. She just wanted to go to the post office.

Why the post office? Because of the money that the Professor had given her. In her relief at escaping from his creepy house, she'd forgotten about the money until this morning, but once she'd extracted it from her pocket, she found that it was two hundred and eighty-five pounds.

I can't keep this, she thought. *It would be like stealing from an old blind crazy person.*

The idea of going back to the Professor's house was out of the question. She would post the money to him. She retrieved, from her schoolbag, the not-too-crumpled blank envelope which had contained her funeral-permission letter. She wrote the Professor's name and address on the front. She got a fresh sheet of paper and started to write:

Dear Professor,
I am returning your £285, because

but then remembered he was blind and wouldn't be able to read it. Also, she didn't know what should come after "*because*." She put the banknotes into the envelope and sealed it up tight. It was quite a fat packet and would need a special stamp.

"I'm just going out for a little walk," she told Malcolm and Ruth.

When you have finished reading this book, you will know how outrageously untrue this statement of Dhikilo's was, but at the time, she meant it.

On the way to the post office, a couple of things happened which were arguably normal but actually, in the circumstances, not normal at all.

Firstly, a man was handing out leaflets about an election. "We must think about where we're going!" he called out to uninterested passers-by. "I mean, where we're *really* going! There's still time to change irection an get on the right track! But we may never get another chance like this!"

Secondly, two ladies were handing out booklets about their religion. They weren't from Somaliland but they were dark-skinned and that made them a rarity in Cawber. The booklets said: THE WORL TO COME—ARE YOU REAY?

Both the ladies smiled at Dhikilo, with big white happy smiles. Dhikilo wondered if her mother's smile had been like that.

The nearer Dhikilo got to the post office, the more doubts she had about the envelope with the money. The Professor's name was full of Ds—did that mean that the post office would refuse to deliver it unless she crossed them all out? And she hadn't put a postcode on the address—Molly's mum hadn't told her that part. And the envelope felt squashy and crinkly to the touch, very much like a wodge of banknotes inside a thin sleeve of paper, so maybe someone in the post office would realize it was money and tell her it was against the rules to send it?

As she walked past the supermarket, two tall old men dressed in identical clothes were going in. She only glimpsed them for a second and maybe they weren't dressed identically at all and maybe if she'd seen their faces she would've found that they actually looked nothing like each other, but she couldn't help wondering if they were a couple of Mrs Robinson's silent ectoplasmic "helpers."

Although, of course, that was all nonsense, just a mad story told to her by the Professor.

FOR THE BEST MUM IN THE UNIVERSE, proclaimed a poster in a gift shop.

She would undoubtedly have wanted to know you, the Professor had said, on that day when she was crying. He was not an evil person and it was no use trying to convince herself that he was. He was a good person, a kind person, and she'd missed him. She was missing him now.

One of the last shops before the post office was a charity shop whose profits went to a sanctuary in Dover for lost and abandoned cats. Its window display was normally full of cardigans and dresses that only a charity-shop dummy would wear, or very popular books that weren't popular any more, or toys that children used to play with years ago.

Today, there was something different in the window. A dummy exactly Dhikilo's size, of dark brown plastic or whatever shop mannequins are made of, wearing the sort of clothes that a thirteen-year-old girl in an extremely cold place might wear, all in white and pale blue. Boots with thick soles and fur inside. Trousers that looked as though they would stay dry if you splashed them with a bucket of water. Gloves with strokeable downy material on the outside and a rough rubbery texture on the palms, for grip. A shiny fleecy jacket with a white star on each arm, just underneath the shoulder. A hat that was halfway to being a helmet, with a generous amount of fur inside it. All of it looking good as new.

Price labels hung off the various parts of the outfit and even though Dhikilo was not as good at mental arithmetic as Mariette, she could tell that the whole lot would cost a great deal less than what she had in the envelope.

YES, WE KNOW IT'S SPRING, said the handwritten sign underneath the display. BUT THIS IS ENGLAN, SO IT WILL BE WINTER IN A JIFFY!

Dhikilo hesitated. A large family of Italian tourists needed to get past her and she stepped out of the way, a little closer to the shop—right in front of the door. There was a small, computer-printed poster taped to the door urging people to adopt a particular cat, a young female, from the sanctuary. *She is a bit wilful and incline to go walkabout*, the text explained, *but she will surely settle in the right home.*

Dhikilo stood reading and re-reading the message until an impatient voice behind her said, "Well? Are you going in or not?"

THE LAND OF LIMINUS

alf an hour later, Dhikilo put down her two bulging parcels and knocked on the door of 58 Gas Hill Gardens. The windows were shrouded with curtains just as before. The front garden was no less dead and still smelled of cat pee.

This time, there was no delay before the door swung open.

"Come in, Miss Bentley!" shouted the Professor from beyond the carpeted corridor. Dhikilo let herself in and hurried to the sitting room, almost tripping in the dark as she shuffled along with her heavy bags.

The Professor's parlour was not quite as gloomy as it had been yesterday because the fireplace was ablaze. The same junk mail that had been delivered to the Bentleys' house this morning—leaflets advertising garden tools, pizzas, sofas and local politicians—had also been delivered here, and was proving very useful as fire-lighters. Mrs Robinson picked up another one—*What's On in Cawber*—with her teeth, padded over to the fire and tossed it in with a flick of her jaw. It went *phizz* and burst into cheerful orange flame.

The Professor looked a bit less tired and dishevelled than he'd looked the day before. His hair and beard were combed and he was wearing proper shoes instead of the tartan slippers.

"Did you bring the snow clothes?" he immediately enquired.

"Yes," said Dhikilo.

"Most excellent girl you are."

"There's lots of change," said Dhikilo.

"Change?" echoed the Professor, puzzled, as she rummaged in her pockets.

"You gave me more than I needed," said Dhikilo, walking up to his chair and tapping him on the coat-sleeve so that he would know she wanted to put something in his hand. He still seemed puzzled as his fingers wrapped around the banknotes that Dhikilo placed on his palm.

"Ah!" he said. "*That* sort of change!" And, to Dhikilo's alarm, he crumpled the money in his fist and tossed it towards the fireplace. His aim was quite good, and at least one twenty-pound note landed in the flames.

"Why did you do that?" said Dhikilo.

"Because money is not what we need in our present circumstances. Not what we need at all."

Sensing that Dhikilo wasn't satisfied with this answer, he sighed and added, "When I was young—even younger than you—I was poor and had to work in a factory. Horrible place! I dreamed of a windfall of money that might rescue me from misery. My dream came true. I got the windfall. I was a very rich man. Still am. But now the whole world is in trouble, and my riches can't rescue it." He paused. "However… I have a feeling *you* can."

"Is this about the D?" said Dhikilo.

"Yes," said the Professor. "It's about the D."

"Do you know why it's disappeared?"

"A letter doesn't just disappear from the alphabet by itself," said the Professor. "The D was stolen. It still is being stolen! Each day, more Ds are spirited away from where they belong. Thousands of them; hundreds of thousands; maybe millions of Ds from all over the world."

"Where are they going?"

"That's what I'm hoping you'll find out."

The fire was putting out a lot of warmth and Dhikilo wished someone would open a window to let some cool air in. The two bags full of winter clothes seemed a very silly idea at the moment.

"Am I…am I going to Switzerland?" she asked.

The Professor frowned in puzzlement. "Switzerland? Why Switzerland?"

"I heard about it in Geography," she said. "It has snow all year round. And huge mountains called Alps."

"So it has, so it has!" agreed the Professor with ardent enthusiasm. "I lived there for a while in the 1840s. Beautiful country. Sublime! You must visit it one day, if you survive this mission! But no, the place you're going is much nearer to hand, and also much, much further away."

Before Dhikilo could protest that she didn't understand, he lurched up from his seat.

"Let me show you!" he said, and stepped confidently across the room, immediately colliding with a lamp and knocking it over. The light bulb went *ping* and the lampshade broke loose and rolled across the carpet.

"Ach, blindness," muttered the Professor, annoyed. "I wouldn't recommend it. Endlessly irritating. Nelly?"

Mrs Robinson padded to his side. Just having the dog there, even without a leash, gave the old man the poise he needed to make his way safely across the room.

"Follow on, follow on," he said, and Dhikilo followed.

They passed through a library filled with yet more books,

and then went up a long wooden staircase to the floor above. It was evident that the Professor owned the entire building and that the impression from the street of a house containing a number of flats was illusory: all of these rooms were part of the Professor's honeycomb-like home. Some of the rooms were extremely shabby and shrouded in cobwebs and smelled damp; rampant mildew added extra texture to the wallpaper. One of the rooms they passed through on the way to yet another staircase was a dressing room full of wooden coatstands displaying very old-fashioned gentlemen's overcoats which had been eaten almost to rags by moths. Other rooms seemed never to have been used at all, and were carpeted in layers of dust that billowed up when you walked across them.

"It's right at the top, I'm afraid," said the Professor, panting with exertion as they embarked on another flight of stairs. A startled mouse dashed between Dhikilo's feet, and even though she wasn't frightened of mice, she yelped with surprise.

"Steady on," said the Professor. "Almost there."

The top room of the building was empty apart from a metal stepladder, some dried-out paintbrushes and a telephone book dated 1983. Oh, and something that looked like a saddlebag, with lots of straps and pouches, slumped in one corner. Through the windows, there were lovely views of Cawber, with the harbour clearly visible despite the cobwebs, and a dramatic vista of rooftops. Mrs Robinson sneezed.

"All my earnest and devoted research," mused the Professor, "looking for a portal between this world and the next. And all the while it was right here, under my nose."

He indicated a door, intricately patterned and deep red. It had no handle and, on closer inspection, Dhikilo saw that it was not a real door but a giant rectangle of cardboard bound in cloth: the front cover of a hardback book, taller than a man. The Professor reached forward, found the right edge with his gnarled fingers and swung it open.

A gush of icy wind blew into the room, as well as a few snowflakes. Light flooded in, but not the light of Cawber: an eerie polar light, cast by a pale chilly sun, reflected off a white landscape with no buildings in it at all, just hills and forests covered in snow.

"And there you have it!" exclaimed the Professor in triumph. "The Land of Liminus!"

A Particularly
Short Chapter

(for a particularly swift decision)

Dhikilo gazed through the doorway at the weather in the world beyond. It had been snowing, and might snow again, but was clear just now. The sun was pale and gave very little warmth—unlike the *other* sun, our sun, visible through the attic window of 58 Gas Hill Garens, which was shining goldenly on the rooftops of Cawber. If the rules of Science applied today, what *should* have been behind this red door was some dusty junk. Instead, three storeys up from the street below, there was the Land of Liminus, its snow-covered earth stretching to a horizon far above the horizon of Cawber. What would Mr Dawkins have to say about that!

The Professor was strapping the saddlebag to Mrs Robinson's back. He seemed to be very pleased with how things were moving ahead now, and was even singing to himself, a sort of tuneless *pom-pi-di-pom-pom*. It suddenly occurred to Dhikilo that maybe there wasn't going to be any more explanation. She'd assumed the Professor would tell her all about where she was going and what she was likely to find there and what to do about it. His *pom-pi-di-pom-pom*-ing as he fastened the straps of Mrs Robinson's saddlebag made her doubt he had any such intention.

"Are we going already?" she said.

"Certainly you're going," said the Professor. "No time like the present."

"But I haven't got my winter clothes on yet."

"Crack on, then: there's a lot of cold air coming through." And he clasped his arms with his hands, miming a shiver.

"My bags are still downstairs."

The Professor looked bemused, as if he couldn't imagine why Dhikilo would be so impractical as to oblige herself to climb all those stairs twice. "Well, you'd better fetch them, then."

Dhikilo hurried downstairs, retracing her steps through the dusty, spooky rooms. When she got to the bottom and back into the sitting room, her bags were right where she'd left them. She'd returned the money and the front door was right near by. This was her last opportunity to run away, back to safety, back to the world she knew—although it didn't seem very safe lately, and it was no longer the world she'd known. She thought about it. But only for a moment or two.

An adventure was waiting for her.

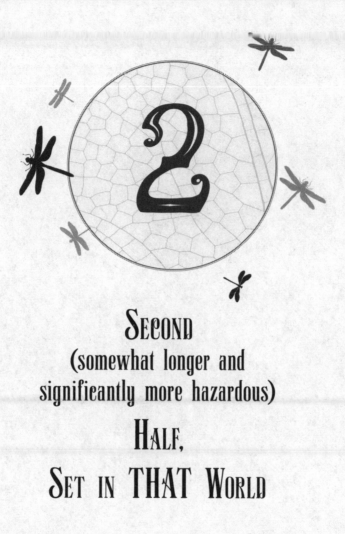

SECOND
(somewhat longer and
significantly more hazardous)

HALF,

SET IN THAT WORLD

What the Shining Objects Were

As soon as Dhikilo and Mrs Robinson stepped through the portal into the other world, England was reduced to a door-sized rectangle, floating in mid-air, its bottom edge suspended a few inches above the snowy ground. It was like a large picture frame hung on the empty space where a wall had once stood, or where a wall might one day be built.

Dhikilo could see the Professor standing near the threshold of the attic room they'd just left, and she could glimpse behind him the empty bags which had contained the snow gear she was now wearing, but it was as though these things were projected onto a thin billboard that might be blown over by a breeze at any moment. The world of Cawber-on-Sands was insubstantial, no longer believable. The Land of Liminus was vast and cold and solid underfoot and endlessly airy overhead. It was the real, true universe, and ours was an illusion.

"Wait!" said Dhikilo, as the Professor waved goodbye and reached forward to shut the door.

"What for?" called the old man.

"How will I know which way to go?"

"Stick with Nelly! She'll steer you right!" He nodded reassuringly, or perhaps his head was merely shaking with cold; it was hard to tell.

Dhikilo opened her mouth to ask another question, but the Professor was in a hurry to get back to the warmth downstairs. "Well, goodbye for now!" he sang out. "Strive to achieve the aim without death or serious injury!" And with that, he closed the door.

For a few seconds, the door remained a door. Then it shimmered and changed into a bare tree. All trace of England was gone and it was too late to tell Ruth and Malcolm that she wouldn't be home for lunch.

They stood for a while, adjusting to the silence and the desolation. The sudden total disappearance of Cawber—of England, of the world she knew—made Dhikilo feel uneasy. It made her wonder if it would still be there when she wanted to get back.

Mrs Robinson made a doggy noise, almost a growl. (Evidently she could only speak when she was a sphinx.) Dhikilo looked at her face, and then looked up into the sky where Mrs Robinson was pointing with her snout.

About half a dozen large dragonflies—or exotic insects that resembled dragonflies—were gliding overhead. Not far overhead, but well out of reach. Dragonflies in snowy weather? Impossible, surely. Where had they come from? Why weren't they hibernating in a pond? And the way they moved was unusual, too: they weren't hovering and helicoptering, the way dragonflies usually do; they were flying in a resolutely straight line, in formation, like migrating birds. That was peculiar.

And what was more peculiar still was that each dragonfly was carrying in its feet a luminous object, an object as big as its own body, an object almost too bright to stare at with the naked eye.

Mrs Robinson barked a warning, or maybe it was the canine equivalent of a shout of anger. The dragonflies took no notice, didn't waver an inch in their progress. They were headed for the horizon, each clinging to its luminous prize.

Just before they dwindled out of sight, Dhikilo realized what the shining objects were. They were Ds.

DREADLOCKS, A DOLPHIN, A PIECE OF DRIFTWOOD

As Dhikilo and Mrs Robinson stood and stared, more and more dragonflies glided by. Sometimes the Ds they carried were shaped "D" and sometimes "d." Sometimes the design was simple and sometimes it was ornate. Jewels of different kinds. But all the same letter, plucked from whatever words no longer contained them.

One careless insect lost its grip and the shining prize fell to the ground. Dhikilo rushed over to where it had landed. It was already dissolving into the snow, but it still glowed. Dhikilo knelt down, pulled off one of her gloves and touched the disintegrating D with her bare fingertips. Immediately, she had a vivid mental picture—like a film projected straight into her brain—of a camel. A camel with one hump. A dromedary.

Then the D shrivelled into nothing and the vision of the dromedary faded from her imagination.

Dhikilo stood up and put her glove back on. All around

her, as far as she could see, was snowed-under scrubland, with a few bare trees shivering in the wind.

Mrs Robinson uttered a sound that wasn't quite a bark: "*Uff.*" She was keen to get moving.

They followed the flight path of the dragonflies. There seemed to be an unlimited supply of them. Five or six minutes might pass when there weren't any flying overhead, but then some more would come along, and sometimes there were dozens at once, a cloud of insects carrying their brilliant trophies. It was obvious that Ds were being stolen in huge numbers. But by whom? Dhikilo had a hunch that the dragonflies were merely providing the transport; insects had teensy-weensy brains and she didn't think they were capable of devising a plot to deprive the English language of one of its letters. A being that was bigger and smarter and more evil must be behind this.

They walked for a long time, maybe an hour, then stopped to have something to eat and drink. Mrs Robinson's saddle-bag was generously stocked with treats, although it was obvious that the Professor had a sweet tooth. There were lots of chocolate bars, and cereal bars, and those so-called "healthy" bars that look like birdseed glued together with baked sugar. There was plenty of water, bottled in thermal containers so that it didn't freeze. On the savoury front, there were packets of salted peanuts and packets of cashews and some weird cheap cheese wrapped in tubes of transparent plastic. And there were six cans of dog food.

Dhikilo wondered if this meant that the Professor expected their mission to be over quite quickly, or if these supplies were intended for emergencies only. In all the time they'd been walking, they hadn't come across any houses or buildings, let alone any shops or restaurants. The Land of Liminus was not a cheerful or welcoming place. It had the sad, impressive beauty that vast desolate landscapes have, but it would definitely have been improved by a friendly log cabin with smoke coming out of the chimney and a sign outside saying, DELICIOUS HOT FOOD. OPEN FOR LUNCH AND DINNER.

Mrs Robinson refused the offer of anything to eat from the saddlebag, and drank only a few mouthfuls of water straight from the flask. It made Dhikilo feel quite self-indulgent eating an entire cereal bar. Maybe Mrs Robinson anticipated travelling for days and days.

"My mum and dad will be worried about me," said Dhikilo as they resumed walking towards the horizon.

"*Ruff*," said Mrs Robinson.

"I wish there was some way of letting them know I'm all right," said Dhikilo.

"*Arf?*" said Mrs Robinson, and looked up at Dhikilo with a frown, as if expressing serious doubt about the notion that they were all right.

They carried on. It's not so easy to walk on snow, especially for a girl who's used to walking on concrete footpaths or on grass. It was a little bit like walking on the shingle beach at Cawber-on-Sands, except of course without the warm sun and the cawing seagulls and the rushing waves and the little pink English children staring at her in wonder. Dhikilo couldn't remember ever having to trudge through snow in Cawber. Council workers promptly swept it away when it fell on pathways where people needed to walk or drive. Liminus didn't look like the sort of place that would have council workers.

Thinking about these things instead of concentrating on her next step made her almost fall over. Her boot had sunk shin-deep into a marshy hole. She needed to focus hard just to keep her feet tramping and her breath coming out in regular white puffs. The exercise kept her toasty warm in her snug winter clothes, but the freezing air stung her nostrils where she breathed it in. The mercilessness of that coldness worried her. As if it was waiting for its chance to do her harm. She and Mrs Robinson were two small mammals in a large empty land-scape and they had no idea where they were going. They were following dragonflies. Following dragonflies didn't qualify as a clever or well-thought-out plan of action.

Every now and then, a D fell from the sky and shrivelled into nothingness in the snow. The first few times, Dhikilo ran over to investigate, touching the D while it was still able to give her a vision of the thing it had been stolen from—dreadlocks, a dolphin, a piece of driftwood. But each time she took her glove off and put her fingers into the snow, it took a little longer for her hand to warm up again afterwards. She should conserve her energy and (as the Professor might say) crack on.

THE MAGWITCHES

As the afternoon wore on, Dhikilo started to imagine she could hear a sound—a sound different from her own footsteps and her own heavy breathing. At first, she thought it must be Mrs Robinson's footsteps, but the dog moved quietly at a steady pace, whereas the sound seemed to be getting gradually louder. She didn't want to look around, because in her heavy winter clothes looking around would require her to stand still and turn her whole body. So she ignored the sound as long as she could. But eventually it couldn't be mistaken; there *was* a noise, a sort of muffled stomping that their own feet couldn't account for.

Dhikilo stopped and turned around. Four dark figures were pursuing them. Pursuing? Maybe just walking in the same direction. Dhikilo waited until they got close enough to be properly looked at.

The four figures were, in fact, four witches.

How did she know they were witches? Because they looked exactly like the witches she'd seen in storybooks and films. Beak-like noses with warts on. Long dirty straggly hair the

colour of the stuff that comes out of the inside of a vacuum
cleaner. Shabby browny-grey robes. They didn't have those
black pointy hats that Dhikilo had always thought would
surely blow off as soon as you flew into the air on a broom-
stick; they had hoods, which was much more practical.

Although…the robes were not so practical for snowy
weather, and none of the women had proper boots on, only
odd raggedy-looking footwear that could've been scraps of
other garments wrapped tight and stitched together. All four
of the women were filthy, as if they'd been smothered in mud,
brushed off a bit and pulled through a hedge not just backwards but also frontwards. And when they started to move
towards Dhikilo and Mrs Robinson, it became evident that
there were chains around their ankles, big iron chains that
dragged through the snow like dead pythons.

"We mean you no harm," said the first witch.

"No harm whatsoever," reassured the second witch.

"A more harmless bunch of gentlewomen you'll never
meet," said the third witch. "Correct me if I'm wrong."

"Those are very warm-looking clothes you've got on," said
the fourth witch.

"But not as warm as our welcome to you, sartorially for-
tunate stranger!" the foremost witch hastened to add.

"I'm Dhikilo," said Dhikilo, wondering if it mattered that
she didn't know what "sartorially" meant.

"We are the Magwitches," said the foremost witch, sounding extremely proud to be able to make this claim. Her fellow witches nodded in agreement.

"Our joy is to welcome all who venture off the path of
safety," the second witch said.

"We strive to protect strangers from the Great Gamp," the
third witch said.

"Because the Great Gamp is not as welcoming as we are.
No, he most certainly is not!" said the fourth witch, casting

a glance over her shoulder, as if worried that some monstrous creature might have snuck into view.

"But let us talk no more of the Great Gamp!" declared the foremost witch. "Let us allow nothing to spoil the pleasure of our meeting with you! Welcome, noble interloper with the covetable clothing!"

"Covetable? My sister meant 'comfortable,' of course."

"Of course. Blessings be upon us all, to have met in peace in such a perilous spot."

"…potentially perilous."

"Potentially, yes."

All four of the witches stood still for a moment, breathing hard from the exertion of their energetic greetings. A bright droplet of snot fell from the nose of witch number three. Gently, fresh snowflakes started spiralling down from the sky.

"It's nice to meet you," said Dhikilo. "But it's cold and we should really keep moving."

"To which we all agree, I'm sure!"

"And we will spare no effort to make it possible for you to keep moving!"

"Although the Great Gamp prefers foreign guests not to move at all. To stop moving permanently, if you follow what I mean."

"Regrettably true."

"He rips little girls to pieces, given half a chance."

"Not that we give him half a chance. We restrain him. It causes us great sorrow to see an innocent girl lying in bits on the snow."

"One leg here, the other leg way over there. Heartbreaking."

Dhikilo looked around the landscape. It was possible to see really far in all directions. She couldn't spot any creatures other than the Magwitches.

"I don't see anyone," she said.

"He is an excellent self-concealer," said the foremost witch. "He seems to spring out of nowhere."

"That's why he's so awfully proficient at tearing unsuspecting travellers like yourself limb from limb."

"If we let him. Which, of course, we try our utmost to prevent."

"For very little payment, I might say, taking into account the enormous trouble we must go to," said the foremost witch.

The other three witches heaved a collective sigh of relief to hear the conversation get to the point at last.

"Fifty silver coins," said the head witch, extending one grimy hand and wiggling her taloned fingers.

"I don't have any silver coins," said Dhikilo.

"We'll accept forty," said the head witch with barely a pause for thought.

"That's only ten for each Magwitch," said the second witch. "A bargain, I'm sure you'll agree, to keep all your limbs neatly in place."

The snow was falling more thickly, making the sky go dim and grey, and the eight eyes of the witches glowed yellow as if lit from within. It was slightly scary, maybe even moderately scary, but at the same time, Dhikilo couldn't help remembering a sentence from the school pamphlet about bullying: *They may, for example, try to steal your lunch money.* These fearsome hags were really just a bunch of schoolgirls gone bad.

"I don't have any silver coins at all," said Dhikilo, loudly and clearly.

There was a pause.

"Well, that's a shame," said one of the Magwitches. She didn't look as if she thought it was a shame: she was smiling.

"An awful shame," agreed her grinning crony.

"A calamity, I might even say," said the head witch. "It seems almost inevitable that we shall be powerless to restrain the Great Gamp from wreaking his grisly violence upon you."

"Although…" said another witch, laying a long bony finger against her chin, in a pose of having just had a fresh thought, "perhaps…a last-minute compromise might yet avert that tragic fate."

"Your boots."

"Your hat."

"Your lovely warm coat."

"Your gloves."

"Those nice thick trousers."

"Even the scarf."

"All very useful to a foursome of poor chilly Magwitches."

"Remove them, unfairly snug trespasser," commanded the head witch. "Give them here." She wiggled her talons again.

Mrs Robinson heaved a deep sigh. A sigh of impatience, Dhikilo thought. And if truth be told, she was in no mood herself to spend any longer with these four annoying old ladies.

"I'm sorry," she said, "but I think I'd better keep my clothes on. I'm not used to this temperature. I think I might die."

"That is certainly your greatest risk at this moment," remarked witch number one.

"Start with the gloves," barked witch number two. "Or the Great Gamp will be upon you."

"I'd better be going now," said Dhikilo. "Thanks for the warning about the Great Gamp. If I see him, I'll… I'll be careful." And she turned around and walked away briskly. Mrs Robinson turned likewise and they walked side by side, heading for the hills.

There was a shuffling and rustling behind them as the Magwitches hurried to catch up, their chains dragging in the snow. Dhikilo hoped that they would soon be left behind but the witches shuffled faster than you'd think, and after a minute or two, their crunchy trudge and increasingly determined panting was louder than ever. Dhikilo moved faster herself, almost running (not an easy thing to do in snow!), but the heavy breathing at her back suggested that the witches were getting closer, not further away.

Finally, when it seemed that the hags might seize hold of them at any second, Mrs Robinson skidded to a halt and whirled round.

The Magwitches were right there, all four of them, red-faced and furious, their matted hair spattered with snowflakes.

Mrs Robinson's tail turned into a snake, her haunches bristled with fresh fur, her body grew larger, luxurious curly hair sprang out from her head like tentacles, and within moments she was a sphinx. She opened her mouth wide, showing the majority of her many sharp teeth.

"Vanishhhh!" she commanded.

Dhikilo wasn't sure if Mrs Robinson meant that the witches should disappear by magic, like a puff of smoke. Could Magwitches do that?

The question was unanswered, because the four bedraggled women flinched, glanced nervously at each other, took a step or two backwards and then slouched away, retracing the long, long gouges their chains had made in the snow.

THE GROWING ATTRACTION
OF LYING DOWN

Dhikilo stood watching the Magwitches get smaller and smaller.

"Maybe they're just homeless old ladies," she said, feeling rather sorry for them as they shambled along in their raggedy boots and dirty dresses.

"They are full of hate and deceitfulnesss," hissed the sphinx. "They asssissst the Gamp."

"The Gamp?" echoed Dhikilo. "Don't you think that's just a story they tried to scare us with?"

The sphinx shook her head, then gazed in the direction they were heading in. "It is not a ssstory. The Gamp is real." And she set off again.

Dhikilo hoped that now the danger was past, the sphinx might transform herself back into a nice friendly-looking dog. But it seemed Mrs Robinson was content to stay as she was.

After a few minutes, digesting what she'd just been told, Dhikilo suddenly had a thought.

"Have you been here before?"

"Yesss," said the sphinx.

"With the Professor?"

"Yesss."

"How did it go?" asked Dhikilo.

"We did not get far," said the sphinx.

"Because...?"

"The Professsor is old. And blind. And he was wearing a dresssing gown and...ssslippers."

Dhikilo laughed before she could stop herself.

The sphinx seemed embarrassed on behalf of the Professor, and the embarrassment provoked her to speak more than she'd spoken before, in defence of him.

"He was excited to dissscover the door to this place. He sssearched for ssso long and did not find it, and then sssuddenly he found it. The ssstealing of the Ds was gaining ssspeed. The Professsor thought he could ssstop it. He thought he could ssspeak to the right perssson, at the right time, ssspeak with passion and truth; make evil sssee reason." Mrs Robinson paused in her explanation. "The Professsor believesss in the power of wordsss. But sssometimes...wordsss are not enough."

She paused again. "Alssso, his feet turned blue."

They walked for a while in silence, apart from the tramping of their feet and the huffing of their breath.

"Did you find the Gamp?" asked Dhikilo.

"No. Only a few of his followersss."

"Are *we* looking for the Gamp?"

The sphinx tossed her hair irritably, or that's how it came across to Dhikilo. "We are looking for where the Ds are being taken."

Again they walked for a while in silence.

"Is it true," asked Dhikilo at last, "that the Gamp tears people into pieces?"

"No," said the sphinx. "He employsss othersss to do it."

A few more dragonflies wafted overhead. It had stopped snowing and the sky had brightened somewhat, allowing the dragonflies' wings to shine, although the most brilliant thing about them was still the stolen Ds they carried in their feet.

"If you and the Professor couldn't stop the Ds being stolen," said Dhikilo, "how do you know I can do it?"

"I do not know," said the sphinx.

"Erm…do you mean…you don't know how you know I can, or you don't know *if* I can?"

Mrs Robinson turned her head momentarily to look straight at Dhikilo. The expression in her inhuman eyes and imperious mouth suggested that they'd reached the limit of how much a human girl and a sphinx could understand each other.

"I do not know," repeated Mrs Robinson, turning her face back towards the horizon. "I only hope."

On and on they went. The wind had died down completely, the sky was clear blue and the sun was so pale it might as well have been a moon. Dhikilo began to feel very keen on lying down for a while on a comfortable bed, or indeed lying down on anything, anywhere. She was pretty sure that it wasn't a good idea to lie down in snow and go to sleep. She vaguely remembered she'd read in a magazine article that people who fall asleep in frozen landscapes without proper shelter don't wake up again.

She wondered if Mrs Robinson was getting tired, too. She didn't know what a sphinx looked like when it was tired. She did so wish that Mrs Robinson would turn back into a dog. Sure, they'd scared the witches away and they'd had a little conversation, but that was ages ago; it would be so much nicer to have Nelly the Labrador padding along beside her, and the sphinx seemed to regret her big outburst of speech and hadn't uttered a word since, so what was the point?

Maybe the point was that Mrs Robinson was a sphinx and therefore more comfortable being what she really was than pretending to be a dog.

The terrain was getting steeper now. Dhikilo estimated that they would reach its highest point by the time the sun set, and then it would be downhill—hopefully not a sheer drop off the edge of a mountain. They really would need to rest when they got there, maybe dig out a little trench in the earth that they could nestle into.

She wondered if Mrs Robinson would let her sleep against her warm body. That's if her body *was* warm, of course. Dhikilo hadn't actually touched it. Maybe it was cold as stone. But she was pretty sure it must be warm, because the snake-tail had stopped waving around and had curled up to sleep on Mrs Robinson's hindquarters, and looked comfortable there.

When rummaging in the saddlebag for food earlier, Dhikilo had noticed a torch in one of the pouches. She extracted it now, while she could still see to find it. Just to make sure, she switched it on and off, in case the Professor's blindness had made him pack a torch that didn't work. How would he know, after all? But it was OK: a beam of yellowish light shone into the gloom. Nowhere near as good as Malcolm's super-duper torch that lived in the kitchen drawer, but fairly impressive for a gadget small enough to put in your pocket.

Anyway, the sun set more slowly than Dhikilo anticipated, and by the time they reached the top of the hill, the sky was not black but still blue, a deep twilight blue like the eyeshadow that Miss Yeats was always forcing Mariette to remove.

Dhikilo and Mrs Robinson paused on the summit and looked down. In the valley below, less than ten minutes' walk away, stood a grand house.

"Ssshelter," said Mrs Robinson.

The Bleak House

The house was so big and stately it was almost a castle. It didn't have pointy turrets on top, but the right side of it was taller than the left and looked as though it might sprout a turret given half a chance. Its stonework was the colour of gingerbread, and the window-frames were painted white. It reminded Dhikilo of the fancy seaside mansions in Cawber which had been owned by very rich families a hundred years ago and were now expensive hotels for tourists.

There were no lights on inside, which made the house appear rather bleak in the deepening gloom, but the building was in good condition (certainly less shabby than the Professor's place in Gas Hill Garens) and also it wasn't covered with snow, which proved it must've been warm only recently. Maybe the owners had just gone to bed early.

Walking towards the house, Dhikilo and Mrs Robinson passed through a garden, a spooky old-fashioned one with a stone fountain and some statues. Unlike the house, the garden seemed to have been neglected for ages. The fountain had no water in it, only some grey snow that was stained with rust.

In the middle of the fountain stood a statue of a horse with icicles hanging off its mouth.

"Do you think this is a good idea?" Dhikilo asked Mrs Robinson.

"Ssshelter," said Mrs Robinson.

They walked up to the mansion's cast-iron gate, which was black between two white pillars. It swung open with a creak. The front door's doorbell was so high off the ground that Dhikilo had to stand on tiptoe to press it. *Bing bong*, it responded.

Dhikilo and Mrs Robinson waited for a couple of minutes, but nobody came and the windows stayed dark. Dhikilo was about to stretch up and do another *Bing bong* when she noticed a small blue plaque with white writing on it.

Dhikilo tried the doorknob and the door opened at once. The hallway was dark, so she had to use her torch to see where to put her feet as she stepped inside. The small beam of light picked out glimpses of ornate wallpaper, dark wooden furniture and carpeted stairs. Also, there was another blue plaque that said: If no light, please pull string. Thank you, The Management. Dhikilo shone her torch above the plaque and found a cord dangling from the ceiling. She pulled it and lots of lights came on: not just in the corridor but further into the house and up the stairs.

If no one at reception, said another blue plaque on the deserted cubicle marked RECEPTION, **please select a room key & make your way upstairs. Thank you, The Management.**

Under the plaque hung many old-fashioned keys on brass hooks. Dhikilo selected one, labelled "The Marshalsea Room." As soon as she had it in her hand, she almost fainted with exhaustion. She'd been walking all day, and now that she'd stopped moving she felt as if she couldn't take another step.

With Mrs Robinson at her side, she ascended the staircase to the first floor, and found that each of the doors in the corridor was clearly named and numbered. The Marshalsea Room was Number 8 and the key fitted its lock as smoothly as could be.

If no light, please pull string. Thank you, The Management, said the blue plaque just inside the door.

The room was very big and very splendid. It had a giant chandelier hanging off the ceiling and loads of ancient wooden furniture polished so thoroughly it shone like syrup. The bed was almost as big as her entire bedroom at home, and dressed up with frilly coverlets and floral-patterned pillows. A handsome table was decorated with a bottle of wine, two sparkling clean glasses and two deluxe-looking chocolate bars. And a note that said: **A member of staff will be with you shortly. Or, if the hour is late, tomorrow morning. Breakfast is from 7am to 9:30am, in the Clink Room. Enjoy your stay! The Management.**

Dhikilo unwrapped one of the chocolate bars and took a bite. It had fragments of real ginger in it and was delicious. She was about to unwrap the other bar for Mrs Robinson, but the look in Mrs Robinson's eyes made her realize that sphinxes don't eat chocolate.

"Would you like some food?" said Dhikilo.

The sphinx nodded once.

Dhikilo lifted the saddlebag off Mrs Robinson's back and rummaged around in it, extracting a tin from one of the pockets. It was ordinary supermarket dog food. She wondered if Mrs Robinson would turn into a dog to eat it. She hoped she would.

There was a tin-opener and a spoon, but the Professor had forgotten to pack a bowl. On one of the tables, Dhikilo found a fancy ceramic bowl filled with dried flower petals; she carefully tipped the petals onto the table and put the bowl on the floor.

"I don't know how much to put in," she said, as she began to spoon out the meaty gunk. "You'll have to tell me when to stop."

The sphinx sat silent until the can was empty. She didn't turn into a dog. Instead, she dipped her paw into the food, squished it around a bit and lifted it to her mouth. Daintily, so that none of the gunk got onto her face, she extended a long pink tongue and started to lick between her claws.

Dhikilo ate an apple. She wished there was some hot food. She was in the mood for cooking. She had a picture in her mind of what she would do: the chopped onions and chickpeas frying in the pan, the chicken sliced into cubes, the lovely fresh green coriander lying ready, the little glass jars of cumin and turmeric…

There was another squishing sound as Mrs Robinson scooped up more dog food. Outside the windows, night had fallen and heavy snow was swirling through the darkness.

"Sssleep," said Mrs Robinson.

Dhikilo lay on top of the bed, without even pulling back the duvet. She didn't feel it was right to make herself fully at home in a hotel room she hadn't paid for, and anyway, she was too tired to get undressed. She simply removed her hat, kicked off her boots, crawled onto the luxurious surface and was asleep within ten seconds of laying her head on the pillow.

The Management

In the morning, bright sunlight beamed through the windows. The house was perfectly quiet, apart from the rhythmic breathing of Mrs Robinson, who'd made herself comfortable on the floor, resting her beautiful human cheek on her furry forepaws. A wisp of her long curly hair fluttered up and down with each breath.

Dhikilo was sweaty from sleeping in her clothes. She would definitely have a bath after breakfast, which was served between seven and nine-thirty a.m., wasn't it? She wandered around the room looking for a clock. There was a handsome antique one in a carved oak cabinet. Its steel hands pointed to twelve o'clock. Dhikilo stared at it for a while and it didn't budge, nor did it tick. It was obviously dead.

She gazed through one of the windows at the landscape. The light was morning-ish. She could see the statue of the horse in the fountain. The icicles hanging off its head twinkled in the sun.

"Barsss," said the sphinx, who'd woken up.

Dhikilo was confused for a moment, thinking Mrs Robinson wanted to eat one of the cereal bars in their supplies. Or maybe she meant that breakfast might be served in a bar downstairs. Then Dhikilo noticed that there were iron bars on the window. She hadn't noticed them last night.

Another thing she hadn't noticed was a little blue plaque next to the window. Its white writing said: **We sincerely regret the necessity of bars. They prevent trespassers stealing or spoiling the beautiful features of this house, which we are sure you are enjoying ever so much. Thank you, The Management.**

Dhikilo pulled on her boots. She estimated that it was probably about nine o'clock and that if they hurried downstairs they would still get some breakfast. Even if they were a bit late, they might be given toast and milk or something. The Management sounded very eager to please.

Dhikilo opened the door, expecting to see the corridor outside. To her puzzlement, she saw another bedroom, just as big as theirs, but with different-patterned wallpaper and different furniture and an untouched bed. She blinked and rubbed her eyes. She'd been exhausted last night and must've misremembered which door they'd entered through. She walked to the opposite end of their bedroom where there was a second door, and opened that. No corridor was revealed there, either. Just another bedroom, different from the others. A piano with a silver candelabrum on it stood near the window, and instead of a double bed there were two single ones.

Dhikilo's stomach felt queasy, from hunger and also from a sort of weird not-rightness. Cautiously, she stepped into the new bedroom. Mrs Robinson padded behind her.

A plaque above the piano said: **We regretfully request that guests refrain from playing the piano. It is antique & fragile. Thank you, The Management.**

On impulse, Dhikilo lifted the lid of the keyboard. Inside the lid was another, very small plaque, which said: **Failure to** take proper notice of notices may result in penalties or other consequences. Thank you, The Management.

At the far end of the room was another door. Dhikilo and Mrs Robinson passed through it, and found themselves in yet another fancy chamber, not a bedroom this time but some sort of dining room, with numerous round tables shrouded with white tablecloths and folded napkins. A large metal trolley stood ready on the patterned wooden flooring. There was no food anywhere to be seen.

A blue plaque said: Throughout the winter months, breakfast is by prior arrangement only. Please apply in writing, stating any allergies. Thank you, The Management.

Dhikilo and Mrs Robinson hurried to the next door, which led into a kitchen. The highest standards of hygiene clearly applied here, and every surface was sparkling clean, even the hobs and knobs on the cooker. The cupboards contained a few essential cooking ingredients like flour, bicarbonate of soda, salt, pepper and vinegar. But certainly nothing that was in any danger of going bad if left for a long time. Indeed, nothing edible. Even the bin was empty and smelled of nothing.

A blue plaque said:

Please note that for health
& safety reasons, guests are
NOT to enter the kitchen.
We will punish infractions severely.
This means YOU.
Thank you, The Management.

"Let's go back," said Dhikilo. She and Mrs Robinson retraced their steps out of the kitchen, re-entering the dining room. Except it wasn't the dining room any more, it was a chamber with many shelves crammed with bed-linen, towels, pillows and spare duvets. The blue plaque said: If you are not warm enough, please contact a member of staff rather than filching supplies from in here. What is WRONG with you people? You're not in your own uncouth primitive country now. Thank you, The Management.

The next room, to Dhikilo's relief, was a bedroom. But, on closer inspection, it was not any of the bedrooms they'd been in so far. Mrs Robinson ran to the window and leapt up, placing her paws on the ledge. She looked out and hissed. Dhikilo stood next to her. The view outside was exactly the same as the one they'd seen from the bedroom they'd spent the night in: the fountain, the stone horse with its beard of icicles. On the door leading to the next room hung a blue plaque that said: Staying in this house is a privilege, not a right. Non-payment is an abuse of our hospitality & we will not tolerate such abuse. Please pay ALL bills NOW. Thank you, The Management.

The next room was yet another bedroom, different again from all the others. The décor had a bird theme: that is, there were bird designs on the duvet, and paintings of ducks on the walls, and little gold robins embossed on the wallpaper, and a woven wicker waste-paper basket in the shape of a swan.

Mrs Robinson ran to the window, jumped up again and hissed. Then she leapt onto the bed and lunged at the wall behind it, knocking a mirror off its hook. The mirror fell behind the bedhead with an ugly crash, while the sphinx tore at the walls with her claws. Scraps and curls of the wallpaper flew into the air, followed by fragments of plaster. For about a minute, the sphinx flailed in a frenzy, before finally falling back onto the mattress, panting. The wall had been gouged deep, revealing solid stone behind the plasterwork.

Then, just as Dhikilo was about to look away, she noticed the edges of the torn wallpaper twitching and trembling. Fresh wallpaper was starting to grow, repairing the damage.

A blue plaque under one of the paintings of ducks said: The Fleet Room is among the most popular with our guests. Many famous personages over the centuries have gone insane here. Prints of the paintings, suitable for framing, can be bought at the gift shop on your way out. Thank you, The Management.

Mrs Robinson was still breathing heavily, licking her lips. She had made herself terribly thirsty with her attack on the wall. Dhikilo looked around the room. To her relief, there was a washbasin in one corner and two clean glasses on a shelf near by. She rushed over and turned the tap on. No water came out: not a drop. A blue plaque said: Please note that taps are for ornamental purposes only. Contact staff for refreshment, or why not try our prize-winning restaurant? Thank you, The Management.

Dhikilo sat down on the edge of the bed. It seemed quite obvious that she and Mrs Robinson would never get out of this house. They could choose to sit still or they could choose to walk from room to room but they would never get anywhere and eventually they would die of thirst and hunger.

What did the house do with the dead bodies of guests? Maybe it ate them somehow? Maybe there was a basement slowly filling up with swallowed people. Or maybe the dead guests just turned to dust and got vacuumed up once every hundred years or so by The Management. Dhikilo felt like running around in a panic and she felt like crying and she felt like lying down on the bed next to Mrs Robinson and just trying to sleep until it was all over.

Then she had an idea.

"Mrs Robinson?" she said. "I have an idea. This is quite a big house. But it can't have as many rooms as we think it does. It just can't. And the way the rooms change: that's impossible."

The sphinx blinked slowly but said nothing. Perhaps, as a creature who could change shape at will, she saw nothing particularly impossible about bedrooms that refused to stay as they were.

"So…" continued Dhikilo, "when we keep thinking that these doors don't lead anywhere, we must be just imagining it. So, we have to find a way to stop imagining it."

The sphinx thought about this for a moment. "We sssee what we sssee," she said.

"Then we shouldn't see," said Dhikilo. "Let's both close our eyes, keep them shut tight and try to find our way downstairs. Can you…erm… I hope this isn't a rude question, but…can you turn into a dog? Maybe as a dog you could smell when we get closer to the outside?"

The sphinx stared at Dhikilo. Her violet eyes glowed and her lips pouted sulkily. Her brow grew wrinkled and knotted; she seemed to be absolutely furious. Then her brow darkened and grew even more wrinkled, and the human face collapsed and bulged and grew brown hairs and suddenly it was the head of a Labrador called Nelly.

Without another word, Dhikilo and the Professor's dog moved forward with their eyes closed. Dhikilo kept one hand at her side so that she could feel for Mrs Robinson's hairy flank and know she was still there; her other hand she stretched ahead of her, waving it around blindly. They made a not-so-good start as Dhikilo almost fell over a chair, but once they reached a wall, things improved. She fumbled for the doorknob and passed into whatever lay beyond.

Two rooms later, Mrs Robinson nudged Dhikilo's leg,

steering her sideways. Another door. And another sideways nudge. A different sort of carpet underfoot. A different kind of echo when she knocked on a wall. A creak of floorboard. The pleasant shock of a banister under her left palm. And, finally, stairs. Dhikilo had to be careful not to rush. It would be a shame to outsmart the deadly house only to break her neck falling downstairs.

A couple of minutes later, one last door, and...fresh air on her face. Stone paving underfoot. And then the crunch of snow.

Dhikilo opened her eyes. The house was just as it had appeared when they arrived here last night. In the morning light, the gingerbread-coloured stonework looked cheerful and inviting, and the white window-frames seemed to celebrate the owners' pride in keeping the building immaculate. A blue plaque on the pillar next to the cast-iron gate said: Scones with jam & cream. Proper English tea. All welcome. Toilets for customers only. Thank you, The Management.

The tips of Dhikilo's ears were starting to sting a little. She'd left her hat inside. Also the saddlebag of provisions. That was very bad news. She considered going back in. She still had the key to the Marshalsea Room. If she entered the house in exactly the same way that they'd entered it last night, grabbed the saddlebag and immediately retraced her steps with her eyes closed, everything would be fine. Probably. Maybe.

Mrs Robinson had turned into a sphinx again. With a scornful toss of her hair she padded away, heading further down the valley, leaving a large dark stain of dog pee on the pillar and a steaming yellow puddle in the snow.

The Wrong Kind of Trees

The flight of a few dragonflies overhead, carrying radiant cargo, reassured them that they were going in the right direction. The only problem was that the right direction for fulfilling their mission might not be the same as the right direction for staying alive. A dense forest lay ahead. The trees looked like the kind that dropped pine cones and needles rather than fruits or nuts.

Mrs Robinson walked with a slight limp, keeping the weight off her front left paw. She must have injured a claw or two during her mad attack on the hotel-room wall.

Dhikilo's ears were stinging so much that she wrapped her scarf around her head. It wasn't as good as a hat, but it was better than nothing. Her body heat was escaping through her scalp, which she knew was not a good thing for a warm-blooded creature in freezing weather. Especially a warm-blooded creature without any food.

At Cawber School for Girls, Mr Dawkins taught all sorts of Science but his speciality was Biology. His lessons were just before lunch, thus giving him the opportunity to announce: "Time for some fuel!" The point he was making was that humans—indeed, all animals—were just machines which needed fuel to keep running. "You can put in high-quality fuel like fresh vegetables and you'll be a luxury car, or you can put in low-quality fuel like doughnuts and you'll turn into a big old van. But if you don't have any fuel at all, you'll grind to a halt and that will be the end of you, girls!"

Dhikilo wondered how long it would be before she and Mrs Robinson ground to a halt. It seemed daft and wrong that all the fun things she might have done in the remainder of a long life could be cancelled just because she didn't get a few mouthfuls of food today.

Before entering the forest, she and Mrs Robinson tried to eat some snow, to quench their thirst. It was hard to tell if this was helpful, because melting the snow inside your mouth made your whole head go very cold and then you had to warm up again. She suspected Mr Dawkins would have a discouraging scientific opinion about the snow-eating idea as well.

In her imagination, she could still taste the apple she'd eaten in the deadly house. It was so delicious! If she could have another apple like that, she'd be a happy person. She recalled how she'd once thrown an apple away after a couple of bites because it wasn't a nice one. If only she could have that apple back now! She would even eat the pips.

They entered the forest and it was indeed the kind that didn't have any fruits or nuts in it, or even any needles or pine cones. It was just a lot of tough spiky trees with gnarly roots that were half hidden underneath the snow, so that you were continually almost tripping over. Their rate of progress had been quite slow already and it was even slower now.

Mrs Robinson managed the terrain better, graceful on all fours despite the slight limp. She kept getting ahead, stopping and waiting for Dhikilo to catch up. Dhikilo felt clumsy and foolish in her thick stiff clothes. She felt she wasn't meant to be stumping about in this sort of environment; she should be in a very warm country, wearing just a T-shirt and shorts, hopping like a gazelle.

But never mind: the ordeal came to an end sooner than she'd feared. After maybe only fifteen more minutes, they emerged on the far side of the forest.

A village lay revealed in front of them. A village consisting of many small dirty huts, arranged in a circle, and, beyond that, one bigger building which looked like a school or a warehouse. The bigger building was made of brick and had grimy glass windows; the huts were constructed of all sorts of bits and pieces—stones, twigs, branches, metal pipes, mud, rubber tyres, empty food tins, lumps of rusted appliances, canvas tarpaulins and so on. There were about twenty of them.

Despite all these habitations, there was no sign of inhabitants.

"I hope this place isn't abandoned," said Dhikilo.

Her hope was immediately fulfilled. In a great eruption of movement and shouting, a dozen or more creatures leapt out of the entrances of the huts. They ran so fast that Dhikilo couldn't tell if they were pigs or overgrown bulldogs or fat monkeys. Only when they'd stopped moving—when she and Mrs Robinson were surrounded—did she have time to see what they really were: a group of dwarfishly short men, dressed in greasy smocks that had once been white but were now dark grey. They were all holding spears—short, stubby spears—and scowling. Their hair was clumped with scabs, their eyes were fierce and their teeth were slimy with yellow gunge.

"We are the Quilps," said one. "What are you?"

The Quilps

"**I**'m Dhikilo," said Dhikilo, but before she could introduce Mrs Robinson, all the Quilps flinched and shivered and groaned as if they'd suffered an electric shock.

"The evil letter!" complained one, clapping his hands to his ears so instinctively that he almost dropped his spear. "Speak not the evil letter, or we will kill you quicker!"

"I'll… I'll do my best," said Dhikilo, triggering another paroxysm of flinching and shivering and groaning among the dwarves.

"I'm sorry!" said Dhikilo. "I really am!" She paused for thought. "My name is… Miss Bentley. My fr…my…erm… companion is Mrs Robinson. We haven't had anything to drink—"

There was another outburst of groaning. One of the dwarves jabbed his spear very close to Dhikilo's chest, so close that it made her heart start beating very hard, for fear of being sliced in two like a tomato.

Dhikilo struggled to think. She mustn't use any Ds! But

talking without using Ds was so difficult. Difficult? Hard. No, *that* had a D in it, too.

"We are very thirsty," she said, speaking slowly to give herself enough time to examine each letter that came to her tongue. "Also, hungry. We were hoping that you might be willing to share some of your…erm…" She racked her brains. "Nourishment."

The nearest Quilp looked miserable as well as angry. The flesh of his face was scabby and blotchy, and much of his hair had fallen out, leaving only coarse tufts.

"We have no nourishment," he said. "We are brought low by the curse of the present time. In the long-lost past, before the Great Calamity, we ate our fill, happy in our plenty. Now we are starving. We ate all the chickens. We ate all the cows. We ate all the sheep. We ate all the cats. We ate all the fruits. We ate all the vegetables. We ate even the flowers. In summer, when there is grass, we make it into soup. In winter, we cook rice, a palmful for each of us. Speak not to us of nourishment, Misspently. You know not what hunger is."

"That's awful," said Dhikilo. "I'm so sorry."

"Your sorryness means nothing," retorted the dwarf. "We want more from you than your sorryness."

Another of the Quilps grunted with impatience, squeezing his spear in a fist that was missing several fingers. "Talk is a waste of energy. Time for action. Time to kill."

Dhikilo glanced sideways at Mrs Robinson. The sphinx's head was turning slowly from left to right; her fur was standing on end and her snake-tail was waving restlessly. Dhikilo could tell that she was doing a kind of mental arithmetic: calculating how many Quilps she could attack before the others ganged up behind her to stab her to death. There was just one sphinx and fourteen Quilps, and no matter how many times you did the sums, the answer didn't get any more optimistic.

"Please…erm…kill us not," said Dhikilo. She wanted to

say, "You wouldn't like being killed, if it was you," but no matter how hard she pondered, she couldn't think of a way to say that without using any Ds.

"It's not fair," she suggested. "We haven't…erm… There has been no trial."

"True," conceded one of the Quilps, a one-eyed one who had not spoken before. "A trial must come before the killing."

"All right," said the first Quilp. He drew a deep breath, gathering inspiration. "I hereby announce the trial of the strangers here before us. The trial starts on the count of three. One—two—three. You are trespassers in our village. Our village is a lawful place. That means we have lots of laws. One of those laws says that trespassing is against the law. So, you are guilty. The punishment for being guilty is that we kill you. So, we will kill you. Amen." He looked round at his fellow citizens. "How was that?"

There was a general murmur of admiration and approval.

"Let's kill the silent animal first," said the Quilp with the missing fingers. "Throw a few spears to make it fall, then—"

"Wait!" said Dhikilo. "If we're condemn—Sorry!…erm… If we're guilty prisoners who you must kill, we shou—erm… the law says we must get a last meal."

"Last meal?" sneered one of the Quilps. "You must think we're complete imbeciles."

"No, it's a real thing," one of the other Quilps said. "I remember hearing about it. In the ancient times, before the Great Calamity. One last meal before the execution, yes. Very lawful."

The first Quilp sighed irritably. "Give them some rice, then."

"Two bowls of rice coming up!" said another Quilp, turning away.

"Wait!" said Dhikilo. "The last meal is meant to be whatever the prisoners want. Their favourite thing."

"You cannot be serious," said the first Quilp.

But his brother said, "No, that's a real thing, too. I remember hearing about it in the ancient times. Their favourite meal, yes. Then execution."

There was a general nodding among the Quilps, and murmurs of "That's fair."

"We have almost nothing left!" protested the first Quilp, scowling straight at Dhikilo. "You cannot *have* your favourite thing!"

"But…erm…" said Dhikilo, "you know not what my favourite thing is."

"Well, for a start, you can't have the tin of mushrooms!" the Quilp retorted. "Those are for February!"

"Of course," said Dhikilo. "I'm not going to ask for your mushrooms. They're for February."

Several of the Quilps who hadn't yet spoken nodded in agreement, looking at Dhikilo with new respect, as if impressed at how well she understood the significance of the mushrooms. Dhikilo was beginning to realize that although these dwarf-like creatures were very dangerous, they were also very, very stupid. They could barely remember what had been said from one second to the next.

"Can I see what you've got?" said Dhikilo. "Please?"

The Quilps whispered and mumbled amongst themselves for a minute. Then they indicated that Dhikilo and Mrs Robinson should walk towards the building that resembled a warehouse.

Dhikilo noted that as the Quilps shepherded them along, they were careful to maintain an ordered circle of spears all around, so that if either Mrs Robinson or Dhikilo attempted to break loose or attack, those spears would be in the ideal position to thrust deep into flesh. Stupid the Quilps might be, but when it came to violence they were clever.

The big building was a combination of larder, kitchen and

canteen. It smelled of rice and beef stock cubes and tomato paste and unwashed dwarf. A large saucepan sat on the bench next to the sink, waiting to be rinsed out after what must have been a recent lunch. It had the frothy pattern around the inside that you get when you boil a large amount of rice. There were three or four slightly burnt grains still stuck to the bottom of the pan, but apart from those, it had been scraped clean.

One of the Quilps opened the cupboards and showed Dhikilo what was available. Nothing was fresh; it was all tins and packets. Even so, there were some useful ingredients: not just rice, but lentils, flour, tinned cabbage, tinned tomatoes, tinned peas and carrots, tubes of tomato paste, vegetable stock and many herbs and spices. There was even a bag of dried chillies which looked as though they were years old but would probably perk up if fried gently in some oil.

"We are wasting time," grumbled one of the Quilps. "They are guilty trespassers. We're going to kill them. Why bother to cook for them? It makes no sense."

"Oh, but we'll cook our last meal ourselves!" said Dhikilo. "You won't have to worry about anything. Just keep watch so that we can't escape. We'll take care of the rest, I promise."

There was more murmuring and mumbling amongst the Quilps, including comments like "She promises" and "That's fair."

Not far from the cooker hung a large black curtain that was shiny with accumulated fat from cooking vapours. It didn't reach all the way to the ground and Dhikilo could see large glass jars in the gap.

"What's behind there?" she asked.

The D in "behind" provoked a cry of disgust in the Quilps.

"Sorry, sorry," said Dhikilo. "But what's on the…erm… reverse of that curtain?"

"Evil things," said a Quilp.

"Evil…nourishment?" Dhikilo guessed.

"Yes," said a Quilp.

"Can I see?"

The Quilp heaved a deep sigh of exasperation. "Eating evil things will kill you."

"But you're going to kill us anyway! Also, it's our last meal!"

The Quilp leered, confident he was about to win the argument. "Yes, but we want to eat you after we kill you. Which means it's best if your stomachs are not full of evil nourishment."

"You can't eat us," said Dhikilo.

"Of course we can," said the Quilp. "Not the—not the portion that contains the skull, the bit that sits on top of your neck. But all the rest. With a little salt."

Another Quilp volunteered, "Cats are very tasty. Your animal is a large sort of cat, yes?"

Dhikilo stared the Quilp straight in his bloodshot eyes. "She's a dog."

The Quilps recoiled in horror at the word, but were not convinced by Mrs Robinson, whose leopard-like body seemed safely edible.

"It resembles not a canine."

"Look again," said Dhikilo, nudging Mrs Robinson's leg with her boot. "Mrs Robinson, you're a dog, isn't that right?"

A few moments later, the Quilps gasped in confusion and revulsion as they beheld the dark brown Labrador suddenly standing in their kitchen.

"All right," said a Quilp. "We will not eat the canine. Only kill it. But we will eat you. You are a human. You are a girl. What you are contains not the evil letter."

Dhikilo thought for a second. "I'm a child," she said.

The cleverest Quilp was not so easily bamboozled. His eyes narrowed as he appraised her mistrustfully. "I think not. You are too tall for a—for an infant."

"Well, maybe I'm an *adolescent*," said Dhikilo. "Also, re-member my name! My name is—"

"Yes, yes," interrupted the chief Quilp. "Waste no more time. Make your last meal." He turned to go; then, struck by a cunning suspicion, he turned back again, reached into the cupboard and extracted the tin of mushrooms.

"Best to keep this out of temptation's way," he said, mo-tioning his companions to follow him to the canteen tables, where they seated themselves about six metres from their pris-oners, spears held firmly in their fists.

Evil Cheese

While Mrs Robinson lapped noisily at a bowl of water, Dhikilo had a think about what to cook for their last meal. She could make a plain tomato sauce to put on top of rice, but the dried specky spatterings of red muck all over the wall behind the cooker suggested that this was the exact same idea that the Quilps resorted to day after day. She could drain the water out of the tinned cabbage and shred it and bake it in the oven with some seasoning. That might be nice. She could roll the vegetables in flour and fry them in oil or bake them. If she had an egg she could make batter. But she didn't have an egg.

She pulled aside the black curtain that shrouded the forbidden foods. The large glass jars on the floor were crammed full of dill pickles. She'd tasted a dill pickle once and it was interesting but quite vinegary and she couldn't imagine it mixing well with other things. She looked higher. The shelves were laden with stuff. Lots of seafood: sardines, marinated haddock, red salmon, salt cod, dressed crab, smoked mussels. Several large tins of duck confit (she didn't know what the word "confit" meant, but there were two drumsticks in each tin). Hot dogs in tins of twelve. Cans of chicken madras and dopiaza. Corned beef.

A packet of dates. She held it in her hand and pondered. Could they be dessert, or could she use them in the cooking? Putting sweet things in a savoury dish was a bit unusual but she had a hunch that dates would work. She could put just *one* in and see what effect it had, and if it didn't make the sauce nicer she could spoon it out again.

Sesame seeds! They were excellent for lots of things. If she made vegetable patties she could add them to the flour. And if she baked the shredded cabbage, they could go with that as well...

There was an entire shelf of cheeses: Gouda, Edam, Cheddar, Leerdammer and Philadelphia. Philadelphia was good for sauces! Dhikilo peeled open the container, but found that the creamy white stuff was tinged with green and pink mould and didn't smell so good. She opened a couple of the harder cheeses and they were fine. Ooh, and there was a jar of stuffed jalapeño peppers! They would be lovely. Maybe she would cut the hot dogs into little pieces and fry them in really hot oil before adding them to a sauce; they would taste almost like proper meat... Then in another pan she could make a seafood stew...

The saucepan with the water in it for the rice was starting to boil already. She put in a few handfuls. Then another few handfuls. Then a few handfuls more.

Ten minutes later, as the smells of Dhikilo's cooking started to drift from the kitchen into the canteen, the Quilps started muttering. She couldn't hear what they were saying, but it wasn't ordinary relaxed conversation.

After fifteen minutes, the mutterings got louder. The word "evil" was mentioned a lot. Also the word "hungry." The

room was getting warmer, and Dhikilo had to unzip her winter clothing to avoid overheating. She resisted the temptation
to take any of her garments off. You never knew when, and
in what sort of hurry, you might need them.

After twenty minutes, Dhikilo put some food down on the
floor for Mrs Robinson. It wasn't any of the special things
she was cooking on the stove and inside the oven; it was just
some mashed-up corned beef and hot dogs and cheese suitable for a dog. This caused an outbreak of louder mutterings
among the Quilps. One stood up from his chair and gazed at
Mrs Robinson wolfing down the gloop.

"We eat worse than that animal!" the dwarf complained.

"Speak not so," warned his brother. "That animal will not
live long enough to enjoy its meal."

Mrs Robinson ate louder. She certainly sounded as if she
was enjoying herself.

After twenty-five minutes, the seafood mixture was ready
and Dhikilo turned off the flame underneath it. The lack of
onions was a shame, but it had turned out quite tasty, after
all. In another pan she had the chicken dopiaza from the tin.
Its sauce had cooked onions in it, which she'd considered
trying to fish out to add to the seafood before admitting to
herself that this wouldn't work. Instead, she concentrated on
making the dopiaza nicer by adding lots of tomato and spices
and the duck drumsticks. Soon it wasn't even a dopiaza any
more but a peculiar thing of its own that didn't have a name
but was interesting.

Meanwhile, at the canteen tables, the arguments were getting more heated.

"Speak not so!" exclaimed the chief Quilp. "Our cook
serves us well! He fills our bellies using almost no nourish-
ments!"

"Yes, that's exactly the problem!"

"Perhaps you prefer to eat evil things? Evil may smell sweet, but the eater must pay the price!"

"How much is it?" enquired an excited Quilp at another table.

"It smells not sweet," another Quilp observed. "It smells like chicken."

"Chicken is permissible, isn't it?"

"We ate all the chickens."

"I am smelling chicken, I tell you!"

"It is evil chicken."

"I am smelling fish."

"It's not fish, it's seafood!"

"Aagh! Use not the evil letter!"

"I used it not!"

"Aagh! Again!"

"I was only explaining why it was evil!"

"Can someone explain to me why I'm sitting here with an empty belly when the whole place is full of the beautiful smell of nourishment?"

"Because you are a Quilp."

Dhikilo opened the oven to check on the baking. The vegetable patties were ready. The sunflower seeds were slightly burnt but the patties hadn't fallen apart as she'd worried they might; they were firm and plump and even a bit crispy-looking. Adding some grated Gouda cheese to the flour had been a good idea.

"I smell cheese!"

"Cheese contains not the evil letter."

"This is evil cheese."

"What foolishness you speak! How can cheese be evil?"

"Not all cheeses are equal."

A fist went *dunf! dunf!* on a table. "You are insane! All of you! Insane!"

"Speak not so of your brothers."

Dhikilo was dishing the food onto plates now. She had already rinsed some cutlery.

"This is torture!" cried a Quilp. "Why must I sit here, smelling these things? I'm going home."

"You can't go home. We must watch our prisoners. It must remain fourteen against two."

"Thirteen is enough. Or even twelve. Oh, my poor stomach! How it begs!"

"You will stay. I am your chief. I have spoken."

Without a word, Dhikilo carried a plate to an empty table very close to the Quilps. It was the seafood paella. The sprinkle of coriander on top wasn't fresh but it was still worthwhile and enhanced the colours. She left the steaming plate on the table to go back to the kitchen to fetch a few vegetable patties and a serving of the dopiaza. Having put these down, too, she mimed a "Silly forgetful me!" thought and went back to the kitchen again, leaving the food on display while she carefully filled a glass with elderberry juice. This, too, she brought to the table. Then, slowly, as if she had all the time in the world, she began to eat.

The Quilps helplessly leaned closer, their nostrils flaring. One drooled, and hurriedly wiped it up with his sleeve.

"My hunger is killing me."

"You ate your ration this morning," the chief Quilp pointed out. "You have no reason to grumble."

"But I tell you, my hunger is killing me!"

"Stop whining, or it will be me and not your hunger that kills you!"

"Aagh! You spoke the evil letter!"

"Rubbish."

"You did! I heard you!"

"Aagh! Aagh!" cried the chief Quilp, and several others cried, "Aagh! Aagh!" likewise.

"I never!"

"You liar!"

Dhikilo ate on as if she was oblivious to the quarrel. She chewed each mouthful pensively, pausing to take sips of elderberry juice.

After some minutes, during which the Quilps continued to growl and snap at each other about the forbidden letter and forbidden foods and unforbidden foods and who was the boss, Dhikilo put down her knife and fork, pushed her plate forward and said, "Well, it was very nice, but I can't eat any more."

She leaned back in her chair. Several of the Quilps craned forwards, almost crawling onto the tops of their tables, to get a closer look at the food that was left on Dhikilo's plates.

"Maybe I'll have something sweet to finish on," said Dhikilo, standing up and walking to the kitchen again. Then, when she got there: "Oh, I'm so sorry. Look at this! How embarrassing. I've…erm…been guilty of a mistake with the recipe. Much too much left over. Such a waste. What was I thinking? I got too enthusiastic, that's what it was."

As she babbled this nonsense, she was quickly ladling the large quantity of food she'd prepared onto a line of clean plates. There were ten more vegetable patties in the oven, still warm. Hardly any of the panful of dopiaza had been eaten yet. There were a good few helpings of seafood paella left. Not fourteen, but four or five at least. Hurriedly, she brought the loaded plates to the Quilps' tables and set them down. Before the dwarves had time to express their astonishment, she was back with more.

"Please," she said. "Feel free."

"Strength, brothers!" declared the chief Quilp. But with a strangled cry, one of the others lunged forward and seized a steaming plate of seafood.

The chief Quilp banged his spear against the tabletop. "I will not tolerate disob—" That was as far as he got before a hairy fist punched him in the face.

Within seconds, the canteen was a hullabaloo of mayhem. Some of the Quilps were strangling each other, kicking each other, pummelling each other. Others were gobbling the food, cramming patties into their mouths, dipping their faces straight into the dopiaza, snatching handfuls of paella, diving to the floor to retrieve drumsticks that had been lost in the rumpus.

There's something about a fight that always tempts bystanders to stand by and look. Dhikilo and Mrs Robinson were certainly tempted to hang around watching what happened with this rioting pack of dwarves. But they didn't. They preferred to sneak to the door and leave the building without a sound.

As soon as they were outside, Mrs Robinson transformed into a sphinx and said, "On my back. Hold the hair."

Dhikilo threw herself onto the sphinx's back and tried to get a grip any way she could, as Mrs Robinson leapt into motion, launching her leopard-like body across the snowy wasteland.

Almost immediately, furious Quilp voices could be heard somewhere behind, bellowing and bawling. A spear landed in the snow right next to Mrs Robinson, causing her to change direction. Dhikilo's shoulder got thumped, as if by a fist, but she knew it must be a spear, glancing off the thick fabric of her coat, miraculously missing her flesh. Mrs Robinson's muscles and bones were like a mighty machine underneath her, pumping and heaving, jolting so hard that Dhikilo had to cling desperately to avoid being thrown off.

Seconds later, the Quilps' shouts faded into the distance. Mrs Robinson slowed her pace and Dhikilo closed her eyes and let out a deep breath.

They were alive. They'd eaten. And they hadn't been eaten. The day was definitely improving.

Scarcely Limping at All

They rested about halfway up a hill. From there, they could survey where they'd come from and make sure that none of the Quilps were still in pursuit. Luckily, there was no sign that they were in any danger—at least not from living creatures.

As the warmth of the canteen and the excitement of the chase faded away, Dhiliko started to feel cold again. Soon her cheeks were numb and her ears were stinging, so she wrapped her scarf around her head once more. Her right shoulder felt as though an icy wind was blowing directly onto the unprotected skin, and when she prodded at it with her fingers, she found that the fabric of her coat had been sliced open, right through to the T-shirt underneath. It was a miracle the spear had missed her flesh. She wiggled her shoulder, trying to find a way of holding it so the cold wouldn't penetrate the rip. A needle and thread would fix this, but even if the Professor had been sensible enough to put such things in a pocket of the saddlebag, they'd lost it and couldn't get it back.

Breathing more slowly now, taking deep breaths while

Mrs Robinson continued to pant, Dhikilo checked again for pursuers. The Quilp village was barely visible in the distance, just a nondescript clump with a wisp of smoke curling up from it. The landscape between there and here stretched white and empty.

Not pure white, though. Dhikilo noticed that there were also some smudges of red. She traced the crimson trail with her eyes and realized, to her horror, that it led straight to the sphinx.

Mrs Robinson's left hind leg had been wounded by a spear! A spear had gone right in! It must've been shaken loose somewhere along the way, but it had left a nasty gash in Mrs Robinson's flesh, which dripped blood onto the snow.

"You're hurt!" cried Dhikilo.

"Yesss," agreed the sphinx calmly.

Dhikilo pulled off her scarf and checked which bits of it looked cleanest. Without even asking permission or explaining what she was going to do, she wrapped the scarf round and round the sphinx's wounded leg, from joint to thigh. She fastened it securely by tearing the last bit of the fabric down the middle and tying the loose strips in a knot.

"Is that all right? Not too tight?"

"Yesss," said the sphinx, in the same tone.

"Can you walk?"

"Yesss." Mrs Robinson glanced at Dhikilo's uncovered head. "We mussst not ssstay." And she walked off towards the top of the hill.

Dhikilo hurried to catch up. Walking alongside Mrs Robinson, she thought at first that the sphinx was scarcely limping at all, which was such good news that she suspected it was too good to be true. Indeed it was: Dhikilo figured out how to glance sideways while pretending to look straight ahead, and as soon as she got the knack of doing that, she observed that the sphinx was limping quite badly, doing her best to carry her weight on three legs only.

The crest of the hill was not far off now. There hadn't been any dragonflies overhead for quite a while. Dhikilo hoped this didn't mean their escape from the Quilps had pushed them off the right path. In the circumstances, getting lost would be extremely unfortunate.

Humanly Possible

When they reached the top of the hill and looked down the other side, they saw that their progress would soon be blocked by a high brick wall that extended for miles in both directions. In the middle of the wall was a checkpoint, like the gatehouse of a castle but much smaller and shabbier. Since the wall was too high for Dhikilo and Mrs Robinson to climb over, they had no choice but to head for the checkpoint, whatever dangers might await them there.

The building's façade was adorned with a number of signs saying, THIS WAY and ASSEMBLE HERE and PLEASE WAIT TO BE SEEN and FORM AN ORERLY QUEUE. A big black door with no handle or doorknob displayed a notice saying, CAUTION: OPENS ONLY FROM WITHIN.

Crudely painted arrows pointed to a large window which was covered with a wooden shutter. The whole building looked like one of those fairground kiosks that sells ice cream or hamburgers or hot waffles, except that this fairground seemed to be closed. There was a long wooden counter sticking out from the wall, set at chest height for not-very-tall adults, so it was just right for Dhikilo.

Despite the window being shuttered up, the counter had been recently wiped clear of snow, and there were several pens laid out on its surface, as well as a laminated warning that said:

STEALING THE PENS MAY ELAY YOUR APPLICATION

As Dhikilo and Mrs Robinson drew near, the sound of snoring could be heard through the shutter.

RING BELL FOR ATTENTION, said a sign next to an old-fashioned brass bell, so Dhikilo rang it. The snoring immediately stopped, replaced by a strenuous snuffle that sounded like some poor fat creature being choked. Then the shutter was lifted, releasing a waft of warmth from within. The gatehouse was, in fact, an office crammed with stacks of paper and filing cabinets and staplers and log books and all that sort of thing. And a plump old man with the thickest glasses Dhikilo had ever seen: they were so thick that his eyes seemed to be peering through a layer of jelly, and they were so heavy that it was just as well his nose was big and sturdy to support their bulk.

"Take a number, please!" he said, pointing to a ticket dispenser that issued little paper tags on a roll. While Dhikilo was reaching forward to tear off a ticket, he quickly attempted to smooth down his sticky-up hair and straighten his tie. His suit could not have been more rumpled if he'd slept in it all his life, which he possibly had.

Dhikilo checked the number on her ticket. It was 1.

"Applicant number one, please!" said the plump old man, consulting a sheet.

Dhikilo handed him the ticket. She noticed, as she leaned over the counter, that the man had his very own engraved brass plaque, proudly displaying his name and profession to all who queued at his office:

WINSTON T. PUMBLECHOOK,
OFFICIAL PASSPORT INSPECTOR
& INGRESSOR INVIGILATOR

"Passports, please!" said Inspector Pumblechook.

"We don't have any passports," said Dhikilo.

"No passports?" said Pumblechook, squinting down at her through his foggy spectacles. "Impossible. How i you get this far?"

"We walked," said Dhikilo.

"Without permits?"

"Nobody told me I needed permits," said Dhikilo. "Just warm clothes."

"Then you are the victim of a shameful, negligent non-supply of vital information!" spluttered Pumblechook. "I suggest you fill in one of these…" And, from one of the many piles all around him, he selected a document and handed it to Dhikilo. ECLARATION OF INSUFFICIENT PREPARATORY ASSISTANCE, it said at the top of the first page.

"Alrighty," said Pumblechook. "Just give me some etails about the forms no one aske you to fill in before coming here, an I'll put in an official request for leniency." He did something with his mouth which he probably intended to be a reassuring smile. A substantial clump of his hair broke free from the smoothing and stood up again.

"Excuse me, sir," said Dhikilo, "but we've been travelling a long way and we're tired and one of us may need a doctor."

Pumblechook craned forward to appraise Mrs Robinson, but gave up almost at once as he failed to make sense of the sphinx's unusual features.

"So, to summarize the situation: two applicants, both in

the process of substantial geographical relocation, without the necessary permits. You are experiencing high levels of fatigue. One of you may require assistance of a meical nature."

"Yes," said Dhikilo.

"I think I have the answer, bureaucratically speaking," said Pumblechook. "A special provisional permit-passport combination! Very rarely given. Almost more than my job's worth. But I recognize the urgency of your circumstances. What are rules for, if not to be bent?" And he clasped his podgy hands against his chest, as if to demonstrate that he had a heart. "Isease or injury?"

"Sorry?"

"The conition for which your travelling companion may require a octor: is it a isease or an injury?"

"An injury."

"Excellent!" cried Pumblechook. "Much simpler, paperwork-wise!" And turning to another pile he whipped off a document titled ECLARATION OF INJURY (SUB-FATAL), and held it out towards Mrs Robinson.

"She can't fill in a form," said Dhikilo. "She hasn't got any fingers."

Pumblechook leaned forward again, in a second attempt to appraise the sphinx. This time, he managed to perceive that she was four-legged.

"Not to worry, not to worry," he breezed. "You can apply to be her legal representative!" And he started rummaging for the appropriate form.

"Is there a hospital anywhere near here?" asked Dhikilo.

"Of course!" said Pumblechook. "Our great country has everything anyone coul want. For those with the correct ocuments."

Dhikilo sensed movement behind her. Mrs Robinson was pacing back and forth, her head tilted far back, examining the top of the wall. It was too high for her to jump over, but maybe she was considering the possibility of leaping high enough to get her claws into the top and hauling herself the rest of the way by sheer force of desperation.

Dhikilo leaned as close as she could to Inspector Pumblechook. "Can't you just give us the correct documents here and now? You have a lot of papers in your office. They must be really useful and important. And you're in charge, aren't you? It must be so satisfying to be the man in charge, making things possible and…erm…earning the huge gratitude of the people he's helped."

"Very true!" affirmed Pumblechook with a blush of pleasure. "Where there's a will, there's a way, I always say." He whipped another piece of paper from a pile, was about to hand it to Dhikilo and then said, "I'll tell you what. Things are a bit quiet here this afternoon, I'm not run off my feet like usual, so…how about I fill in your application *for* you?"

"Erm… OK, thank you," said Dhikilo.

"Full name?"

"Dhikilo Saxardiid Samawada Bentley."

"Uh-hmm," murmured Pumblechook with serene concentration, busily writing.

"Would you like me to spell that?" asked Dhikilo.

"I am passably fluent in many languages, ma'am," said Pumblechook, still writing. "Arabic among them. 'Bentley' is with two Es, I take it?"

"Yes," said Dhikilo. "Are you putting the Ds in?"

"Hmm?" The inspector seemed not to have heard the question.

"The Ds in my name," said Dhikilo. "Are you putting them in?"

Winston T. Pumblechook raised himself to his fullest possible height while remaining seated. He glanced to the left, he glanced to the right, he peered over Dhikilo's shoulder and he peered behind him, through a small window in the back of his office.

"A passport must always be correct," he declared tremulously, as if fearing he might be brutally punished for saying so. But there was pride in his voice, too. "There are proceures to be followe; noble historic proceures which are, in my humble professional estimation, more important than the whims of…of…of whoever might be the country's current ruler."

"You mean the Gamp?"

Behind the thick lenses of his glasses, the inspector's eyes swivelled around in fear, like startled fish in a goldfish bowl. "It's not in my job escription to iscuss in etail any aspects of government beyon my own epartment," he said carefully.

"What's the Gamp doing with all the Ds?" said Dhikilo.

"Let's push on with this application," said Pumblechook, in a stern voice that warned her not to mention the Gamp again. "I haven't got all ay. Ate of birth?"

"Sorry?"

"Ate of birth?"

"I'm not exactly sure," said Dhikilo. "I'm sort of an orphan."

"Uh-hmm," murmured Pumblechook, applying his pen to the paper again. "I'll put 'unknown.' Place of birth?"

"Somaliland."

"Let's see here…" Pumblechook consulted a wall chart: an alphabetical list of dozens of names, each with its own code. "Saint Kitts… Samoa… Serbia… Singapore… Slovakia… Ah! Yes! Somalia."

"It's actually Somaliland," said Dhikilo.

Pumblechook raised one eyebrow, which caused yet more of his imperfectly smoothed hair to flip up in sympathy. "I think you'll fin it's Somalia."

"It's Somaliland," insisted Dhikilo. "But nobody believes it's a real country. Except the people who live there. They have their own flag, their own money, their own football team and everything."

Inspector Pumblechook thought this over. He consulted

another wall chart. "Ah—here we have it, as a member of the Confeeration of Inepenent Football Associations!" He chewed the end of his pen, pondering. He scratched the top of his head, thus releasing the last of his hair into free formation.

"I'll put 'not applicable,'" he said at last, and traced his finger down the boxes on the form. "Which takes us straight to the last page! What a jolly well-esigne ocument this is! It's a cracker!" He tilted his head admiringly. Then: "Reason for visiting Liminus?"

This one took Dhikilo by surprise. She considered saying, "Getting the D back," but resisted the impulse and said, "Holiday," instead.

"Uh-hmm," said the inspector, scribbling. "I'll put 'vacation,' if it's all the same to you. How much money are you travelling with?"

"We don't have any money at all," said Dhikilo.

"Well, you won't have much of a vacation, then!" smirked Pumblechook.

"We just want to see the…erm…beautiful sights," said Dhikilo.

"Quite right! Quite right!" exclaimed Pumblechook. "Liminus has the most *magnificent* sights. Peerless natural beauty! Rolling green hills! Fertile valleys! Ripe fruits falling off the trees! Every imaginable type of flower! Joyous newborn animals gambolling in the meaows!" As he was making this speech, he scurried around his office, excitedly gathering glossy brochures. But then he came to an abrupt halt, looked down sadly at the colourful leaflets in his hands and let them fall out of sight.

"At least," he continued in a despondent tone, "that's how it *was* before the Great Calamity. Since then, nothing has grown. We have snow, but no rain. Frost, but no thaw. Every plucky green thing perishes beneath the ice. Famine has riven us to the brink of esperation. Liminus has become a frozen wastelan!"

He took his seat again, and seemed almost to be muttering to himself. "I'm partial to a nice shrub, myself. I like roses. Chrysanthemums. My wife grew vegetables in our little plot, bless her soul. It's tragic what's befallen this country. Think of the impact on tourism, for a start." He drew a melancholy breath. "Anyway, back to the present task. In the box for how much money you're bringing in, I'll just put 'zero,' shall I?"

"Yes, please," said Dhikilo.

"Ever been in prison?"

"No."

"Carrying any weapons?"

"No."

"Any mechanical tools that might be mistaken for weapons?"

"I've got a torch," said Dhikilo uncertainly.

"Let's have a look at it," said Pumblechook.

Dhikilo handed her dinky torch up to him and he measured it solemnly with a rusty steel ruler.

"Well within the allowable range," he declared, and handed it back. "Any poisonous spiers?"

"No."

"Smuggling enangere species of bir or animal?"

Dhikilo glanced at Mrs Robinson. "Erm...no."

"Recently been in a country that's got an outbreak of Somersaulting Rabbit Flu?"

"I don't think so."

"I'll put 'no,' shall I?"

"Yes, please. Look, I don't mean to be rude, but is this going to take much longer? There's a person here with a wound in her leg."

"We're getting to that, we're getting to that," said Pumblechook, snatching another form off a pile. "Escribe in ten wore or less your lawful relationship to the entity for which or whom you are applying to act as legal representative."

Dhikilo felt a giddy surge of headache. Was it the freezing cold or a flash of anger? She wasn't sure. Maybe Winston T. Pumblechook and his border barrier were a bit like the evil guesthouse with its endless inescapable rooms. Maybe exhausted travellers got detained here, filling in forms for hours and days until finally they dropped dead.

"I'm sorry, I don't think I understand the question," she said.

"Woul you say," said Pumblechook, "that she is your pet? Your aughter? An animal that you are transporting for the purpose of slaughter? Your sister? Your niece or aunt? A frien? A total stranger on whom you have taken pity?"

"Friend," said Dhikilo, after a moment's hesitation.

"Right-ho," murmured the inspector, scribbling. "Name?"

"Mrs Robinson. Nelly."

"Ate of birth?"

Dhikilo hesitated. The sphinx raised her head above the counter. "Sssunday the third of March," she said. "Eighteen thirty-nine."

"Place of birth?"

There was a pause. "England," said the sphinx.

Pumblechook scribbled for a couple of seconds longer and was satisfied.

"Almost there, almost there," he assured Dhikilo. "Time for the photograph." He fetched a bulky old camera out of a cabinet and balanced it on the counter. Waving his hands in the air, he indicated where Dhikilo should stand.

"A fraction to the left. A fraction forwar. No, too far. Yes, just there. Lift your chin slightly. Eyes open. No smiling." He pressed the button on the camera and it went *clunk*. Briskly, Pumblechook removed the camera from the counter and busied himself in his office for a little while. Then, with a flourish, he handed the completed forms to Dhikilo. "Just your signature now, in the places where I've put an X."

Dhikilo wrote her autograph several times, feeling odd. She was far too young to sign any sort of official paperwork, at least back home, but maybe the laws worked differently here.

"Many thanks," said the inspector as he took the signed forms back into his possession. "Your passport shoul be reay for collection in…" (he consulted another wall chart) "… twenty-four to forty-eight hours. However, the Eclaration of Insufficient Preparatory Assistance may slow things own a bit. To be safe, I recommen allowing…two to three weeks."

Mrs Robinson hissed furiously. If Dhikilo hadn't been so cold already, a cold chill would have passed down her spine. All of this had just been a cruel game, like a cat playing with a mouse before biting it to death. It was all the more hurtful because she'd decided that Pumblechook was a decent man, after all—a bit crazy, perhaps, but genuinely well-meaning.

"I thought you were going to help us!" she said to him, almost crying. "You said you would."

"I've given you as much assistance as I'm at liberty to give," said Pumblechook stiffly. "I've set the wheels in motion, so to speak. You'll be able to pick up your passport from the White Hall as soon as humanly possible."

"The White Hall?"

"That's where they make the passports. They have a proper passport-making factory there. I am only a humble inspector, a lowly pen-pusher, a mere link in the chain."

"But where's the White Hall?"

The inspector seemed taken aback by her ignorance. "It's in the capital, of course," he said, gesturing behind him, at the part of Liminus that his gatehouse and the high wall were stopping Dhikilo and Mrs Robinson from reaching. "Gampalonia. Or, as our capital city was known until quite recently, Amistat."

Once again, Dhikilo felt a pang of indignant distress, but before she could start crying, the inspector ducked out of view. A moment later, the big black door with the OPENS ONLY FROM WITHIN sign opened from within. The landscape beyond was revealed. There was even a road.

"On you go!" said the inspector, motioning them to come through. He was even smaller, tubbier and more rumpled than he'd looked in his office. "If you walk at a regular pace, you'll reach the next village well before nightfall. You have nothing to fear from the people there; they will assist you if they can."

As Mrs Robinson and Dhikilo passed through the door, Dhikilo reached out to shake the inspector's hand, but he turned his back on her. This time, she barely had a chance to feel disappointed before he turned towards her again, hold-ing a bottle of water in each hand.

"For the journey," he said.

Dhikilo took the bottles and smiled. "Thank you so much, Mr Pumblechook! You're a star!"

The old man's ugly face was lit up by the most beautiful, beaming grin. He waved at his two departing clients as they grew hazy in his sight.

When Dhikilo had already taken a dozen steps up the road, she remembered something and called out to the inspector before he disappeared back into his little office.

"By the way, what does the 'T' stand for? In the middle of your name?"

Winston T. Pumblechook glanced left and right and ahead and behind him. "Theodore!" he shouted at last. "Theodore! The name my dear departed mother Theodora gave me, God bless 'er! Theodooooore!"

And with that, he was gone.

THE DROOD

It was a relief to be on a proper road at last, rather than hiking clumsily across frozen fields. Much easier on the feet: almost as good as having a rest.

Also, before long, they saw several more dragonflies passing overhead, each carrying a luminous D. That was reassuring. They weren't lost. (Unless the dragonflies were lost, of course.)

The sun was at its brightest, which wasn't particularly bright but at least took the worst chill off the air.

And—best of all!—they'd been promised that the next lot of people they met wouldn't try to kill them.

All of these things made Dhikilo feel they were finally making good progress, even though, to be honest, they hadn't achieved anything yet, mission-wise, apart from staying alive and walking in the same general direction as some weird insects.

Mrs Robinson was no longer trying to disguise her limp. The bandage was still in place but had a red stain in the middle of it. Dhikilo imagined Ruth emptying the dirty clothes basket, holding up this scarf and saying, "What a shame. I'll wash it, but that stain will never come out."

"Does it hurt?" she asked the sphinx.

"Yessss," said Mrs Robinson.

"Shall we stop?"

"I will ssstop," said the sphinx, "when I mussst. Not before."

As Pumblechook had promised, they reached the next village before the daylight faded. It was a more cheerful-looking place than the Quilps' garbage-heap of hovels, and the houses were larger, although not in the best condition. Holes which should've been repaired with proper plaster or specially cut lengths of fresh wood were patched over with mud and ill-fitting fragments of this or that. The thatched roofs were impressive at first glance, but parts of them were dark with rot. It was clear that the villagers were houseproud, tidy people who'd been forced to make do with too little for too long.

"Hello-o!" called Dhikilo as she and Mrs Robinson approached the nearest house.

"Hewwo!" came an answering cry from inside—a rich, melodious holler.

A person emerged from the front door. Dhikilo was expecting a human, so she was a little surprised at what stepped forward instead: a tall elegant female creature whose sole garment was a long sleeveless white dress, exposing bare feet and slender arms and delicate shoulders. Her skin was actually a pelt: she had downy black fur all over. At the top of her long neck was a startling sight: the glossy black head of a cat, as big as a human's, and with a somewhat humanish mouth.

"Welcome," she said. As she spoke, others of her kind emerged from the houses near by. Three…five…twelve… thirty. They were all tall and graceful, all dressed in long white dresses (the females) or shorter white robes (the males), all with glossy-furred black hides and feline heads. There was some variation in the shapes of their ears and noses and brows and so on, but they were all equally sleek and well groomed, and their clothing was spotless.

"I'm Dhikilo," said Dhikilo, "and this is Mrs Robinson."

"We are Roo," one of the male creatures said, laying his charcoal-black hands first on his white-clad chest, then pointing to his companions all around. "Aw of ush. We are Roo."

"Roo?" echoed Dhikilo.

"ngo, *Roo*," corrected one of the females, contorting her mouth in effort.

"Roo?" tried Dhikilo again, in a slightly different accent, in case that helped.

"ngo," said the female, shaking her head. She stretched out one of her hands, making a curly gesture in the air in front of her. *"Roo."* Again she made a curly hand gesture, the same as the first. Dhikilo thought for a moment that it might be some sort of magic sign or ceremonial greeting. Then she realized the hand was tracing the shape of a D.

"Drood?" she guessed.

The whole community of cat-headed people whooped and applauded. They smiled broadly, and their bright white teeth were not fangs, but almost human.

"Roo! Roo!" they affirmed.

One of the Drood came forward from behind the others, her brow wrinkled with concern, and pointed straight at Mrs Robinson's bandaged leg.

"Yook!" she said. "Bwah!"

Everyone looked to see the blood.

At once, the community sprang into action, running off to fetch various things. Dhikilo and Mrs Robinson were ushered into the nearest house, a cosy bungalow whose sitting room was painted red, white and green. A pot-belly stove in the shape of a giant vase stood in the centre of the room, giving out warmth and a delicious smell. Mrs Robinson was urged to sit near the fire. She didn't sit, but stood where she was directed, holding her head high. Within minutes, she was surrounded by white-robed strangers holding bowls of steaming water and metal trays of glittering instruments. She appeared unconcerned. It was as though she could sense that these creatures meant her no harm. Dhikilo wondered if the fact that Mrs Robinson was kind of lion-ish or cheetah-like and the Drood were kind of pantherly made a difference.

One of the Drood kneeled at Mrs Robinson's flank and carefully unwrapped the scarf. Dried blood had glued the fur to the fabric, so one of the other Drood handed down a pair of scissors for the matted hair to be snipped free.

"Shpear. Quiwp shpear!" someone said as the wound was revealed.

The Drood worked fast. With a sharp blade they shaved off the fur around the wound, revealing pale pink skin. They washed the wound gently, then sewed it together with a silver needle and black thread. Mrs Robinson shut her eyes and bared her fangs while the needle was passing through her flesh, and made a noise of pain: *"Aarrrrrrrrrrrrrrrrrrrrrr…"* But she kept perfectly still until it was over.

The Drood stepped back, appraising what they'd done. Mrs Robinson understood that they were waiting for her to say how she felt. She lifted her leg, flexed it to and fro and stamped it hesitantly on the ground.

"Better," she said.

Afternoon tea with the Drood was the nicest afternoon tea Dhikilo had ever had. Or, at least, the nicest she could recall. She must've had nicer ones in the past—after all, the Drood could only offer mugs of hot water flavoured with dried spice, and small bowls of sweet sticky rice with cinnamon—but she badly needed some comfort and pampering now, and it was heavenly to be sitting in a warm house with friendly people, being fed. Also, the sweet rice was exactly the right thing to be eating because she hadn't had time for dessert in the Quilps' canteen, and even though there'd been a good reason to leave in a big hurry, she still regretted not having those yummy dates.

Warm and safe for the first time since the start of her journey, Dhikilo took off her winter gear. One of the Drood had noticed the rip in her jacket, and immediately fetched the garment into his own lap, examining the damage carefully yet decisively, just as he'd examined Mrs Robinson's wound. Another sewing needle was handed over, this time with white rather than black thread in it.

Dhikilo leaned back against a cushion, almost laughing out loud with pleasure at the luxury of relaxing. She only hoped her sweaty T-shirt didn't make the cushion damp and smelly. Mrs Robinson walked over to one of the walls and sank down against that, still flexing her leg gingerly. One of the Drood softly strummed a beautifully carved musical instrument that resembled a guitar but had a more muffled, melty sort of sound.

"Make yourshelf a home," beamed the creature who was sewing up Dhikilo's jacket. And thus began a long conversation.

The Drood were an ancient people—the most ancient in Liminus, they said. "Five foushan yearsh ago" they'd ruled the whole land, and other lands beyond, in a magnificent empire. They'd sailed the seas and cultivated the deserts, built palaces and schools, waged wars and made peace, invented solutions for every conceivable problem and laws for every conceivable crime, produced artists and athletes whose achievements were legendary and composed unforgettable music that was passed down from generation to generation.

Then their empire had fallen, as all empires do, and new empires had sprung up, ruling Liminus for centuries in turn until they, too, fell.

Finally, when too many centuries had passed and the supply of wise rulers had temporarily run out, the Gamp had come along and seized control.

When mentioning the Gamp, the Drood didn't talk about him as if he was a fearsome enemy, but more as if he was like bad weather or pollution in the sea or an earthquake or a wildfire—something that happens sometimes because of the way the world is.

"What does he want?" asked Dhikilo.

The Drood, descendents of emperors who'd been worshipped as gods, looked at her in pity for her childish ignorance of the attractions of power.

"He wamsh *everyfing*," explained the one who'd knelt at Mrs Robinson's side to wash the wound. "Everyfing."

"But what does he want it for?"

Again the pitying look. The Drood obviously believed that if Dhikilo didn't understand already, there was no point trying to explain.

"Why is he stealing the Ds?"

"He shealsh everyfing."

"But why Ds?"

"Ish jush uh beginging. Shoong he will scheal uffer ye-ursh."

Dhikilo listened to these words, unable to figure them all out, and then she kind of played them back to herself in her mind until they made sense. "Did you say, 'This is just the beginning'?" she ventured.

"Yesh," said the Drood.

"And, 'Soon he will steal other letters'?"

"Yesh," said the Drood.

"But why start with D?"

A few of the Drood looked infinitely weary in their sadness. "He haych ush evem more vam he haych uffer people."

"Hates you?" echoed Dhikilo. "Why would the Gamp hate you?"

"Becaush we are"—the Drood contorted his mouth—"Roo…"

Dhikilo thought this over. Then, remembering how Pumblechook had found courage to speak the forbidden letter, and how the Quilps were too stupid to prevent themselves using the forbidden letter once they lost their temper, she wondered why the Drood were making things so difficult for themselves.

"Can the Gamp hear everything?" she asked. "Like, does he have a way of listening in to us as we talk?"

The Drood signalled no.

"Then why don't you speak the D? Why can't you just say, 'We are the Drood'?"

The Drood looked around at each other, as if seeking each other's permission for a naughty action. Then, turning their faces straight towards Dhikilo, they all opened their furry black mouths simultaneously and stuck out their tongues.

Dhikilo was a little taken aback. For a moment she felt as if she was surrounded by a bunch of spiteful schoolgirls intent on teasing her. But then she noticed that all the tongues were strangely blunt: the tips were missing. Pink and healthy-looking, sure, but...cut short.

"Oh! How awful!" she cried, understanding. "I'm so sorry. How did it happen?"

The nearest Drood, a mature female, reached out her hand and laid her velvety palm against the side of Dhikilo's face. She shook her head slowly.

"You are...choo young," she said.

"I'm not a baby," protested Dhikilo. "I'm old enough to know."

The motherly Drood looked at Dhikilo with an expression of profound love. Tears welled out from her eyes and glittered briefly on the fur of her cheeks before falling off.

"Choo young," she repeated, stroking Dhikilo's face tenderly.

And no more was said about the tongues that could no longer say D.

The Purportedly Magic Weather-Changing Song

Dhikilo's coat was soon mended. It looked just as good as before; it only had a neat white scar. The Drood who'd sewed it displayed it proudly, then handed it over to his guest.

"Wow!" said Dhikilo, a bit louder than she really needed to, so that some of the Drood in the further parts of the room could hear how grateful she was. But several of them put a finger to their lips to signal "Shush!" then pointed to Mrs Robinson. The sphinx had fallen fast asleep against the wall. Her abundant hair—matted and in bad need of a brush—had dropped across her face, and fluttered with each breath. Her cheek lay heavy on one forepaw. Her soft underbelly, with fur almost as short as the Drood's, was exposed, rising and falling slowly. Her snake-tail was stretched straight out like a dead thing. Every few seconds, her injured leg twitched irritably.

In quieter voices, Dhikilo and the Drood continued their conversation. The Drood's speech remained difficult to comprehend but Dhikilo got better at it as the afternoon went on, and the Drood were smart—they could instantly tell when she'd missed something, and repeated themselves until she got it. They managed to make clear to her that what made them sad was not their mutilated tongues, which they'd learned to live with and which hadn't destroyed their pride or their enthusiasm or their courage. No, what made them sad was the dismal decline of their country since the coming of the Gamp.

Pumblechook had spoken the truth: once upon a time, not so long ago, Liminus had been green and fertile, producing plentiful food for all its citizens. It suffered occasional bad weather like any other place, and each year snow would fall and animals would hibernate and people would huddle indoors eating soup by the fire. Then spring would come and the snow would melt and the landscape would turn green again.

One year, the snow didn't go away. It lay obstinately where it had fallen, growing denser and dirtier but never melting. The sun was pale and feeble, and remained pale and feeble for so long that people forgot what a warm sun felt like. The calendar said it was summer but it wasn't summer; the seeds in the ground waited for the spring rain but they waited in vain; harvest time came but there was nothing to harvest.

The old ruler of Liminus, when called upon by his subjects to do something about the crisis, confessed that he had no idea how to make the snow go away and the sun return and the rain fall once more. This made him very unpopular with the people, and he was soon replaced by a new ruler who promised he would make the good weather come back. That ruler was the Gamp.

The Gamp had been in charge for quite a few seasons now, and the good weather still hadn't come back, but he blamed this on the evil deeds of various people he disliked. If it wasn't for these terrible evil people, he would have brought the sun

back ages ago, but wrestling with the threats of his enemies
was taking up all his energy, he said. The Gamp had an army
of strong and merciless men supporting him, and the popula-
tion soon learned that these men could make life even more
difficult than it already was. It was important to like the same
people the Gamp liked and hate the same people the Gamp
hated, if you didn't want to become one of the people the
Gamp hated, which would lead to dreadful punishments.

"Rule by fear," said the Drood bitterly. It was one of the
few sentences for which his tongue could form all the words.

"Can't anybody stop him?"

The Drood shrugged. "Emperorsh come, emperorsh go.
Real probwem ish uh wevver. We mush chage uh wevver."

"Change the weather?" echoed Dhikilo.

"Chage uh wevver," affirmed the Drood. Suddenly his
eyes lit up with enthusiasm. "Come choo our chemple. Ish
chime for our richual! Come!"

He motioned for Dhikilo to stand. Dhikilo checked on
Mrs Robinson, who was still deeply asleep, and then she put
her boots back on and followed the Drood out of the house
into the cold of late afternoon.

About a dozen of the Drood escorted her towards a churchy-
looking building which she supposed must be the temple. Was
it foolish of her to leave her companion and accompany these
strange creatures to a "ritual"? What if the ritual was human
sacrifice? The Drood had been very kind so far, but rituals in
temples to change the weather sounded a bit weird, like the
bloodthirsty rites of ancient civilizations.

The temple, on the inside, was not what she was expecting.
There were no altars or statues or paintings. It was unheated,
so rather chilly. Also quite dim, as dusk was fast approaching, the windows weren't big and there were no fancy lamps
or candles or any other kind of illumination that you might

expect in a temple, just a single naked light bulb dangling down from the ceiling way up high. It reminded Dhikilo of her school hall, where they put on plays and had the yearly prize-giving. Big and boxy and slightly gloomy and a bit echoey, with a stage that was shrouded with a huge moth-nibbled curtain.

Two of the Drood pulled the curtains aside to reveal the stage. The polished wooden floor was crowded with musical instruments.

There were two large keyboards—one looked like a grand piano but bright green and with no lid; the other looked like a harpsichord or harmonium. There were guitars and mandolins and an autoharp and an oud. There was a double bass so tall that only the tallest Drood would be capable of reaching the top of its neck. Cushions were laid on the floor in case anyone fancied playing the sitar. Lots of woodwind instruments nestled upright in special stands—flutes and clarinets and bagpipes and so on. And over there: was that a xylophone or a vibraphone or a marimba? Even in England, Dhikilo wasn't sure she would be able to tell the difference, and this beautiful sculpture of metal blocks and mallets might be unique to Liminus. And so many percussion instruments! Drums of every conceivable kind, including African ones like the djembe, Japanese ones like the o-daiko and the Indonesian kendang.

"This is brilliant!" exclaimed Dhiliko, so excited she couldn't help jumping on the spot. "It's like at my school, but ten times better! You've got everything!"

The Drood smiled their white smiles. One of them spread his arms in pride. "We are mugishamsh!"

"Musicians?"

"Mushishamsh, yesh," grinned the Drood. "Alsho magishamsh!"

"Magicians?"

"Yesh!" And he raised a triumphant fist in the air.

"We make magical mushic," explained another Drood. "Or mushical magic. For making uh shmow go away. For making uh raih fall. For making uh shum come back."

Another Drood, one of the stately females, lifted her chin imperiously and declared, "Evewy eveming we make magic here. We shall pwevail."

Through the nearest window, the feeble sun and the stubborn snow were plain to see. Dhikilo naturally felt like asking whether the weather had ever taken the slightest notice of the Drood's magic music. But she guessed that the answer would be no, and she could tell that the ritual was nevertheless very important to these people. It brought their community together, and it made them feel they hadn't given up hope.

"Will you pway wiv ush?" said the stately female Drood, extending a furry black hand.

"Pray with you?"

The Drood laughed. "ngo! Pway! Pway!" And she pointed towards the stage.

One by one, the Drood ascended six steps at the side and took their places, picking up clarinets and flutes and drumsticks. Someone took a seat at one of the keyboards, then someone else took a seat at the other one. Dhikilo felt a little pang of regret that she hadn't leapt up there first.

Then she leapt up there anyway, to the welcoming applause of the Drood. She chose the xylophone–vibraphone–marimba thing. It was the next-best thing to a piano because instead of hitting keys that operated mallets, you held mallets in your hands and hit keys. Sort of.

"Wung choo free four!" announced the Drood with the oud. And they were off.

It was a beautiful noise they made together. It wasn't like any kind of music that got played at Cawber School for Girls or on the radio or in movies. It was more ancient and weird and sad and yet also cheeky and frisky. It was all the feelings people can have, swirling around like waves in the ocean.

Dhikilo hit the bars of her xylophone-vibraphone-marimba thing very softly at first, to work out which notes were wrong and which were right. Then when she got the hang of it, she hit one right note quite firmly whenever its time came round, and then she made up a little tune of four notes and hit them whenever they fitted in with what the Drood were doing. The Drood were delighted. Not only did they nod their approval, but they added harmonies to Dhikilo's tune with their own instruments. "Shing wiv ush!" called the Drood at the bright green piano, and the Drood all began to sing, in deep dignified voices, just *oooh*s and *aaaah*s, no words.

Dhikilo *oooh*ed and *aaaah*ed for a while, but the performance went on and on, and even though it was beautiful and pleasurable, she wondered how long it would last. It was a ritual, after all. Were they supposed to keep going until they collapsed in exhaustion? She didn't fancy that.

After a few more minutes, she had an idea. If the whole point of this performance was to change the weather, maybe she should just tell the weather what was wanted?

So she lifted her hand towards the window, making the same shape with her fingers as she made when doing her "Sun!" trick for Mariette, Fiona and Molly.

"*Snoooooooooow,*" she sang, pretending she was an opera singer.

"*It's really time for you to gooooo.*

"*So things can hurry up and groooow.*

"*What to sing next I do not knooooow…*"

After a moment's hesitation, she added:

"*Hallelujah! Hallelujah! Ha-lay-lu-jaaah!*" from the old song by Handel.

It seemed to fit.

The Drood tootled and fluted and strummed and hummed for a few seconds and then motioned to her to sing some more.

"*Suuuuuuuuun,*" she sang.
"*It would be nice to have some suuuuun.*
"*It would put smiles on everyoooooone.*
"*Some sun would def'nitely be fuuuuun.*
"*Hallelujah! Hallelujah! Ha-lay-lu-jaaah!*"
Then:
"*Raaaaaaaaain.*
"*We'd like to see some rain agaaaaaain.*
"*In, erm, this place that isn't Spaaaaaain.*
"*Too long this snowy snow has laaaaain.*
"*Hallelujah! Hallelujah! Ha-lay-lu-jaaah!*"

Dhikilo's singing inspired the Drood to even more joyful playing. The piano and the various drums got louder and louder, and everyone was looking at everyone else, waiting for the signal to stop, and finally, with one last exultant flourish, they all finished at once.

"Bravo!" shouted the Drood with the oud, and everyone laughed and applauded.

Outside, the sun glimmered and went ghostly grey, and snowflakes started spiralling down from the leaden sky.

Nothing Like a Comb

As night fell, everyone went to their own homes. The house where Dhikilo and Mrs Robinson had been welcomed grew quiet. A mattress and some well-used but clean bedding were brought out for the guests to make up as they wished. No evening meal was offered; presumably there wasn't enough food for that. The Drood were so grand with their long slender legs and arms and necks, but Dhikilo wondered if the slenderness was really the beginnings of starvation.

"Shleep well," said their hostess as she backed out of the room. Dhikilo waved her goodnight. It seemed a shame not to spend more of the evening talking.

Mrs Robinson had woken up. She was still in sphinx form, her violet eyes glowering. She yawned, showing most of her fangs.

"I thought I'd let you sleep," Dhikilo said. "I hope that was all right."

"Yesss," said the sphinx.

"I was singing and playing with the Drood. They do a magic ritual every day to make the normal weather come back."

"Yesss," said the sphinx.

"Is there anything I can do for you?"

"Yesss."

A few seconds passed, and Dhikilo thought that maybe the sphinx had lapsed into the habit of saying "Yes" to anything anyone said. Then she noticed that Mrs Robinson was blinking irritably against the tangled strands of hair that hung in front of her eyes. All the running and escaping and sweating and being snowed on had not been good for her grooming.

"My hair," said the sphinx.

"Oh! Yes," said Dhikilo, and reached for her jacket, then remembered that actually there was no comb or brush in her jacket or anywhere else. Back in her house in Cawber, she had a special comb for her type of hair, a comb that Ruth urged her to take with her wherever she went. It lived mostly on top of the chest of drawers in her bedroom, and sometimes in her schoolbag. But not in her pocket when she was just nipping out to the post office.

Did the Drood use combs? They were impressively sleek, but maybe they just licked their fur, like cats. In any case, their hostess had gone to bed and Dhikilo didn't want to disturb her. Instead, she walked around the room checking all the surfaces, hoping that a comb or brush might've been left lying about.

It hadn't, and that was bad news. Some tasks can be done easily enough when you haven't got quite the right tools. For example, all sorts of things can be achieved if you're forced to use a substitute for a ruler or a hammer or a mop. But there's nothing like a comb, really.

Except...

She sat down in front of the sphinx and held up what she'd found: a fork. An ordinary metal fork, for eating with.

Mrs Robinson looked at the four-pronged implement. Her face betrayed no reaction.

"Shall we try it?" said Dhikilo.

The sphinx nodded once.

Dhikilo set to work. The fork would only do a few strands at a time and got stuck frequently. Dhikilo teased out little clumps of dirt (there was even a fragment of twig) and, little by little, the worst of the mess got fixed. But each time the fork got stuck, she pulled at Mrs Robinson's scalp in a way that would've *really* hurt if Mrs Robinson was a human.

"Let me know if this is uncomfortable," said Dhikilo.

The sphinx remained silent. The fork pulled her head askew again. A tangle untangled. One tangle among hundreds. This might take all night.

When the fork got stuck for the umpteenth time, Dhikilo said, "Can I… Would it be all right if I used my fingers?"

The sphinx did not reply, but tilted her head back in submission. With her eyes and mouth closed, she spared Dhikilo the sight of those weird eyes and those sharp fangs. Instead, she just resembled a middle-aged woman who was very, very tired.

Dhikilo inserted her hands into Mrs Robinson's hair. It was soft like a human's, yet strong as twine. The knots and matted locks came loose much more easily when nudged with fingers and nails. As the minutes passed, Mrs Robinson regained the proud beauty that the arduous journey had taken away. Eventually, Dhikilo felt free to stroke the hair, smoothing it back from the sphinx's cheeks and forehead, fluffing it out so that some of its proper volume was restored. It was actually very nice hair. Brushing it with a proper brush would probably be a very satisfying activity.

"I suppose the Professor usually does this for you?"

"Yesss."

"I suppose he does it much better."

The sphinx didn't answer.

Finally, Dhikilo's arms were aching and Mrs Robinson looked fabulous, and Dhikilo said, "That's the best I can do."

The sphinx shook her hair, seemed content with the way it fell around her shoulders.

"Yesss," she said. "Yessss."

Dhikilo made up the bed and switched off the light. The room had grown colder and she was glad to get under the blanket, which was a knitted one in green, orange and white wool. When she got back home to Cawber—*if* she ever got home— she would ask Ruth if she could have a blanket like this, instead of the puffy duvet with the princesses on it. Malcolm had been dropping heavy hints that for Christmas she might be getting an iPad. She didn't want an iPad. She wanted a blanket whose weave she could feel with her fingertips.

After a few minutes, her eyes adjusted to the dark and she could see Mrs Robinson's eyes glowing as though they had little purple lights inside them. She wondered if the sphinx would ever change into Nelly the Labrador again, or if that lovely dog had never been anything more than a disguise, which was now discarded.

The edge of the mattress rustled and Dhikilo felt its shape altering. The sphinx settled down beside her. The room was growing colder by the minute. Mrs Robinson kept herself to one side, except for one curve of her furry flank which rested gently against Dhikilo's hip through the blanket. The creature uttered one deep sigh—a sigh as deep as any dog's—and then her breathing settled into the rhythm of sleep.

Outside, the wind died down and there was a faint pattering noise, like the footfalls of tiny animals. Dhikilo hoped that the house wasn't being surrounded and overrun by rodents of some sort. Quite enough nasty things were being inflicted on the long-suffering Land of Liminus already. Then, just as she was getting properly worried, she fell asleep.

ALL HALLELUJAHING

When Dhikilo woke in the morning, she was too warm. Far too warm! For lots of reasons…

First, during the night, her body had come to a fine agreement with the blanket, sheets and mattress; they'd all got on really well and found the perfect balance of natural blood-circulation and cosy wrapped upness. She was snug as a caterpillar in a cocoon.

Second, there was a big brown Labrador sleeping next to her, which was like having the world's biggest, most luxurious hot-water bottle. Nelly's breath was quite hot, too, puffing gently onto Dhikilo's shoulder. Her furry flank rose and fell, and her mended leg had laid itself across Dhikilo's ankle through the covers.

Also, the sun had come up. The Drood's houses must be really cleverly designed, because there seemed to be oodles of light beaming in, despite the early hour.

Also, the room had heated up considerably. Someone must've snuck in very quietly this morning and lit a fire, so that the guests wouldn't have to get up in the dawn chill. The

Drood really were wonderfully hospitable. But Dhikilo worried they might be using up all their precious fuel.

She slipped out of bed and walked over to the window. The sun hadn't risen far off the horizon yet. It was big and warm and yellow, too bright to stare at. She rested her eyes on the dark brown patches of earth that had been exposed by the melting snow. The gutters of the house opposite were dripping rainwater onto the ground, quite loudly, although the rain had stopped. There were puddles everywhere, reflecting blue sky.

"Mrs Robinson!" she shouted.

Mrs Robinson jerked awake and leapt off the mattress so quickly that she fell and rolled over onto her back. Comically heaving herself right-way up again, she rushed to Dhikilo's side, ready to attack any enemy that was threatening them. Instead, she saw golden sunshine and the silvery aftermath of a night full of rain.

When the Drood discovered what had happened, they went half-mad with joy. They dashed around, embracing each other, lifting each other aloft, legs kicking in the air.

"Magic!" they cried. "You are magic!"

One by one, and two by two, they rushed up to Dhikilo to kiss and embrace her. Within a few minutes, she'd rubbed faces with so much cat fur that her cheeks were getting itchy.

"It was *our* song," she protested. "We did it together!"

Or maybe, she thought, *the right time just came for things to change.*

Dhikilo got dressed and joined the Drood in their exploration of the shining new world outside. There was no doubt that spring had come: the sun was now as warm as any sun she'd ever felt in England. Could this be summer, not spring? Summer shouldn't come straight after winter, it wasn't natural, but then the winter that Liminus had suffered wasn't natural, either.

"Shpwing!" shouted one of the Drood, and "Shpwing!" another responded, and that seemed to settle the question.

The whiteness of the landscape was melting away before Dhikilo's eyes. Clods of snow fell off the houses, scattering into slushy fragments which immediately sank into puddles. Sheets of ice creaked and cracked and collapsed into ditches, and the ditches trickled into small streams.

The dark tracks made by Dhikilo and the Drood as they ran about grew bigger, losing their resemblance to footprints, joining up in unpredictable patterns of colour. Patches of grass came into view, clammy and clumpy at first, but then, as the sun warmed them, perking up and looking more alive.

"Hawwa-woojah!" sang one of the Drood who'd been at yesterday's concert. "Hawwa-woojah! Hawaaay-woojah!" She was imitating Dhikilo's imitation of Handel's tune. It didn't sound much like the original that Mr Berger had got the students at Cawber School for Girls to practise, but it sounded good.

Soon all the Drood were singing it, the ones who'd been at the concert and the ones who hadn't, all hallelujahing to welcome the spring, swaying in the sunshine that had been cold for so long and now, at last, was mellow.

Dhikilo joined in, copying their tune even as they imagined they were copying hers. And, as she sang, she spotted Nelly coming back from somewhere behind the houses, where she'd gone for a pee, and she was still a dog.

All things considered, it was one of the best days ever.

Why Seek Evil?

Among the creatures cheered up by the sunshine were the dragonflies. A fresh flurry of them flew overhead, still carrying the stolen Ds, although the radiance coming off the letters was more difficult to see now that the entire sky was bright.

Dhikilo was feeling so encouraged by everything that she felt encouraged, too, by how swiftly and industriously the dragonflies were flying. For a moment, she got muddled and guessed they must be travelling in the opposite direction from before, carrying the Ds back to the wounded words that had lost them. But no. They were still heading straight for the city of Gampalonia (not so far away now), and the mild weather only meant that the theft of the Ds could be conducted more efficiently.

"Go back!" she called up at the insects. "Things have changed!"

But the insects ignored her. Whatever method or magic spell the Gamp had used to compel them to follow his orders, it was still working, and one little human girl shouting up at them from the ground wasn't going to change their minds. Did dragonflies even *have* minds? Their brains were the size of breadcrumbs.

Dhikilo took off her jacket and held it by one of the cuffs, then she *fwapped* it in the air above her, like a whip. She was hoping to disturb the dragonflies' flight path, maybe confuse them, but all she managed to do was flick one unfortunate insect with the tip of the sleeve. It fell to the ground, dead. She rushed over to the patch of slush where it had landed and touched the dainty D that lay there, disappearing in front of her eyes, diminishing and dwindling and finally fading away. She stuck her forefinger into the last vestige of its glow, right between the limp dead legs of the dragonfly. No picture flared up in her imagination of anything that had a D in it: no dromedary or dolphin or desk or duffel coat. Only a vague, formless impression of something dark and big and nasty that was somewhere out of sight but might harm her at any second.

Danger.

Mrs Robinson padded up to Dhikilo's side. She was walking well, not really limping, just being careful with her newly mended leg.

"We should go," said Dhikilo, looking around. The Drood were still dashing about, celebrating. It would probably take quite a long time for them to calm down.

Mrs Robinson nodded. She'd already had to run away from an excited young Drood who'd tried to embrace her. Fooling about in playful exuberance was all very nice but it was not Nelly's natural disposition. She was a working dog. (Or a working sphinx?) And there was work to be done. The world they'd come from—so distant from Liminus, yet so closely connected—was in deep trouble, and the Professor was waiting for them to complete their mission.

"We need to get the Ds back," said Dhikilo. Again Mrs Robinson nodded.

A few minutes later, Dhikilo explained to the Drood why she must continue her journey. A wise old leader of the tribe, whose fur was peppered with white hairs, looked sad.

"Schay wif ush a while wonger," he pleaded. "You are weary. Be welcome. Shweep, wake, shweep, wake, grow shronger."

"That's very kind of you," said Dhikilo. "But we need to find out what's happening to the Ds. We need to find the Gamp."

The old Drood shook his head. "Why? Why sheek evil? Gamp will isshapear evemchually. Emperorsh come, emperorsh go."

"Yes," said Dhikilo, "but I don't think we can wait a hundred years."

The old leader laid his furry hand gently on Dhikilo's shoulder. "Gamp ish powerful," he fretted. "You are shmall girl..."

But another Drood objected: "She ish powerful! She chage uh wevver! She brough' back uh shum! Behol her power!" And he waved his arms all around, to call everyone's attention to the miracle of spring.

Soon enough, the Drood accepted that Dhikilo and Mrs Robinson must go. The community sprang into farewelling action. Dhikilo was given a beautiful new scarf in green, orange and white, to replace the one she'd sacrificed for Nelly's bandage, and an elegant, wide-toothed comb for Mrs Robinson. Cheery yet strangely doleful tunes were played on the mysterious carved guitar-like instrument, and the Drood explained that these melodies were ancient songs especially designed to confer "chavewwing mershiesh" upon friends who were about to embark on a risky voyage and might benefit from some travelling mercies.

There was a marvellous breakfast, at which all sorts of delicacies were brought out that hadn't been available the day before, as though the change of weather was already having an effect on Liminus's famine. The Drood even served up an unidentifiable treat for Mrs Robinson which wasn't meat but which she devoured with great enjoyment.

Then, just as Dhikilo and Mrs Robinson were setting off, the sunny sky unleashed a brief shower of fresh rain, which created the first rainbow the Drood had seen for years. This made them even more excited and grateful, and Dhikilo felt embarrassed, because a rainbow was a scientific thing, a combination of light rays and moisture, and not the magical result of a girl's song. Or was it?

"Come back awive!" called the wise old chieftain after them as they stepped onto the road out of the village. It wasn't the most encouraging parting wish, although it was hollered in such a majestic, musical tone that it felt more upbeat than the Professor's "Strive to achieve the aim without death or serious injury!"

"Are we walking the right way for Gampalonia?" asked Dhikilo.

"I fear sho!" quipped the old Drood. And indeed right at that moment some more dragonflies flew overhead, easily overtaking the girl and her dog.

The Real Eal and Other Impressive Artefacts

(as emonstrated by the eitizens of littlegampton)

They didn't have to walk far before there was no need to wonder any more if they were heading the right way: the city of Gampalonia grew visible on the skyline. It was looming up to meet them.

And "loom" was the right word, because "loom" has a gloomy, doomy sound to it and the cityscape had a gloomy, doomy appearance. Even from a long distance, it looked like the sort of place you would rather not be going to; a destination you'd rather not reach. It wasn't a magical-looking city like the ones in fairy stories. There were no castles or minarets or turrets. Just huge rectangular towers made of something dull-coloured, like cardboard boxes. A horizon littered with packing material. And if you stared long enough, you could glimpse a faint pall of smoke rising from somewhere behind the foremost rows of buildings.

Apart from that, Liminus was getting more cheerful every minute. Much of the snow had melted and grassy fields twinkled in its place. Under the warm sun, boggy puddles became patches of mud and then stretches of rich, moist earth, ready to sprout whatever seeds had been trapped below the surface for too long. The eerie quiet that had reigned since Dhikilo and Mrs Robinson first stepped through the portal in Gas Hill Garens was dispelled. The land was full of noises. Water trickled along fresh channels. Insects buzzed. There was a pleasant sort of creaking or croaking which might be the sodden, steaming ruins of abandoned buildings drying out, or might be frogs. Also, subtle squeaks and twittering which sounded like birds, even though no birds could be seen and there hadn't been enough time yet for any to be born.

"Isn't it wonderful!" said Dhikilo, turning to Mrs Robinson, then remembered that she couldn't respond while in dog form. She hoped Mrs Robinson wouldn't change back into a sphinx just to say "Yes." But no, the dog did no such thing. And, in a way, Mrs Robinson said "Yes" by wagging her tail. That meant "Yes" in dog language, didn't it? Or, at the very least, it meant that Mrs Robinson was in good spirits.

There was one last village to be passed through before the big city. It was signposted with a large wooden placard screwed on to a pole.

LITTLEGAMPTON

A few steps further on, there was another pole with another placard.

ALSO KNOWN AS GAMPVILLE

A smaller sign was tacked on to the same pole, about halfway down, very crooked, so that Dhikilo had to tip her head sideways to read it:

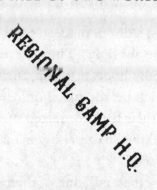

Littlegampton, or Gampville, was as sad a place as the Quilps' village, with squat grubby buildings that were crumbling from neglect. The only reason it didn't look quite as miserable as the Quilps' village was that the sun was shining brightly and it's difficult for even the most dismal buildings to look grim if the sun is bathing them with golden light.

It occurred to Dhikilo that the Drood had not given her any advice or forewarning about the inhabitants of this village—whether they might be friendly or homicidal. If there was a risk of being speared to death, surely the Drood would've mentioned it? But maybe they'd been so preoccupied with celebrating the magical end of winter that it had slipped their mind?

Peering at the grimy, steamed-up windows of the houses ahead, Dhikilo could see the silhouettes of their restlessly moving inhabitants. It seemed unlikely that she and Mrs Robinson could sneak all the way through the village without being noticed, so she decided she might as well announce their arrival. Getting stabbed in the front seemed less unpleasant than getting stabbed in the back, somehow.

"Hello-o!" she called.

In the nearest house, a round ugly face pressed up against the window.

"Hello-o!" he called back. He didn't seem startled or suspicious. Just very short.

Within seconds, a dozen modest-sized men had emerged, blinking, into the sunlight. They were as furry as bears, naked, wearing only boots. On top, they were all perfectly bald, but with thick beards and shoulder-length hair at the back; it was as if their fur had started melting off at the uppermost point and they'd somehow managed to stop it halfway down their faces.

"We are the Spottletoes!" one of them proclaimed.

"Pleased to meet you," said Dhikilo. "I'm Dhikilo, and this is Mrs Robinson." She looked aside, just in case Mrs Robinson had changed back into a sphinx, but no, she was still a dog. Her eyes were calm and she was breathing normally; the small crowd of hairy strangers didn't seem to alarm her at all. If dogs have an instinct for dangerous creatures, that instinct had evidently not been triggered by the Spottletoes.

"You are welcome in our humble shrine to all things Gamp!" said one, waving his arm towards the village in general.

Another boasted: "There is no place, other than the Gamp's own mansions, where so many artefacts in honour of our great ruler are on free isplay!"

"Many times, we've thought of charging entrance fees to view these treasures, but each time, we realize: everyone must have the opportunity to experience—"

"...or even *own*—"

"...these high-quality souvenirs."

The Spottletoes looked at each other, nodding in vigorous approval, before realizing that they hadn't yet shown their guests any treasures.

"Please, please, come with us," said a Spottletoe. "I hope you have plenty of time to spare. An entire afternoon is barely long enough to take in everything we have here."

"We're...just passing through, actually," said Dhikilo.

"A pity," said the Spottletoe. "But we'll give you the abbreviate version of the full tour. You'll just have to let us know if the sheer ensity of excitements is too much for you to stan!"

"OK," said Dhikilo, as she allowed her hosts to lead her and Mrs Robinson to a house festooned with signs mentioning the name "Gamp" as many times as possible. An ornate G, made of papier-mâché and painted gold (or, in truth, yellow with some glittery spangles mixed in) was hung on the door.

"That's not for sale," said a Spottletoe, noticing Dhikilo glancing at it. "Although we can make one specially for you, almost the same."

The door was swung open, but just before Dhikilo and Mrs Robinson were ushered in, a Spottletoe asked, "Your og is safe, I hope?"

"Safe?" said Dhikilo.

"He won't break anything?"

"She's a she," said Dhikilo. "I'm sure she'll be very careful. She's a guide dog."

"…because all breakages must be pai for," the Spottletoe added.

"You're not blin, are you?" enquired another Spottletoe.

"Blind? No," said Dhikilo.

"Because you'll appreciate these wonerful sights a lot more if you can see 'em," said the Spottletoe. "They are highly visual."

With that, they were in.

The museum, or gift shop, or whatever it was supposed to be, wasn't exactly fancy. It reminded Dhikilo of the indoor market that was held several times a year in the Cawber Methodist Church, where tough-skinned poor people would banter with each other while trying to sell ugly plastic toys, slightly worn-out shoes and almost-complete jigsaw puzzles. The Cawber Methodist Church didn't pong, though. The

Storehouse of Gamp smelled musty, like a basketload of wet washing that someone had meant to hang out to dry but forgotten about.

"Welcome!" declared a Spottletoe. "You will notice, I'm sure, that the carpet on which you walk is ientical to the one in the entrance of the Gamp's own banquet hall!"

Dhikilo looked down. Under her muddy boots was a length of threadbare red fabric, much dulled by constant traffic from previous visitors' dirty feet. On closer inspection it was decorated with many small Gs, which she'd mistaken for stubborn smudges of darker dirt.

"And here is a replica," said one of the Spottletoes, pointing to a large chair painted fake gold like the G on the door, "of the exact chair that the Gamp sits upon when he sits in thought. All his best ecisions have arisen while his bottom was given support in a seat of precisely this esign."

Dhikilo looked at the chair and didn't know what to say. She looked at Mrs Robinson. The dog was nodding solemnly. So Dhikilo turned back towards the esteemed chair and nodded solemnly, too.

"We live in hope," said a Spottletoe, "that the Gamp may visit our humble shrine at some point, when his busy timetable permits. Then, he will no oubt oblige us by sitting in this chair, which will increase its value a thousanfol."

Next, the Spottletoes called attention to a trestle table on which lay half a dozen objects that looked like dead squirrels. With the utmost dignity, a Spottletoe picked up one of these furry clumps and positioned it on his bald head, tying it round his neck with a couple of bits of dangling shoelace. It was a wig, it seemed, or maybe a hat. A sort of hairy bonnet.

"These are for sale," said the Spottletoe.

"Amazing hats, the ultimate in comfort," said another Spottletoe, tying on his own equally fluffy specimen. "Just the thing to stop the ears freezing in the current conitions. As you see, there are special ear-shape flaps that fit snugly over the most sensitive parts. Protect yourself from frostbite while being stylish!"

"Very nice, but we don't have any money," said Dhikilo.

"No one has any money any more," sighed the Spottletoe, glum-faced. "It's a miracle our country keeps going."

"It keeps going thanks to our great ruler," his friend reminded him.

"Yes, but sooner or later, we're going to nee—" the glum one began, only to be hastily interrupted by a colleague.

"And here we have a comprehensive range of the Gamp's anti-winter equipment." The Spottletoe pointed to a jumble of oddments. "Everything anyone might want in the struggle against the isaster that has befallen us."

"Not such a isaster, thanks to the Gamp!" interjected his friend breezily. "Really, life is a hunre times better since he took us into his care. The Spottletoes are earer to his heart than any other race. He's more than just a ruler to us—he's like a father! The best, wisest, lovingest father imaginable!"

The other Spottletoes nodded uneasily, aware that the praise had gone a little over the top, in the circumstances.

"A special broom," said the first Spottletoe, pointing to a pink and yellow broom-shaped object, "for sweeping the snow away from your front oor. Each inivual bristle mae of high-quality plastic, hence the higher price than orinary brooms.

"Surprisingly warm plastic gloves," he said next, indicating some thin pink gloves which looked as though they would be cold and clammy, "available in size Small, lined with luxurious flock paper."

Dhikilo figured that, for politeness' sake, she should probably take an interest in one of the items before it was formally pointed out to her. She leaned forward to examine a folded-up scrunch of white paper, daintily balanced on the table on two of its pointy edges. If you squinted a bit, it resembled a duck or a swan. Dhikilo had been in a Thai restaurant once where the napkins were folded to look like birds. It had seemed a shame to unfold them and wipe your mouth with them, but Ruth had assured her that it took the staff only a few moments to make each one.

"It's a tissue," explained the Spottletoe. "A tissue into which the Gamp himself blew his nose, three years ago. We have our previous curator to thank for this exhibit, bless his soul. He saw a work of art where others might've seen a snotty scrap of rubbish. With each year that passes, it grows lighter, more elicate. You can almost imagine it taking wing, can't you?"

"Yes," said Dhikilo, and she actually could. But if by some magic it did take wing, she hoped it might fly away from her rather than towards her.

"Moving right along," said a Spottletoe, in haste to enthuse about more artefacts, "super-luminous flashlights for those long ark nights." He grabbed one, switched it on, nothing happened, so he grabbed another, switched that on, and a pale yellowish glow leaked out from the bulb.

"I've already got a flashlight," said Dhikilo, trying to sound informative rather than exasperated.

"I'll bet it's not as goo as these."

"The long dark nights are over anyway," Dhikilo observed, nodding towards the world outside, which was radiant with summery sun.

"Maybe. Maybe not. There's been no official statement about that yet. The Gamp has not yet spoken."

"But can't you see the sun's out?" said Dhikilo.

"We're waiting for confirmation on that issue. In the meantime, these are the best flashlights money can buy."

Dhikilo nodded again, wishing the Spottletoes would stop

talking for just a few seconds, so that she could think of a less offensive way to say she'd had enough of their Gamp-related rubbish than "I've had enough of your Gamp-related rubbish."

"Not getting quite enough nourishment in these times of famine?" babbled one of the Spottletoes. "Gamp vitamins give you everything you're missing!"

"Taste great, too!"

"Teeth falling out? Plug the gaps with Gamp tooth replacements! No nee for surgery, they slot right in! Urable plastic, white 'n' bright! Get your bite back! Time to smile again!"

"This all looks very…impressive," said Dhikilo, a little louder than she'd spoken so far, in case it made any difference. "But we really must be going. We've been travelling a long time and we've had some delays and it's time we got to Gampalonia."

"Unerstoo! Unerstoo!" cried the Spottletoes. "After all, who wouln't want to go to Gampalonia?"

"I suppose you go there all the time," remarked Dhikilo.

"How happy that woul make us!" said the Spottletoes. "Unfortunately, the hotel prices are quite beyon our meagre buget."

Dhikilo thought of asking why they didn't simply stay with their old friend the Gamp, but she had a feeling she knew the answer.

"Tell us," said a Spottletoe, "how have *you* foun the hotels in our country? Afforable?"

"We've only stayed in one so far," said Dhikilo. "I can't remember the name of it. It was huge, almost a castle, with a statue of a horse in front. The rooms changed all the time and we couldn't get out."

"I know the one you mean!" exclaimed a Spottletoe. "Bleak House! Bought by the Gamp himself! Lovingly restore! It has a marvellous reputation. Five stars. The cream scones are suppose to be absolutely heavenly! Not to mention the luxurious rooms with all their fancy history! How I woul love to stay there just once before I ie! But it's quite beyon the means of a humble Spottletoe."

Another of the hairy men asked, "What about last night? I suppose you staye at the Royal Bog Inn? Although some-one tol me a while ago that the place has finally sunk into the marsh. Is that true or just a rumour?"

"We didn't see any hotels," said Dhikilo. "We stayed with the Drood."

"The Roo?" echoed a Spottletoe with barely concealed re-vulsion. "You are lucky to be alive. Terrible people. Savages. Harly better than animals."

"They were really nice to us," said Dhikilo. "Much nicer than the Quilps, who tried to eat us."

"The Quilps? We have no quarrel with the Quilps. Sure, they're not the smartest of creatures, but they're har-working. Own-to-earth, ecent toilers. The sort that have kept this country going, if I may say so. Nothing wrong with them that a bottle of Gamp bath-soap wouln't fix."

"As for the cannibalism thing," added another Spottletoe, "I can see why some people might think it was a problem, but they're hungry. It's natural. We're all hungry. Personally, I think eating passers-by is the wrong solution. But I uner-stan where the Quilps are coming from."

"They just nee to have a little more faith in the Gamp, that's all. Soon enough, Liminus will be a lan of plenty once again. Then the Quilps will be top-rate citizens, you'll see."

"I suppose you like the Magwitches, too?" ventured Dhikilo.

"The Magwitches!? Irty isgusting evil emons!" exploded the nearest Spottletoe, amid general indignation from his brothers. "The Magwitches are half the reason things went wrong in the first place! The Gamp was *never* their frien, never! Where is the proof for that accusation?" He paused for a fraction of a second, as if to give Dhikilo ample opportunity to come up with some proof. Then: "See? There isn't any."

"Ignorant people say the most outrageous things," complained another Spottletoe. "They say that the Magwitches are the real power behin the throne, that they whisper into the Gamp's ear, that he relies on them for all his opinions! Imagine that! The greatest, most magnificent genius in the history of our civilization, the lone pioneer of our triumphant rescue, epenent on the avice of a bunch of filthy shabby little tramps! What makes people invent such insane stories? You won't see a Magwitch within a mile of the Gamp. Not within a hunre miles! Not within a thousan!"

The stress of being furious had brought the Spottletoes out in a sweat. Big droplets of perspiration ran down their bald heads and got absorbed in the fur below.

"Well, I'm sorry I offended you," said Dhikilo. "I didn't mean to. Now, we really must—"

"Yes, you must be going," said a Spottletoe, calming down rapidly and resuming a benevolent tone. "But let us show you just one more treasure before you leave."

All the Spottletoes hummed and nodded in approval: they knew exactly which treasure was being referred to. Dhikilo and Mrs Robinson were led to a podium on which a glowing object was draped with a white cotton shroud. Proudly, the Spottletoe removed the shroud, to reveal a transparent glass sculpture with many stalks or legs, illuminated by a single light bulb screwed into the base.

"It's a moel," said the Spottletoe. Dhikilo assumed he meant model, as this thing did not look like a mole; it looked like a jellyfish.

"It looks like a jellyfish," she said.

"Clueless foreigners always say that," sighed the Spottletoe. "It's a scale moel of…" (he paused for effect) "…the Tower of Light."

There was a hush, during which it became obvious that he was not going to volunteer any further explanation.

"The Tower of Light?" echoed Dhikilo, doing a thing with her eyebrows that she hoped would get results.

"The Tower of Light," agreed the Spottletoe. "The greatest builing ever built. The architectural pinnacle of civilization. All previous builings were nothing more than ress rehearsals for this. This is the real eal."

Dhikilo gazed at the sculpture, imagining tiny people walking about in it. Try as she might, it still looked like a jellyfish to her. Or maybe a spider with unusually fat legs, standing on its tiptoes.

"Is it the Gamp's palace?" she asked.

"Palaces are for kings," pronounced the Spottletoe. "The Gamp is more than a king, more than a sultan, more than an emperor, most efinitely more than a mere prime minister or presient. The home of such a being must be as unique as the Gamp himself. Hence this." And he gazed down in worship at the jellyfish-spider-lightbulb-ornament thing.

To Dhikilo's relief, the Spottletoes at last ushered them out of the museum, back into the fresh air and sunshine. The hairy men looked up at the sky, their bald heads rimpled with frowns, as if the warm weather was a puzzling and perhaps even inconvenient phenomenon, a development that might in some way spoil everything. However, at that moment, a small swarm of dragonflies passed overhead, carrying the usual freight of luminous Ds. The Spottletoes grunted in satisfaction, reassured that one thing, at least, was proceeding as normal.

"We wish you success in your journey, whatever its purpose may be."

"Well, actually," said Dhikilo, "we're...erm...curious to know what's happening to those Ds." She pointed up at the dragonflies, which were already dwindling into a twinkle, heading straight for Gampalonia.

"They're serving a terribly important purpose!" a Spottletoe told her. "They're making a great sacrifice for a vital cause!"

"Sacrifice?"

"A great sacrifice, yes."

"Why do they need to be sacrificed?" protested Dhikilo. "D is a letter of the alphabet. It's important!"

The Spottletoe's eyes narrowed. "I beg to isagree," he said. "This letter is isposable. This erisory, iminutive squiggle, which was scarcely any use to man or beast, has foun its true value at last!"

"But what's it being used for?" said Dhikilo.

"It is fuel," said the Spottletoe. "Most excellent fuel. It fees the Ynamo of our inustrial engine!"

"I don't understand," said Dhikilo. She'd heard about dynamos in Science class. "You mean the Ds are being burnt?"

"It's their estiny! Haven't you hear the Gamp's speeches on this subject? Ever since the Awn of Time, one letter was chosen for sacrifice, so that in our hour of nee we all might be rescue from isaster! It was foretol from the beginning! We mustn't think of it as losing a letter, we must see it as the fulfilment of a prophecy!"

Dhikilo thought this over for a moment. "But do you mean the Ds are being burnt?" she asked again.

The Spottletoe clasped his hairy hands together and assumed an expression of utmost gratitude. "Thanks to them, the Tower of Light lives up to its name! Thanks to them, this shining beacon of our empire never grows im!"

"But…but you're burning the Ds!" cried Dhikilo, clenching her fists.

Mrs Robinson butted her head against Dhikilo's hip. "*Muffle*," the dog growled warningly, her nose pointing towards the exit.

A Sound without Any Meaning

Hurrying away from Littlegampton after a hasty good-bye, Dhikilo and Mrs Robinson once again had the grim cityscape of Gampalonia ahead of them. It looked grimmer than before, and the pall of smoke hanging over the buildings now had a sinister significance.

"That smoke…" said Dhikilo. "That's the Ds, I bet."

Mrs Robinson didn't look up, but trotted onwards at a steady pace.

"They're burning the language," said Dhikilo. "And they're not even ashamed!" She didn't care if Mrs Robinson changed back into a sphinx now. She was angry and upset.

Overhead, some more dragonflies flew past, carrying their trophies.

"Stop it!" Dhikilo shouted up into the sky. "*Stop* it!"

But of course the brainless creatures took no notice.

Dhikilo marched on. "I suppose this means that the words that've already lost their Ds have lost them for ever," she muttered to herself. "Which means… Dolphins are stuck with being olphins. Ducks will always be ucks. Female deer will be oes. Or eer! Those lousy dragonflies will be ragonflies—serves them right!"

She marched faster, thumping her feet on the ground in agitation.

"I don't even know why we're carrying on. What's the point? What can we do now? How many words are left with Ds in? Not many, I bet. Probably all the best ones have already been ruined."

The more she thought, the more upset she got; and the more upset she got, the less able she felt to stop herself thinking.

"People will just pretend the ruined words were always like that. Or they'll just replace them with something else, something totally rubbish. There won't be such a thing as donkeys ever again, only those stupid onkey toys they had at the Derby. All sorts of things won't be things any more. They'll be dead as a dodo and it won't even be possible to say so. *Ehh as a oh-oh!* We'll all sound like babies!"

She tramped some more, almost in tears.

"And the girls at school will call me Icky, even the nice ones."

She was crying now.

"And if I ever find my real dad, what will he be? Just a sound. A sound without any meaning."

As angry people often do, she looked at the person nearest to her and tried to think of a way to make that person angry, too.

"And *you*—you'll just have to be an og, won't you? Just an og."

"*Oof*," said Mrs Robinson gently.

AN APOLOGY

Walking and crying don't go well together. Eventually you will stop doing one of them to concentrate on the other. Dhikilo and Mrs Robinson walked, and the warm sun dried Dhikilo's tears and made her wish she had lighter clothing to wear, because the polar jacket was making her sweat. And her furry boots, though comfortable, were getting damp inside, and she could feel the skin between her toes getting mushy and flaky, which couldn't be good for the feet.

When you've said an unkind thing to somebody because you were angry about something that wasn't their fault, the wrongness of it sits in your stomach like bad food. After about ten minutes, Dhikilo said, "I'm sorry I said you'd have to be an og for ever."

Mrs Robinson glanced up briefly as she trotted along, chiding Dhikilo with her soulful Labrador eyes.

"*Orfl*," she replied.

An Exciting New Evelopment

An odd thing about city skylines is that they always appear closer than they really are. It's got something to do with geometry. Anyway, when Dhikilo and Mrs Robinson set off from the Spottletoes' village, the gloomy doomy buildings of the capital seemed just a short hike across the wasteland, but then it took them hours to cover the distance.

Another odd thing about skylines is that you seem to be heading towards one for ages and then suddenly you realize you haven't seen it for a while because you're already there.

WELCOME TO GAMPALONIA, said the sign on the archway of the city gates. The archway was made of concrete fashioned to resemble ancient stones, carved (or, more likely, moulded) with the letter G in every conceivable style. The gates were open and there were no guards, which encouraged Dhikilo to think that her fears of danger might be exaggerated.

As soon as they stepped through the gates, the wealth of the city became obvious: the streets were paved with gold.

Or, at least, gold paint. Each paving stone (or concrete imitation of a paving stone) was painted glittery yellow. In dull wintry conditions, it probably looked handsome and a bit mysterious, but in the full light of sunshine it was lairy and glarey and made you squint. Dhikilo looked around to see how the other people on the streets might be responding to the excess of reflection, but there didn't seem to be anyone else around. Which was odd, because Gampalonia was a big city and it was late afternoon on a nice day.

All the buildings she could see were ugly grey square things which could be offices or maybe warehouses or maybe department stores that hadn't yet opened. It was hard to tell because the windows were tinted and nothing was visible inside.

COMING SOON: AN EXCITING NEW EVELOPMENT! said a billboard on one of the buildings.

Another billboard, in a little side street that was barely wide enough for it, said: KEEP THIS SPACE CLEAR! NO UNAUTHORIZE VENORS, TRAERS OR PANHANLERS. On the ground beneath it, much trampled by feet, was the soiled remnant of a handwritten cardboard sign, fluttering in the breeze. Dhikilo bent down to read it.

LOVELY BIG VINTAGE BANANA, FROZEN SINCE PURCHASE, REASONABLE OFFERS ONLY

They walked on, and as they ventured deeper into the city, a few of its elusive inhabitants were revealed, scurrying down lanes and turning corners. Some of them resembled Quilps (except better dressed), one of them looked as if he might be from the same tribe as Mr Pumblechook, and there were a couple of tall thin ones, too. But they all behaved the same. Their heads were hunched into their shoulders as they hurried to wherever they were going. They appeared not to notice the presence of newcomers in their city. However, if Dhikilo and Mrs Robinson were walking on the same footpath as them, they crossed over to the other side of the street.

This happened over and over.

Once, turning a corner, Dhikilo almost ran into a stout little man walking in the opposite direction.

"*Gah!*" exclaimed the stout little man in surprise. His open mouth had only a few brown teeth in it, and his heavy overcoat was threadbare.

"Sorry," said Dhikilo. Then, while she had him there: "Nice afternoon, isn't it?"

The stout man looked up at the sky in worry.

"I on't know," he said. "Maybe. There's been no announcement yet. Excuse me; mustn't illy-ally." And he was gone.

After another five minutes or so, Dhikilo and Mrs Robinson came upon a pole which had several helpful direction markers bolted on, pointing the way to various Gampalonian attractions.

OWNING STREET, said one marker. THE WHITE HALL, said another. HIGH SECURITY PRISON, said another. NON-SPECIFIC PENITENTIARY, said another. PUBLIC ENJOYMENT AREA, said the fifth. Another arrow, pointing in exactly the same direction, said TOWER OF LIGHT.

They followed the arrow to the Public Enjoyment Area. I will tell you about it in a minute, but to be honest Dhikilo barely noticed that she'd got there because all her attention was sucked up by the spectacular amazing thing just behind it—the Tower of Light. It overshadowed everything.

Overshadowed? Precisely the wrong word. Overluminated? The Tower of Light lived up to its name, towering and radiant, a magnificent edifice of pure white brilliance, casting no shadows, only casting light. There must have been a thousand lamps inside it, all switched on, even though dusk was some way off yet. So many lamps that it made you wonder if they'd replicated themselves like mindless deep-sea organisms, proliferating until they clung in clusters to every ceiling and wall, from the ground floor to the domed roof. The Tower of Light had been erected in the spot where you might expect the city's cathedral or town hall to be. The capital's brightest jewel, created to provoke gasps of awe from all who beheld it for the first time.

And yet…it still resembled a spider or jellyfish. And that resemblance, which had been almost cute in the Spottletoes' titchy scale model, was actually rather alarming in a building the size of a cathedral. Its monumental tentacles, which had staircases and rooms inside, looked like the legs of some huge creature that might start marauding its way through the city at any minute, kicking smaller buildings in its path to smithereens.

Also, it didn't look safe. The giant windows that Dhikilo had at first assumed were made of glass were, she was now almost certain, made of ice. They glittered and gleamed lustrously, almost blinding with the reflections they threw off. The gleam and the lustre came from moisture. The windows were sweating in the sunshine. A subtle haze of vapour rose from the whole structure. Dhikilo could see a few tiny people inside the tower, making their way up and down the staircases, and she instinctively wanted to call out to them: "Get out of there! Quick!" But they were much too small and much too far away and much too high up.

The Public Enjoyment Area was a market square, similar to market squares in most big cities in other countries and other worlds. Except that such squares usually have crowds of people hanging about in them, whereas this one was eerily uninhabited. The gold paint on the paving stones had mostly worn off, which, in truth, was restful on the eye. There was a fountain, sputtering water from the mouth of a giant fish. It needed a good clean, but at least it was working again, in defiance of the sign that said, OUT OF ORDER. There were some sculptures scattered about, including a realistic family of stone ducks which would be ideal for small children to stroke or run in little circles round. That was nice. What wasn't so nice was the large rectangular wooden structure which she recognized from Professor Dodderfield's history lessons about the French Revolution. It was a guillotine.

Dhikilo stared up at the fearsome iron blade, which was held suspended high above the chopping block by strong ropes. She could tell that this wasn't a dummy replica created for educational purposes. This was the real thing.

A large billboard near the fountain said:

ANNOUNCEMENT ABOUT WEATHER, THIS SATURAY. BE THERE!

FREE NUTS & BERRIES
FOR FIRST 100 ATTENEES.
"STATE OF THE NATION" SPEECH BY

OUR GREAT LEAER.
ALSO, TRIALS & EXECUTIONS
(SUBJECT TO AVAILABILITY).

"I wonder what day it is," said Dhikilo. She'd lost count. Mrs Robinson sighed.

A small swarm of dragonflies passed overhead. They flew slowly, sluggishly. Tired out by their long journey, perhaps, or made sleepy by the sun, or maybe they were just taking it easy because they'd almost reached their goal.

Dhikilo and Mrs Robinson followed in the dragonflies' wake. This took them right past the Tower of Light, walking so close to the nearest leg of it that they could see the droplets trickling down the windows. Those windows really *were* made of ice! The hum of refrigeration motors was quite loud when you walked close by; it made a nagging, groaning sound that must surely be driving the people inside the tower crazy.

Looking up, Dhikilo caught sight of an old woman standing at one of the windows. She was wearing a uniform and waving down at Dhikilo. Well, not waving, exactly. Gesticulating, in a manner that was not at all relaxed. She seemed to be pointing at Mrs Robinson, and then shaking her head strenuously. Dhikilo waved back, knowing full well that this was not the response the person in the Tower of Light wanted of her, but figuring that a friendly wave was better than nothing.

Large puddles had formed at the base of the tower, shining silver. The concrete was painted pure white, with little glittery bits mixed in, making it look beguilingly like snow. A clever architectural idea, she had to admit. Unless…unless it *was* snow? Unless the entire framework of the tower was made of frozen water, like an igloo stretched incredibly high? No, that was ridiculous. Nobody whose job it was to build buildings could possibly make such a foolish decision. Could they?

The Tower of Light was so enormous that it took them several minutes to walk past it. The dragonflies had long since disappeared from view, but their direction had been clear and Dhikilo followed them, choosing the widest of the narrow streets that lay behind the tower. Pretty soon, she could smell burning.

NO TRESPASSING. ANGER OF EATH, said a sign at the end of the street.

And then they saw what they'd been looking for for so long: the end of the journey for the dragonflies and their stolen cargo—the power plant which the Spottletoes had referred to as the Ynamo.

It was a factory made of red brick, or of brick that would've been red if the chimneys hadn't been belching so much smoke. It was a soot-soiled, solid, low-roofed, largely subterranean structure, almost opposite in design from the miraculous Tower of Light whose power it supplied. The fumes stank of a weird mixture of diesel oil, deodorant, detergent, dhal, dried dung, digestive juices, drains and dead things.

A fresh swarm of dragonflies flew into view. They headed straight for the one chimney that wasn't spewing smoke. The top of the chimney sucked them in like the nozzle of a vacuum cleaner. The Ds twirled like tiny fireworks and the dragonflies' wings whirled in helpless resistance against the fatal suction of the factory. Then they disappeared within.

Dhikilo turned to Mrs Robinson to say something. But at that moment, there was a funny *pFFt!* sound behind them, and Nelly shuddered violently as a dart thudded into her flank, piercing deep.

Dhikilo was too surprised to understand what had happened, too shocked to reach over and pull the metal dart out of Mrs Robinson's flesh. But it didn't matter anyway. The dog reared up in fury, and the Labrador-brown of her eyes changed to the unearthly violet of the sphinx—but that was as far as she got before the poison sped through her system. Still very much a dog, she collapsed to the ground.

"Hans up! On't move! Or you'll get the same!" shouted a harsh, hoarse voice.

The Law Must Be Obeyed

Three hefty men in yellow uniforms and black leather boots emerged from the shadows and marched up to Dhikilo. They wore helmets that hid their faces and they were carrying rifles of various kinds. One of them had a large sack slung over his shoulder. Dhikilo knew she could easily outrun them, but only if they didn't shoot her, and they looked totally like they would be pleased to shoot her on the slightest pretext.

One of the men nudged Nelly's body with the toe of his boot, just to make sure the tranquillizer had done its job. Dhikilo almost said, "Don't kick her!" but then she became aware of that feeling which defenceless people always get when they're being pushed around by heavily armed bullies—fear that the bullies will do exactly the thing that you beg them not to do. So she shut up.

"Can you rea?" said one of the yellow-clad men.

"Read?" said Dhikilo. "Yes."

The yellow-clad man stiffened with disapproval at her use

of the forbidden letter. But after a deep breath, he carried on: "So, you in't bother to rea last week's new law, then?"

"I wasn't here last week," said Dhikilo.

"You won't be here *next* week, neither," remarked one of the other goons, but his colleague shushed him with the edge of a gloved hand.

"I'm talking about the law against ogs," he said sternly.

"I'm sorry," said Dhikilo. "I di—I wasn't…erm…aware that there was a law against ogs."

"Well, wake up. There is. And you was breaking it."

"I'm sorry," said Dhikilo. "What's going to happen to my friend?"

"You mean the animal? It'll be taken away to the Og Clearance Facility. Experts will examine it for isease. It will be purifie. Then…we'll estroy it."

Dhikilo thought of saying several things that she didn't say. Finally she asked, "Why?"

"Because it's a og. They're irty, isgusting beasts. They eat the foo we haven't enough of ourselves. This law was long overue."

The man with the sack busied himself shoving Mrs Robinson into it. He seemed to be more accustomed to handling dogs who weren't quite so big, and he grunted and heaved, muttering in annoyance at the way he would get one of Mrs Robinson's legs into the sack only for another leg to slip back out.

Dhikilo was forming a plan. She would apologize some more, and eventually these horrible men would send her off with a warning. They would take Nelly somewhere and she would secretly follow them to find out where, and then she would rescue Nelly somehow.

"Ignoring the law," said the first yellow-clad man, "is against the law."

"I'm really honestly truly sorry," said Dhikilo. "I'm new here."

"We can see that," said the man. "Little fuzzy wrong-colour thing you are, long way from home. You shouln't have come here. Better off staying wherever you was born."

"She looks a bit like the Roo," commented his colleague. "Maybe she's a half-bree? No fur on her, but she's black like them."

"Show us your tongue."

Dhikilo obeyed, wishing she could kick these nasty brutes instead, or bite them, or shove them into a bottomless pit of their own horribleness. But they had the guns, so she stuck out her tongue.

"On't look like a Roo to me," said the man who'd thought she might be. Meanwhile, his pal had finished stuffing Mrs Robinson into the sack.

"Anyway, as the sheriff of the Gampalonian Guar, I place you uner arrest," said the head goon. "Og ownership, for starters. Also, we've strict orers to etain any stranger who might have some connection with a espicable act of vanalism to our Glorious Leaer's valuable property."

"But I just got here!" said Dhikilo. "I haven't had time to vandalize anything!"

The sheriff of the Gampalonian Guar lifted the visor of his helmet, exposing tiny piggy eyes. Dhikilo could tell from one glance at those eyes that there would be no point arguing with him about anything, ever.

"Ever spent the night in Bleak House?"

Dhikilo didn't reply.

"Luxury hotel in the heart of Liminus's rural playgroun? Seventy-five silver coins per person per night? Each room ifferent? Tell me, little fuzz-top: is this ringing any bells in your memory?"

Dhikilo didn't reply.

"Let's go, little monkey," said the sheriff.

"Where to?" asked Dhikilo.

"To prison, of course." He seemed impatient at her slowness to catch on. He gestured with his gun and they started walking. The goon with the sack tried lifting it onto his back, but Mrs Robinson was too heavy, even for a strong man. So he dragged the sack behind him, pulling it over the paving stones.

Dhikilo tried not to panic. She told herself that the plan she'd made a few minutes ago was still a reasonable one: the only change was that she would have to escape from custody herself first before she could rescue Nelly. But her legs were trembling as she walked, and for the first time since rejecting the Drood's offer of safety and hospitality, she felt cold.

"How long… ?" she began to ask.

But the sheriff already knew what was on her mind. "You're in luck!" he barked. "Tomorrow's Saturay. We all know what happens in Gampalonia on Saturays, on't we? Lots of fun in the Public Enjoyment Area!"

His colleague felt compelled to pour a little caution on this enthusiasm. "It's tight timing," he pointed out. "She may not get put forwar till next week."

The sheriff grunted with optimistic impatience. He jabbed Dhikilo in the shoulder with his rifle to make her look up at him. "On't let him isappoint you. I'm sure we can rush an investigation through this evening, or first thing in the morning. With luck, you'll be on trial by lunchtime. Especially since there hasn't been an execution for a while. We've been running out of lawbreakers!"

"Every person," remarked the second man, "shoul have the thrill of seeing the Great Gamp at least once in their life. You'll get your wish."

"This animal weighs a ton," complained the third man. "I'll pull my poor arm out of its socket at this rate. Can't we just estroy the creature now?"

"Oi!" shouted the sheriff. "None of that! The law must be obeye!"

They walked on in silence then, with only the sound of the sack being dragged along the ground to accompany them on their march to the prison. Every bump of the sack against a cobblestone or kerb went through Dhikilo like a blow to her own body. She tried walking slower so that the men would walk slower, too, and maybe there'd be less chance of Nelly getting all bruised and broken.

"Stop ragging your feet," snarled the sheriff. "It's an offence to elay the Gampalonian Guar in the execution of their uty."

"Execution!" echoed another of the guards with a snigger. "One of my favourite wors!"

THE MARSHALSEA ROOM, NO. 8

The High Security Prison was one of those nondescript square buildings that could've been an office or maybe a warehouse or maybe a department store that hadn't yet opened, with tinted windows that made it impossible to see what was going on behind them.

"Your new home," joked the sheriff of the Gampalonian Guar. "But not for long."

A large metal door swung open and the sheriff escorted Dhikilo inside. The other two men didn't come in. Looking over her shoulder as the door swung shut, Dhikilo got one last glimpse of the sack that contained Mrs Robinson being dragged across the paving stones to wherever dogs got analysed and destroyed. She felt like crying out or falling to her knees, but she was too frightened to do anything except stand stiffly upright and do what she was told.

"This way," said the sheriff. With one hand—the other still holding the rifle pointed at her back—he pulled off his helmet, revealing a very red sweaty face. His uniform was designed for much colder weather than Liminus was experiencing right now. Dhikilo tried to imagine how she might be able to take advantage of this in some way to allow her to escape, or at least make friends with this piggy-eyed, uncomfortable, sweaty man. She couldn't think of any way. Her store of clever ideas seemed to be all used up.

"What have we got here?" said a woman sitting behind a desk—a Quilp woman who looked exactly like the murderous ogres in the Quilp village, except with slightly cleaner teeth and lurid scarlet lipstick.

"Og owner," said the sheriff. "Foreigner. Up to no goo at the Ynamo, sniffing aroun. Possible perpetrator of vanalism. Check her out, then brief the Gamp for trial tomorrow. I want her up there on that square. We've been three weeks without an execution."

The woman shrugged. "Maybe that proves people are learning to behave themselves."

"Maybe," said the sheriff. "But even the best-traine citizens nee a reminer sometimes of the consequences of misbehaviour."

The Quilp woman bent over her desk to write down some words on a piece of official paper. There was a big scab on the top of her head, with coarse dark hairs growing out of it.

"Empty your pockets," she said. She was still looking down at her paperwork and Dhikilo was slow to realize who the command was addressed to. But a gentle jab from the rifle prompted her.

One by one, she laid the following things on the table: her torch, the plastic wrapper of a chocolate bar, the comb given by the Drood for Mrs Robinson, the plastic wrapper of a snack-size piece of cheese and a small slip of paper that had been handed to her by Mr Pumblechook, confirming that Dhikilo Saxardiid Samawada Bentley had formally applied for a Special Provisional Permit-Passport Combination.

"That all?" said the Quilp woman.

Dhikilo nodded, swaying a little in terror.

"Come here," said the Quilp woman, flipping open a hatch in the desk and ushering Dhikilo into the passageway that led to the cells. But before allowing her to walk on, she clapped her paw-like hands on Dhikilo's shoulders, then her waist, squeezing the jacket in her taloned fingers.

"You forgot something," she remarked sourly, as she hauled something else out of Dhikilo's right pocket. It was a brass key with a little ornamental tag dangling from it. The Quilp woman held it up and squinted to read the engraving on the tag. But Dhikilo already knew what it would say: The Marshalsea Room, No. 8.

Just a Story Someone Had Told Her

The evening and night that Dhikilo spent in Gampalonia's High Security Prison were the loneliest and most unhappy hours of her life so far. And they were made even worse by the awareness that her life might soon be over.

Her cell was at the end of a long corridor of cells, all of which were unoccupied. A jail full of miserable prisoners is undoubtedly a sad place, but even sadder is a jail in which you are the only captive, locked away in one small corner of a large silent compound from which all other human beings have been removed.

The cell was small—barely big enough for the bunk bed that also served as a chair—and had nothing else in it except a toilet and a sink. A previous occupant had written **AMISTAT WILL RISE AGAIN** on one of the dirty grey walls. On another wall, a different prisoner had written **I'LL SAY D IF I WANT TO**—except that the defiant D had been scrubbed away so that it was a shapeless smudge. Another piece of graffiti was **EVERYONE HATES THE GAMP**, except that the word GAMP had been rubbed away so thoroughly and violently that the plaster had crumbled to reveal bare brick. On the opposite wall, yet another long-departed prisoner had scrawled **WHO WILL TAKE CARE OF MY BABY?**

There was just one small window, much higher than Dhikilo could reach, and she spent her first hour of confinement watching a ray of afternoon sunshine gradually fade away until it was replaced by darkness. There were no artificial lights in the room, so the only vague hint of illumination came from the faraway reception area where the Quilp woman presumably still sat keeping watch, or nodding off to sleep. Or maybe she had gone home, leaving Dhikilo utterly alone in this giant pen!

Time passed—very slowly, it seemed, although she had no way of telling how slow. Normally she was a girl who didn't need to look at clocks because she was busy doing things. But here in the dark, in prison far from home, she wished she could see the seconds ticking by, to know how much longer it might be until dawn. Under her breath, she counted to sixty, but she had a feeling she was counting too fast, distracted by her heartbeat.

After a long time, she shuffled over to the door of her cell and took hold of the bars and rattled them gently, just to see if the Quilp woman had been absent-minded or careless and not shut the door properly. Such a thing must surely have happened once or twice in all the thousands of years that jails and jailers had existed. But it hadn't happened here tonight.

Even though the cell was locked tight, she rattled the bars again anyway, this time in anger. How had all this happened? Why had she allowed herself to get led into this trap? Only a few days ago she'd been OK, safe under a duvet in her own home. It was the Professor's fault she wasn't under that duvet now. She was just a kid and should never have been put in so much danger. She wasn't even old enough to see a scary movie at the cinema without being accompanied by a parent.

Dhikilo sat in the dark for a long time and then she sat in the dark for a long time more, and then she walked a few steps this way, and a few steps that way, in the dark, and then she sat down again.

She remembered reading an article in a magazine about some English people who'd been kidnapped by bandits in one of those countries whose name ended in -stan, and they'd kept their spirits up by drawing a sort of mental map of their home town. They'd started with their own house and then the neighbours' houses and their street and the shops round the corner and so on. Dhikilo tried to do this for her own house and its surroundings in Cawber, but she had trouble picturing anything.

Her duvet with the blonde princesses on it: she could picture that. The kitchen, more or less, complete with toaster and a vague impression of Ruth hovering around the coffee-pot. The door to the corridor. How many steps from the house to the footpath? She wasn't sure. What did the end of the street look like? She couldn't remember. The school? She had a hazy impression of its front gates, but not the shape of the building, what it was made of, how it was laid out inside. It was as if she'd been wandering around in Liminus for years, gradually losing her grip on everything she'd left behind. It was as if there had never been any such place as Cawber, no such place as England. It was just a story someone had told her when she was little.

Darkness and this prison: that's what her world was now.

Tired of sitting up, she stretched out on the bed and covered herself with the blanket. She felt the hope she'd once had, of growing up to be a well-educated, well-respected woman, being crushed inside her chest. Her heart was so young and fit, and it beat so bravely, and was so perfectly suited to helping her have a thousand more adventures, but soon it would be forced to stop. All the things she'd learned and thought about and been delighted by would be extinguished. The more she thought these things, the faster her heart beat and the more shallowly she breathed, until she thought her body would burst.

"Breathe deep, child," said a voice.

Dhikilo jerked to attention. She looked round in the darkness but could see nothing.

"Breathe deep." The voice was low, with a strong accent that wasn't English.

Dhikilo took some big gasps.

"Not like that. You sound like a hyrax caught out in the noonday sun. Breathe like a human. A human at rest in a safe place."

Dhikilo protested, "This isn't a safe place."

"Trust me," said the voice wearily, "compared to some places, it's pretty safe. No one is doing anything bad to you right now, are they?"

Dhikilo had to admit this was true. She breathed deeply, then breathed deep some more. She was feeling better already.

"Are you a prisoner?" she asked.

There was a pause. "Not any more," said the mystery man.

"Can you help me escape?"

The voice chuckled. "That's a big thing to expect of me."

"I mean, can you let me out of this cell?"

Again there was a pause. "Have a little sleep, child. There's a bed here and you need some rest. It's dark and you can't do anything now anyway. In the morning you can think again."

"In the morning," said Dhikilo, "I think they're going to kill me."

The voice chuckled again, a little sadly. "It's not morning yet."

Dhikilo pushed her head back against the pillow and got settled. She pulled the blanket up to her neck.

"In the morning," she said, "will I be able to see you?"

"No, aabo," said the voice. "But we'll be watching you."

"'We'?" echoed Dhikilo. "Who's 'we'?"

But there was no answer, and eventually she fell asleep. She dreamed of being carried by strong hands through an agitated crowd, and finally being thrown through the air to safety.

ASKING FOR MORE

In the morning, the tiny window of her cell glowed bright blue, and there were noises filtering through from the streets outside the prison—the soft hubbub of a gathering crowd. It was Saturday and the citizens of Gampalonia were heading for the Public Enjoyment Area.

Dhikilo lay on her back, still breathing deeply, listening. She wasn't frightened any more. Her aabo and hooyo were watching her, somehow, somewhere, wishing her to be all right. She would do her best to be all right, and if it didn't work out—well, that was just…unlucky.

There was a harsh clunk of metal on metal. A guard was standing at the door of her cell. Not the Quilp woman from yesterday, but a man twice as ugly, holding an ironware mug so big it was almost a dog dish.

"You slept like an innocent baby," he sneered. "Which is funny, for someone as guilty as you. Here, take this."

He flipped open a hatch in the bars and handed the mug through.

"What is it?" said Dhikilo.

"Water, of course," said the jailer. "What were you expecting, eggs on toast?"

"I'd like that," said Dhikilo.

The jailer laughed. "You won't nee a full stomach where you're going."

"Where am I going?"

"To stan trial."

"But I might get…erm…" She couldn't think of the word. The word for being put on trial, and saying things that won the sympathy of a jury, and everything turning out OK so that you walked away free.

The jailer, guessing what she meant, looked at her as if she was the stupidest fool he'd ever seen.

"The Gamp's trials on't muck about," he informed her. "Why bother to have a trial if you ain't gonna follow through? Waste of everyboy's time. Spen ages investigating a prisoner, igging up evience, rawing up the arguments, only to let them go? Pointless. Nah, the people know what they're gonna get this morning. First, the trial. Then the tribulation." He grinned broadly. Dhikilo understood that he'd just made what he thought was a witty joke.

Dhikilo's stomach rumbled. She glanced into the mug. There were specks of dirt floating in the water.

"But don't I get a last meal?" she asked. (She figured she might as well try this one on again. It had worked in the Quilps' village, after all!)

"Forget it," said the jailer. "This ain't a luxury hotel. Although you know all about those, eh?" This was the last of his witticisms. He was no longer in the mood, it seemed, for conversation. Peering disdainfully at the mug Dhikilo was holding, he snarled, "Are you going to rink that or what? 'Cause if you ain't, give it back."

Dhikilo swirled the water around a bit, trying to make the

dirt specks float away from where her lips would go. She took a big swig and handed the mug over.

Having had the meal that wasn't a meal, Dhikilo sat on the bunk for a little longer, until the yellow-clad sheriff arrived to escort her to her dire appointment. He was carrying his rifle just as before, and Dhikilo could tell that he took very, very seriously his responsibility to escort her to her final destination without any slip-ups.

"OK, little fuzz-top, let's go have some fun," he said.

Dhikilo felt a wave of outrage, just like she'd felt the day she hit Kim the bully with a big history book and knocked her flat. But that was in a different time and place, and she was empty-handed now.

The Smallest Possible Cage

Despite everything, it was a beautiful morning. All Dhikilo could think of as she was being led along the streets towards the town square was how fine the weather was, and that, if you *must* go on trial and possibly be condemned to death, it was much pleasanter to do it on a day of brilliant sunshine and gentle breezes than in the middle of a miserable dark sleety squall.

The city of Gampalonia, which had seemed so deserted yesterday, was full of people this morning, all heading in the same direction. Large placards had been fixed to lamp posts proclaiming STATE OF THE NATION SPEECH THIS WAY, but the placards weren't needed because everyone was following everyone else, and the Tower of Light kept them on course, a monstrous beacon pulling them onwards.

The citizens came in many shapes and sizes and facial types, including some that Dhikilo hadn't yet seen on her travels, suggesting that Liminus was a big complicated country with many communities in it. The capital city was where all these different folk mixed together: the short hairy ones and the long bald ones, the lumbering soft ones and the sharp-faced darting types, the solid muscular ones and the frail specimens who looked as if a puff of wind might blow them over.

None of them looked very cheerful, though. They looked hungry and anxious. Dhikilo guessed that they were attending the meeting because of the free nuts and berries that the big advertisement on the fountain had promised, and because the Gamp was going to make a speech and they'd probably get in trouble if they didn't show up to listen. Oh, and maybe also because they fancied seeing some poor girl's head being chopped off.

The sheriff took no chances of his prisoner suddenly sprinting away and hiding in a dense crowd. As the main streets filled up, he led Dhikilo through a special side-lane that was closed to the public. At the end of that, a narrow alleyway— barely more than a tunnel—brought them to one side of the town square, right near the fountain.

Everything looked remarkably different from the day before, and not only because there were lots of people. A set of large wooden structures—including a stage—had sprung up overnight, like a travelling circus or the Cawber Donkey Derby. The sheriff escorted Dhikilo up a creaky wooden ramp to a box-like coop some distance off the ground. With every step, Dhikilo felt the understanding grow heavier that there was nowhere else to go but where she was being led.

"Goo luck," said the sheriff as he pushed her to take her place inside the pen, but she could tell he was convinced that the luck she was going to have wouldn't be good at all. He swung a hatch shut against her legs and bolted it, so that Dhikilo was left standing inside a sort of crate whose bottom half was made of wood and whose top half was made of wire mesh. And there she was: displayed like a zoo animal in the smallest possible cage.

Through the mesh, she had a good view of the many hundreds of people who'd gathered in the Public Enjoyment Area today. She had an excellent view of the stage—a better view than anyone in the crowd below, not because she'd been given a special treat, but because she was on trial and they weren't. The stage, which she guessed would also function as the courtroom, had several empty chairs and a fancy gold throne on it, and a tent behind it, and a length of red carpet laid out between the tent and the throne.

What else? She had a decent view of the Tower of Light behind the square. It was shinier than ever and seemed to be giving off a cloud of steam, but perhaps that was only an optical illusion, because the sun was in her eyes when she looked in that direction, and the tower was radiant with reflections and haloes, which forced her to look away.

Last, but not least, she had a very fine view of the guillotine, ready and waiting right near by. Indeed, she was in the shadow of it.

Although the official proceedings were not ready to kick off yet, a man in a dark blue smock leapt onto the stage and shouted through a megaphone, "There are no more nuts 'n' berries! I repeat, the nuts 'n' berries are all gone! They've all been hane out!"

"There never was any!" cried a voice from the crowd.

The man in the blue smock ignored this allegation. "So, take note, my friens: next time, come early!"

He scurried off, and the stage was once again unoccupied. It stayed that way for the next five or ten minutes, as the crowd swelled even bigger. A brass band started playing military-style music, cheerful *humpa-pumpa* tunes that you could probably march to if you were in the mood, although by this time there were so many people crammed into the square that marching might be a bit difficult. A pink balloon floated by, then a white one. Someone must be inflating them somewhere and letting them go.

The blue-smocked man with the megaphone jumped on-stage again.

"For you latecomers who haven't got the message, I repeat: the nuts 'n' berries are all gone! Stop asking for nuts 'n' berries! Those of you who got the nuts 'n' berries: congratulations! Enjoy! Those of you who got none: commiserations! Maybe in future you'll bother to stir your lazy bones a bit earlier!"

There was a murmur of displeasure in the crowd, nothing out-loud enough to get any individual onlooker in trouble, just a sort of muttery mumbly rumble. A purple balloon floated along the stage and bounced off the head of the man with the megaphone.

"Enough frivolity!" he barked through his loudhailer. "Our Great Leaer is about to speak! Prepare to listen! Prepare to listen!" And again he jumped off.

From the tent behind the stage, three small figures emerged. They stepped onto the boards, shuffled quickly over to the modest wooden chairs and sat down on them, virtually shoulder-to-shoulder. They wore bright yellow, ill-fitting caps emblazoned with a G, and dark sunglasses. Apart from those details, they looked awfully familiar to Dhikilo.

Underneath the bright yellow caps, the hair of these ancient females was straggly and dirty grey, like wisps of dust swept up from under a long-neglected cooker or wardrobe. They wore shabby browny-grey robes, from which bony white hands poked out like overgrown rat paws, and their boots seemed made of random bits of old leather stitched together. Their faces were not easy to make out behind the dark glasses and the matted hair, but their chins were pointy and they had beak-like noses with warts on.

Dhikilo was pretty sure that this threesome was a different bunch of Magwitches from the rather more bedraggled foursome she and Mrs Robinson had met at the start of their journey. But Magwitches they unmistakeably were.

At Last, the Gamp

The brass band stopped playing *humpa-pumpa* music and, instead, a lone trumpet blared out a solemn fanfare. The flap in the tent behind the stage parted wide and an extraordinary figure stepped into view.

At first glance he was a tall, powerfully built man, but that impression lasted only a second or two before you noticed that his shoes had absurdly thick soles and his head was topped with an absurdly puffed-up wig and a big yellow cap perched on top of that, so that the actual person in between these two artificial extremities was only of average height, or even a little shorter. And the rippling muscles? They weren't muscles at all, but a quilted puffer jacket, made of silvery nylon, with matching quilted puffer trousers. Over this already substantial outfit, he wore a long fur coat so luxurious and bulky that it resembled several dozen small furry animals who'd leapt onto him and were clinging in desperate fear of falling off.

"All rise! All rise!" hollered a courtier, even though everyone in the crowd was standing up already. "Rise for the Gran Emperorial Chief Prime Minister of the Unite Commonwealth of Liminus! Also Mayor of Gampalonia, By Perpetual Popular Ecree! Also Worshipworthy Captain of All Gamps! Also Legal Overmonarch of All Non-Gamps!"

There was a rustle of applause and a few half-hearted cheers from the crowd. Dhikilo was reminded of the annual Prize Night at Cawber School for Girls when all the parents were supposed to applaud every two minutes whenever yet another girl went onstage to accept her brass trophy or book token for being top in Year Seven Mathematics or whatever. You can't expect people to clap like mad for two hours on end. And the citizens of Gampalonia sounded as if they'd been required to clap for years and years.

The Gamp took his seat on the throne, next to the three Magwitches. This involved a fair amount of fidgeting and shrugging and adjusting bits of his clothing and body, because he stuck out so much in various directions, and the throne—generously throne-sized though it was—had not been designed for quite such an excess of garment and girth. Dhikilo wondered how the Gamp could bear to have so much gear on, given the new weather conditions in Liminus. She was feeling quite hot herself.

But the Gamp was hot, too: that became obvious when he finally got settled in his seat. Sweat dripped down his pudgy face, and his elaborate wig was drooping at the front, weighed down by perspiration from his forehead. His nose was red and swollen, and his eyes were moist. His lips were pursed and puffing, like a cross between a baby and a fish.

And cross he certainly was.

"This weather is an outrage," he complained to the Magwitch nearest him, leaning so close to her that their two caps collided and went slightly skew-whiff. "It's not *your* work, I hope?"

"Of course not," snapped the Magwitch. "What you think we are, supernatural?"

"On't give me that false moesty," bickered the Gamp in return. "Your magic is what I employ you for. Those ragon-flies on't sacrifice themselves for the fun of it."

"You wante fuel for your Ynamo," said the Magwitch. "We organize fuel for your Ynamo. We are not in charge of the weather."

"So who *is*?" demanded the Gamp, and the Magwitches shrugged, which almost made their ridiculous yellow caps fall off.

Dhikilo was surprised that they would speak this way in hearing of the crowd, but then she realized that the crowd couldn't hear. Dhikilo could hear because her box was suspended right next to the stage, in easy earshot of the Gamp and the Magwitches (although they were ignoring her entirely, as though she was some sort of inanimate object). The crowd was kept further at bay, cordoned off by a barrier of ropes and chains and armed guards. To be heard by them, the Gamp would need to use a megaphone.

As if responding to Dhikilo's thought, the courtier who'd made the announcement about rising for the Grand Imperial Chief Minister of the Blah-Blah-Blah walked over to the Gamp and handed him the loudhailer. He took it without saying thank you, not even a nod, and put the mouthpiece to his pursed little lips.

"Citizens of Gampalonia!" he exclaimed, and his husky whingy voice was amplified into a grand bellow that resounded around the square. "Once again we are gathere here to celebrate the glory of our empire, as it conquers new pastures, goes over fresh limits, pushes onwars unaunted espite all obstacles, sails into eeper waters!"

He paused for applause, which was so slow to come that he was talking again by the time it arrived.

"Citizens, I ask you to poner how lucky you are to be alive at this juncture. Yes, lucky, I say! This is the best of times, this is the best of times, this is the age of knowing everything worth knowing, this is the epoch of belief, this is the season of light, this is the spring of hope, we have everything before us, we are all going straight to Heaven."

There was clapping and some cheering, but, considering the great size and noise-making potential of the crowd, not a very impressive amount.

Once again, the Gamp lowered his megaphone and leaned sideways to speak to the Magwitches.

"Last week was better," he said.

"True," agreed the nearest Magwitch.

"Last *year* was better still," the Gamp recalled. "I almost went eaf from all the cheering."

"Last year was last year," shrugged the furthest Magwitch.

"They're hungry," remarked the middle Magwitch. "Mention the meat."

The Gamp lifted the megaphone to his lips again.

"The best of times!" he hollered. "No empty boast, my friens! For I have news for you—mouth-watering news! I know that lately there has not been quite as much choice of foostuffs as you might wish. Well, it gives me the utmost pleasure to announce a breakthrough on that front! Yes, citizens, from next week onwars, each citizen of Gampalonia is entitle, on presentation of a voucher available from the White Hall, to one frozen portion of premium-quality meat."

A roar of genuine enthusiasm rose from the crowd, as well as some excited whooping. The Gamp smiled broadly. Dhikilo wished he hadn't, as his smile was even more repugnant than his scowl.

"Now on to other business! I'm sure you're all aware of the new policy on ogs which became Law last week. Public-health notices have been posted everywhere, warning against the primitive practice—which no moern society can tolerate—of harbouring these filthy, isease-carrying vermin. Any citizens still in possession of a og were urge to eliver the offensive specimen straight to the relevant authorities. Espite this, *some inivituals*"—and here he nodded towards Dhiklio, acknowledging her presence for the first time—"have taken it upon themselves to flout the Law, putting all of us at terrible risk of og-borne germs!"

Dhikilo wondered if her trial had now begun, and if she should start trying to defend herself. All she could think of was poor Nelly inside that sack, being dragged across the cobblestones. Where was Nelly now? Was she even alive? Dhikilo was pretty sure that the guards' talk of checking captured dogs for diseases was all just a pile of lies. The Gamp was promising meat for everyone. Where was that meat going to come from?

"The spring of hope!" the Gamp thundered, and that last word echoed round and round the Public Enjoyment Area. "For as long as I've been your protector, I've been working tirelessly to banish the big freeze. I gave you my cast-iron promise that I woul bring back the sun, re-install the rain for the benefit of our agriculture, restore the seasons! I have kept that promise!"

Again the crowd cheered—the loudest, most enthusiastic cheer so far. The Gamp wiped his forehead on the sleeve of his fur coat, and the clammy hairs of his wig almost got stuck to the fur, as if one fluffy creature had momentarily considered leaving its perch in order to join a community of other fluffy creatures.

"But let us not forget what brought the unnatural weather to Liminus in the first place! Our enemies! Those evil, conniving, paranormal Magwitches! It has taken all my effort—with the help of your citizenly sacrifice—to rescue the weather from their clutches."

The Gamp's speech was interrupted by a strange noise—a squealing sort of creak, from somewhere not so far away. From the direction of the Tower of Light, Dhikilo thought, although when she looked at it, it seemed exactly as it had been before, monumental and still.

"But it has come to my attention," continued the Gamp, "that there are rumours, vicious rumours, being put about that I, the Great Gamp, have gone soft on our enemies—in fact, that I am in cahoots with the Magwitches! Imagine that!"

Dhikilo looked at the Magwitches to see how they reacted to this. They remained perfectly calm. As for the crowd, there were a few listless cries of "Boo!" and "Shame!" but these did not seem to be directed at anyone in particular, certainly not the three thinly disguised Magwitches.

The Gamp lowered his megaphone, leaned across to the nearest crone and said, "How's it going, you think?"

"Fair to reasonable," replied the Magwitch after a moment of thought.

"A bit more righteous inignation might improve things," said the middle witch.

"Maybe mention some more enemies?" the witch at the far end suggested. "Other than us, that is."

Again the Gamp lifted the megaphone to his lips and did some more yelling.

"Me? In league with the Magwitches? This vicious slur upon my integrity hurts me, oh my faithful followers! Hurts me like a knife stuck in my heart! I ask myself…who, *who*, WHO in this great nation is so spiteful as to accuse me of this? WHO is nasty enough to invent such outrageous lies? I can only think of the Quinions, the Heeps, the Ogers, the Roo, the Barnacles, the Chuzzles, the Nubbles, the Guppies, the Squeers…all the people who quite frankly on't belong in Liminus, who on't eserve to live in Gampalonia, who woul be wise to pack their bags for the journey back to where they came from!"

The crowd made harsh noises of approval, even though, in all likelihood, some of them must be members of the groups the Gamp was threatening. Dhikilo could still barely believe that nobody had noticed that the crones sitting onstage were the evil doers being vilified in the speech. Dark glasses and a silly yellow cap were evidently all that was required for the Magwitches to conduct their business with the Gamp as brazenly as they liked.

Dhikilo tried to see the faces of the people in the crowd below. Her cage was up above their heads and she could only see a few through the mesh, but they didn't look very smart. Hungry and thirsty and fed up and frustrated. But not very smart.

The Gamp lowered the megaphone and leaned sideways again. "Can I ask them for money yet?"

"Not yet," said the nearest Magwitch. "Entertain them first. Give them the execution they've been waiting for. Start the trial."

The Gamp turned his face towards Dhikilo, and narrowed his already tiny eyes.

"But now, my friens," he barked into his megaphone, "the moment you've all been waiting for! We have a criminal here, an uneserving outlaner, an intruer into our fine city— in short, exactly the sort of unesirable I've just been talking about!" He flung forward his free hand, pointing one rigid pink finger straight at Dhikilo. "YOU!"

Dhikilo straightened her back.

THE TRIAL

The trial of Dhikilo was quite a lot shorter than the State of the Nation address that preceded it. It seemed the Gamp had already used up his best words on the speech, and he was hot and bothered and in no mood for further exertions.

"You know why you're on trial, I presume?" he challenged her through his loudhailer.

Dhikilo opened her mouth to speak, but nobody had given her a loudhailer of her own and she realized that, without one, only a handful of the nearest members of the crowd had any chance of hearing what she might say.

"Can I have a megaphone, please?" she said, as loudly and clearly as she could without shouting.

The Gamp cupped a hand to his ear, pretending he was doing his best to hear the question, then shook his head in amazement. "The prisoner says she oesn't know why she's here!" he exclaimed in mock-exasperation. "Let me refresh her memory of her crimes!"

From the pocket of his preposterous puffer trousers, he extracted a piece of crumpled paper and consulted it. "First of all, she was in possession of a og, a full week after the last remaining ogs were require to be surrenere to the authorities."

"My friend's not really a dog!" cried Dhikilo as loud as she could. "She's a sphinx!"

For the benefit of the crowd, the Gamp mimed an expression of astonishment. "The prisoner claims that her og is not a og!" he marvelled, his voice so full of sarcasm that he reminded Dhikilo of Mr Dunstable at school. "How *convenient* for criminals, if they can simply eny the realities that are plain for the rest of us to see!" Again he shook his head, as though dumbfounded by the shamelessness of the riff-raff brought before him. His wig was quite soggy with sweat by now, so when he shook his head, the pile of fake hair swivelled around almost independently.

"But I am a merciful juge!" he bellowed on. "I wouln't conemn a lawbreaker for just one crime!" He consulted the paper. "So here are the others!" Triumphantly, he jabbed his finger towards Dhikilo. Finger-jabbing was evidently one of his favourite things.

"Fact! The prisoner snuck into Liminus without any official permission to be here! Yes, my friens, she was smuggle through the gates by a corrupt passport inspector, a crook by the name of Pumblechook, who obviously has no interest in keeping us safe from ingressors! I've ispatche my men to arrest him without elay! You can expect to see him on trial next week! He won't be making any more aministrative errors when we've finishe with him, believe me!" For emphasis, he slammed his fist onto his well-padded knee. The nearest Magwitch flinched, and scratched herself in irritation.

"Also!" roared the Gamp. "The prisoner has been proven to've spent a night at the Bleak House hotel, one of the most luxurious establishments in all of Liminus. I'm sure many of you ecent har-working people *ream* of staying there just once

in your lives, if you can only save up enough of your har-
earne coins! But the prisoner here preferre not to pay! Yes,
it's true—she snuck away without paying!"

"That horrible house almost killed me!" cried Dhikilo, but
her protest was lost in a hubbub of boos and hisses.

"Also!" pursued the Gamp. "She cause malicious amage to
the premises, scratching at the priceless vintage wallpaper like
some sort of animal! Also! In a final act of barbaric isrespect,
she… I hesitate to even utter this in public, my friens, for I
know that we have impressionable youngsters in the auience…
She left a pool of urine, my friens, right uner one of the ancient walls!"

There were a few gasps and murmurs of indignation from
the crowd. A balloon popped in the heat.

"Get on with it," remarked one of the Magwitches irritably. Sweat was dripping off the end of her pointy nose.

"So, my friens!" concluded the Gamp. "The case against
this irty foreigner is crystal clear! She has emonstrate her
complete contempt for our Law! Therefore, we are left with
no choice but to bring the fullest weight of that Law upon
her neck!"

The squealy creaky sound from not so far away could be
heard again. The Tower of Light was now wholly enveloped
in mist. Dhikilo thought she saw, through the haze of steam,
the lights swaying from side to side.

"I think your tower is melting," she said, as firmly and
loudly as her fear-shaken voice could manage. "I think if
anyone's in it, they should get out."

But the Gamp wasn't listening. "Executioners!" he yelled.
"Escort the prisoner to the guillotine!"

Trumpets blared another fanfare. The trial was over. Four
tall men in the distinctive yellow clothing of the Gampalonian Guar emerged from the crowd and marched slowly up
the ramp. Their faces were invisible inside their helmets, and

this, along with their relentless, synchronized advance, gave them the appearance of robots. Pleading with them would be as much use as pleading with the guillotine itself.

The tall men reached her cage and one of them unbolted the hatch. Without a word, they hauled Dhikilo onto the ramp and pushed her to walk.

All the D-Words She Could Think Of

As Dhikilo passed in front of the Gamp and the Mag-witches, she felt suddenly angry. Angrier than she'd ever felt in her life, now that her life had been dismissed by this ridiculous conceited thug, and her brave amazing friend Mrs Robinson was probably being slaughtered so she could be fed to all these stupid Gampalonians, who were too dopey to stand up for themselves.

"You're a dictator!" she called out to the Gamp. "A dreadful dirty dictator!"

Each word made the Gamp flinch, and each time he flinched his wig wiggled and droplets of sweat flew off different parts of his puffy red face.

"You're domineering!" yelled Dhikilo, racking her brains for all the D-words she could think of before she lost the head with which she could speak them. "And dishonest! And dodgy and…and deplorable! And…a despot!" She was pleased she'd remembered that word; it was quite an unusual one.

The four men ushered her off the ramp and directly towards the guillotine.

"You're a deceiver!" yelled Dhikilo over her shoulder. "Disgraceful! Disgusting! You haven't got any dignity! And you're…erm…derelict in your duty!" She was running out of D-words to insult the Gamp with. No doubt there were lots more in the dictionary, but she could see that awful rust-speckled blade ahead of her and thought she might faint.

Not that there would even be room to faint, because the four guards surrounded her tightly as they marched, almost squashing her between them. Dhikilo couldn't help noticing that their yellow uniforms were ill-fitting, as if made for much shorter men.

"How can you *do* this?" she berated them, even as they led her up the steps to the execution platform. "You know it's wrong! Why don't you say something?"

At that, the four men did indeed speak.

"Marmalade," said one, in a dull, distant monotone.

"Soft-grain bread," said another, in exactly the same voice.

"Coconut macaroons," said the third. "Maybe a couple of bananas, if they're ripe."

"Oh, and something that's not on the list," said the fourth. "Surprise me."

They'd reached the place where Dhikilo was supposed to get on her knees and lower her head into the wooden trap so it could be clamped around her neck. One of the men reached forward to grasp the rope that held the great iron blade suspended.

"I've brought my own bag, thank you," he said, and released the rope.

With a fearsome *THWOKK!* the blade fell into the blood-stained slot below. Hundreds of people in the crowd gasped simultaneously—a huge communal intake of breath— "Ooohh!"

The only odd thing was: Dhikilo's head wasn't in the trap yet. She was still standing. There must have been some mistake?

The four men grabbed her—eight long rubbery arms—and lifted her off her feet. With a mighty heave, they tossed her forward, over the heads of the crowd. The people she was going to fall on top of went "Ooohh!" again, but instinctively threw up their hands—and caught her. For a moment she was almost upside-down, but then—clumsily but gently—the people turned her the right way up and set her feet-first on the ground. The whole thing—seeing the blade slam down, being seized and thrown into the air, being caught and landing on her feet—took just a few seconds.

Dhikilo glanced back up at the guillotine, just in time to see the four tall men deflate like balloons. Their flesh just vanished, leaving their yellow garments and helmets to fall to the ground with a *fwopp* and a clunk. Then the people around Dhikilo pulled her back from the stage, tugging her deeper into their midst. For a moment she feared that they were angry and would tear her apart, but no, their hands were gentle and she could see on their concerned sweaty faces that they were glad she'd survived. They were only trying to hide her.

"Gaurs! Guars! Get her!" bellowed the Gamp through his megaphone. But before any of the soldiers could respond to his command, the air was filled with a noise like an enormous cotton sheet being torn in half, a squealy, whiny, fraying sort of sound, and all eyes turned towards where this noise was coming from.

The Tower of Light shivered one last time, and then, with a colossal crash, it collapsed. It shattered into a thousand icy fragments, some of which bounced and skittered all the way to the square. The crowd surged out of the way. The whole Public Enjoyment Area dissolved into a great hullabaloo.

"Treachery! Treason! Foul play!" roared the Gamp, as the

Magwitches scurried back into the tent behind the stage. Then he began to retreat, too, waddling clumsily in his inflated clothing. A few of the townspeople started to clamber up onto the stage, and, in terror of being caught by them, the Gamp yanked off his heavy wig and headgear, kicked off his ludicrous boots and hastily, even as he ran, discarded his burdensome clothes.

Divested of all the layers of bombastic pretence, the naked creature that scampered towards the tent was revealed to be an unimpressive pink thing, similar to a Spottletoe but hairless. Free of his trappings, he moved as fast as a pig, scooting out of sight. The crowd roared in anger and glee.

Frightened of getting accidentally trampled underfoot—for she knew that such things can happen when people are running in a panic—Dhikilo tried to swerve and avoid any heaving creature that might be about to collide with her. When something solid pushed against her bottom, she cried out, scared that it would knock her to the ground.

"*Sssstop!*" commanded an unearthly voice. "On my back! Hold the hair!"

Dhikilo clambered onto Mrs Robinson's back, and the sphinx sprang at once over the tumult of bodies, strong and sure.

An Explosion of Fed-upness

The sphinx's instinct was to get them to a high place, out of danger's reach, so that was what she did. Having ducked and weaved through the mob of panicking Gampalonians, she leapt onto a stone barrier, then a low balcony, then a higher balcony, then a still higher balcony. Dhikilo clung on as tightly as she could, barely able to keep herself from being flung loose. It would be a shame to get saved from having her head chopped off only to break her neck in a fall.

After a couple more mighty leaps, they came to rest on the roof of an abandoned shop, a nice flat roof far above the street. Mrs Robinson was breathing heavily, but other than that, she was uninjured, in full control of herself and rather magnificent.

"You're alive!" cried Dhikilo, hugging Mrs Robinson hard. "You're alive!"

"Yesss," agreed Mrs Robinson, indicating with a shrug that Dhikilo should get off now.

"I thought they'd killed you!" cried Dhikilo, scrambling

onto her hands and knees, a bit giddy from being slung about. "I thought they'd made you into meat!"

Mrs Robinson blinked her purple eyes slowly. "Not ssso easssy," she said. Her lips drew back slightly over her fangs. Was that a smile Dhikilo saw?

"But how did you get away?"

Mrs Robinson was silent for a few moments before answering. "With sssome force," she replied. "And disssadvantage to the men."

Dhikilo could tell that Nelly would not go into details about her escape. But she figured that somewhere in the city, in a grim place called the Og Clearance Facility, there must be four clobbered members of the Gampalonian Guar stripped down to their underwear and wondering what had become of their stolen uniforms.

The sphinx walked to the edge of the roof and looked down. Dhikilo crawled to join her there. Their rooftop was very near the ruins of the Tower of Light and just a couple of hundred metres from the Public Enjoyment Area, so they could see the aftermath of the collapse clearly.

The Tower of Light was no longer recognizable as a thing that had once been a tower. It was more like a gigantic smashed egg, a pile of broken shards melting so fast that every time you blinked they became a little more like a vast mound of slush. Dhikilo couldn't see any bodies in the wreckage, so the people who'd been inside the tower must have made their getaway before it fell. She was glad about that. And she was glad to be alive to be glad.

A skeletal remnant of staircase that was still upright keeled over with a *ploff*. So even the staircases had been made of ice! How stupid was that? How deeply, dreadfully *dumb*! Those were D-words she could've shouted as she was being led to the guillotine, if she'd thought of them. Soon, maybe even before sundown today, the Gamp's grandiloquent citadel would be nothing more than a lake-sized puddle in the middle of the city.

Where was the Gamp! Where were the Magwitches! Dhikilo peered into the distance to see if she could spot them anywhere. They certainly weren't hiding in the tent behind the stage, because the townspeople were busy pulling this tent to pieces, scattering the bits all around. The whole Public Enjoyment Area was a scene of lively uproar. The citizens of Gampalonia, having retreated from the square when the tower first collapsed, had surged back again. The listless good behaviour they'd exhibited during the State of the Nation speech was completely swept away now: they were dashing around energetically, and seemed excited and angry.

At first Dhikilo thought they were angry because they'd been promised an execution and hadn't got one. But then she realized what was going on: she was witnessing a revolution! Or, as the Professor used to explain it when he gave history lessons about revolutions, an "explosion of fed-upness." The citizens of Gampalonia had been bullied for much too long, and now that the weather had changed and a public display of power had gone wrong and a tower had collapsed, they sensed that the moment had come for things to be different.

The townspeople were now doing their best to topple the guillotine. Dozens of them were pushing at it, but it weighed a ton and they only managed to tip it forward slightly. Dozens more people joined the crew and at last, when enough arms and shoulders lunged at the giant contraption, it swayed, overbalanced and crashed to the ground. Everyone cheered, a proper hurrah.

There were some children in the crowd, too, and their parents invited them to step up onto the toppled guillotine, and together they danced on it. The townspeople shouted joyfully and, after a while, Dhikilo realized that the shouts weren't just any shouts, but "Long live Amistat! Long live Amistat!"

So Gampalonia was getting its old name back. Yesterday, the Gamp had been lord of all Liminus; today, his capital city wasn't even called Gampalonia any more. Watching the crowd celebrating in the wreckage, as the once-great tower continued to melt into slush, Dhikilo understood that history sometimes progresses extremely slowly, and sometimes amazingly fast. This morning, she was an eyewitness to one of the amazingly fast bits.

As if to join in with the general mood of violent change, a piercingly high whistle started up, and the air began to stink of diesel oil, deodorant, detergent, dhal, dried dung, digestive juices, drains and dead things. The noise and the smell were coming from the direction of the Dynamo, though the Dynamo itself was invisible behind the maze of streets and buildings.

Looking again at the ruins of the Tower of Light, Dhikilo noticed that the pipeline which had supplied refrigeration to the tower, and which was now not attached to anything, was not coping well. The pipe thrashed about feebly like a giant snake in the throes of a health crisis, thumping on the ground, puffing gasps of frigid white vapour into empty air. The high-pitched whistle became almost deafening, and then there was a tremendous BANG.

No lights or flames were visible, but Dhikilo knew at once that the explosion must have happened at the Dynamo. A cloud of dark grey smoke rose from behind the buildings in that part of town, and the stench got ten times worse. The dark cloud expanded at frightening speed, billowing up to block the sun, drifting in all directions. Bright silvery embers swirled around inside the smoke, falling slowly down from the dismal sky. They fell everywhere, including on the roof where Dhikilo and Mrs Robinson huddled. Dhikilo flinched as one of the bright embers fell on her head, and her hand flew up to flick it away before it could set fire to her hair.

But it was not an ember. It was a D. And when her fingers collided with it, even for the fraction of an instant that it took to send the D spiralling sideways, Dhikilo was buzzed with a kind of electric shock, a strange thrill that went straight to her brain.

Dove, the thrill said. She had a vivid vision of a white bird, with the palest blush of yellow on the top of its head, and pure black tail-feathers, taking flight.

Another D landed on her, tumbling off her shoulder and onto her forearm.

Drowsy, her brain responded, and she saw a baby in a pram struggling to stay awake, its eyes falling shut. No sooner had the vision blossomed in Dhikilo's imagination than the brilliant little letter vanished.

She looked up into the smoke cloud, which was dissipating now. A few more Ds were still floating down towards the roof, and instead of flinching back from them, she reached out to catch them.

Dénezé-sous-Doué. A mysterious cave full of spooky sculptures holding hands.

Dilapidated. A wooden house in a dusty shanty town, mended with bits of rubbish and cloth.

Downpour. Dhikilo fancied she could feel the cool raindrops splashing on her, but when the D disappeared, she was still dry.

The next one she caught was damaged, scarcely recognizable as a D, and when she touched it, she thought at first she was seeing a dark field scattered with *dandelions*, but then, no, it was the shoulders of a man wearing a black coat, speckled with *dandruff*.

Next to spiral down was *delectable*. She thought she knew what this word meant but the vision was confusing: a long wooden table outside a restaurant, big enough to seat about a dozen people. The restaurant was painted in vibrant colours: red, white and green. The vision faded just as the door swung open.

There were other Ds, but they were fluttering quite close to the edge of the roof. Dhikilo reached her arm forward, but Mrs Robinson's voice called her back.

"Ssstay."

The sky was clearing rapidly, as if the smoke was being sucked away into a further universe beyond this world.

The city grew quieter and quieter as the crowd drifted away from the Public Enjoyment Area. The people were going home with their emboldened hearts and their souvenirs of destruction. The Gamp had fled to wherever it is that defeated dictators go when they're no longer wanted. The only sign of the Gampalonian Guar was a few torn-up shreds of the yellow uniforms borrowed by Mrs Robinson's ectoplasmic helpers. The remnants of the tent in which the Gamp had primped himself for his grand entrance lay littered all around like confetti. The stage on which the Gamp and his Magwitches had presided so disdainfully had been dismantled and carried away in pieces, to be used by kinder people for better purposes. The throne was smashed to splinters. The cage in which Dhikilo had been judged, and the ramp that led up to it, had likewise been demolished. The guillotine lay like a defeated dinosaur that would never rise again.

Mrs Robinson touched Dhikilo's shoulder with one gentle paw.

"We alssso ssshould go home."

An Adventurer of Considerable Experience

And so they left the city and set off for home.

The journey *back* was so different from the journey *there* that Dhikilo might almost have been a totally different person travelling through a totally different country. But then, she sort of was.

On the way to Gampalonia, she'd been bewildered and clumsy, thickly wrapped against the perilous cold, worried that her ability to complete her mission might be hampered by not having a clue where she was going or what she was supposed to do when she got there—*if* she got there, because she might die along the way, struck down or swallowed up by a hundred unpredictable horrors waiting for her just over the next hill or in the next village. And her only companion was a dog who wasn't really a dog but a creepy monster with purple eyes and wicked fangs.

On the way back from Amistat, Dhikilo was an adventurer of considerable experience. She'd survived some dangers and encountered some very strange people and helped to make some big changes. She was walking through a landscape that was unrecognizable from the one she'd passed through only days before, she was lightly dressed under a summery sun and the person walking next to her was Nelly Robinson, her dear, brave friend.

"What do you think will happen to the Ds now?" she said.

"We ssshall sssee," Mrs Robinson replied.

"I mean," said Dhikilo, "do you think they might be able to sort of…grow back? Now that they're not being stolen any more?"

"We ssshall sssee," Mrs Robinson replied.

Homewardly Re-Encounter 1:
The Spottletoes

They crossed the wasteland without any problem and reached Littlegampton by early afternoon. The sign on the outskirts said: LITTLEGAMPTON. MUSEUM, GIFT SHOP, TOURIST ATTRACTION, TOILET, REFRESHMENTS.

Dhikilo read the words carefully in case any Ds had popped up in them, but there'd never been any to begin with.

Mrs Robinson slowed down, looked around mistrustfully.

"On my back," she said. Dhikilo couldn't tell if it was a command or a suggestion or a question.

It might indeed be wise for her to climb on to Nelly's back, and for the two of them to move through the village swiftly, avoiding any contact with the Spottletoes. After all, the Spottletoes were the Gamp's biggest fans, and they would not be pleased to hear the latest news from the city-formerly-known-as-Gampalonia. Nor were they likely to give Dhikilo three cheers and a big round of applause for her role in reducing the Tower of Light to a puddle of slush.

And even if the Spottletoes suspected nothing, they might still try to drag their weary guests into another long tour of their exhibition of Gamp-related rubbish. So, yes, straight through the village without stopping was best. Except…

"We need water," said Dhikilo.

It was true. They hadn't had a drink for a long time and it was hot and they were walking and it would be evening before they reached the Drood.

"Yesss," said Mrs Robinson, and, with a sigh of acceptance, changed herself into her Labrador form.

They found the museum with ease (there were about fifty THIS WAY TO THE MUSEUM signs scattered around the village) and Dhikilo knocked at the door. A lone Spottletoe was minding the shop, sleepy-eyed with boredom. He was glad to see them, and fetched them water at once.

"You saw the Gamp?" he enquired, as Mrs Robinson lapped loudly at the dish.

"Yes, we saw the Gamp," said Dhikilo, sipping from her glass. "But not for long. He…had to be off." She was determined to handle this encounter with another very important D-word: diplomacy.

"Lucky you!" exclaimed the Spottletoe, his eyes shining with the imagined thrill of beholding his hero in the flesh.

"Yes," said Dhikilo. "We're…erm…lucky to be able to tell you about it."

"What news have you from the capital?"

"Erm… There's lots going on," said Dhikilo, waving her hand in a way that she hoped would convey a general sense of big-city thrivingness. "Events. Excitement."

"We saw smoke this morning," mentioned the Spottletoe, a little nervously. "Over the Gampalonia skyline."

"Yes, there was...erm...some serious pollution," said Dhikilo. "But it's gone now."

"Also, there's a rumour," said the Spottletoe, "that there's going to be more foo for everyone."

"I'm sure that's true!" said Dhikilo. "Look at the weather! All sorts of things will be growing. You must be thinking of recipes, I suppose?"

"Recipes?"

"Nice things you're going to make."

The Spottletoe's eyes went misty as he imagined creating something marvellous.

"If there are ever pumpkins again," he mused, "we will carve them into the shape of the Gamp. Ozens of them! We will put lights insie them; they'll be visible from afar. Then he is sure to come an visit us. On't you think?"

Dhikilo made a humming noise that could mean either yes or no. "Or you could roast them," she suggested. "With garlic and paprika. Thanks for the water!"

Homewardly Re-Encounter 2:
The Drood

It was still broad daylight when they reached the village of the Drood. They were greeted like conquering heroes, even before Dhikilo had a chance to let the villagers know what had happened in the capital.

"Emperorsh come, emperorsh go," nodded one of the elders sagely, when he heard the news. But Dhikilo could tell that underneath his dignified veneer of weary wisdom, he was bursting with happiness. And the younger Drood were so excited that they collided with each other as they danced about.

"Avencher! Avencher!" cried the little ones, who'd never had an adventure and were very excited at the idea of it.

"It was really uncomfortable and dangerous and frightening, actually," said Dhikilo, not wanting them to rush away from the safety of their village and their families. "I almost got killed."

"Never!" said the children, refusing to believe it. "You are vewy powerful witch! Mosh powerful witch of aww!"

Dhikilo laughed. "I'm not!" she protested.

"You are!" they giggled back.

Well, she thought, *if I am a witch, I hope I'm the sort of witch who's allowed to play music and maybe run a restaurant and doesn't have to have huge warts on her nose.*

The children wanted to make a fuss of Mrs Robinson, too. Nelly put up with their pats and strokes and squeals for as long as she could, but then she got irritable and tired. Dhikilo hoped she wouldn't lose her temper and bite somebody. But instead, Mrs Robinson found a different solution: she created four more of her ectoplasmic helpers and sent them out to play with the children. Without clothes to disguise them, they looked less convincingly human—Nelly put a reasonable amount of effort into giving them faces and hands, but didn't bother much with the rest, so their bodies looked like they were made of big twigs, except rubbery and pale. But the Drood children liked them, and climbed fearlessly onto the creatures' weird rubbery shoulders.

"Marmalade," one of the helpers would say.

"Marmaway!" the children shouted.

"Coconut macaroons."

"Cocowa macawooooo!"

Eventually Mrs Robinson began to doze off and the helpers grew smaller and finally evaporated, and the Drood children fell to the ground, but it was like jumping off a playground swing.

The rest of the day was spent eating and talking and singing. The temple where Dhikilo and her fellow musicians had performed their weather-changing ritual was turned into a sort of banquet room, and with brilliant sunlight beaming in through the windows it was no longer chilly and dim—not at all like Cawber School for Girls' gloomy prize-giving hall any more. In honour of their guests, the Drood sang their version of Dhikilo's Hallelujah song, although of course by now it had changed into something else entirely, unrecognizable except for the enthusiasm. *"Hááá-wa-wa-wah!"*

When it was time for bed, the family who'd opened their home to Dhikilo and Mrs Robinson made a formal, solemn request:

"Come yiv wiv ush. Make our viwwage your home. You will grow chall here."

But I have school, Dhikilo thought. Also, she knew she would grow tall no matter where she lived, because she was still young and she was from Somaliland and the people there were pretty tall, as far as she could tell from pictures.

"That's very kind of you," she said. "Maybe one day."

HOMEWARDLY RE-ENCOUNTER 3: MR PUMBLECHOOK

In the morning, the Drood gave Dhikilo a clever back-pack made of white cloth, as light as a fleece but sturdy enough to hold bottles of water and other supplies. Everyone in the village waved them goodbye, sad but not too sad. The Drood had plenty to get on with. Tiny green buds and leaves were pushing up from the muck all around. Liminus would soon burst into bloom.

Mr Pumblechook's checkpoint, when Dhikilo and Mrs Robinson got there a couple of hours later, looked abandoned. They walked back and forth beside the gatehouse, listening for signs of activity, or even of snoring, but the building was silent. The big black door through which Pumblechook had let them pass was shut. And the wall was still too high to climb.

A sign said:

WE ARE CURRENTLY EXPERIENCING A HIGH VOLUME OF APPLICATIONS

"Hello!" called Dhikilo. "Hello!" But even as she called, she was resigned to getting no answer. The Gamp had claimed that Pumblechook had been arrested. Everything that came out of the Gamp's mouth was a lie, so Dhikilo had assumed this was a lie, too, but evidently it was true. Pumblechook must be in prison right now! Maybe the citizens of Gampalonia, in all the excitement of their revolution and in all their delight at turning their city back into Amistat, had totally forgotten to check the prisons and let the prisoners out! Maybe Pumblechook would be stuck in a stifling hot cell for days and days without water or food, until—

"Just a minute!" called a voice from somewhere inside the building. "I'm currently experiencing a high volume of applications!"

Sixty-two seconds later, the door swung open and there he was, wild-haired and wide awake. His suit was just as rumpled as before, or perhaps even a little bit shabbier, because he'd accidentally ink-stamped his sleeve when aiming for a document.

"Miss Bentley, if I recall correctly?" he said, peering at her through his slightly fogged glasses. He peered at Nelly, too, blinked and peered harder. "But what became of your fellow applicant? A Mrs Robinson, I believe? This looks to me very much like a..." He glanced around nervously. "I hope you're aware that ownership of ogs is illegal."

"This *is* Mrs Robinson!" said Dhikilo. "She can choose what she wants to be!"

Pumblechook frowned sternly, as if to let her know he was not so easily fooled. "Regrettably, from a bureaucratic point of view, that is not how it—"

"I'm so glad you're OK!" Dhikilo burst out. "The Gamp said you were under arrest!"

"It seems not," said Pumblechook, pondering the possibility. "But who knows? The ay is young." He lifted the edge of his hand to his bristly brows and gazed towards the horizon, looking for any yellow-clad figures that might be approaching in the distance. "The Gampalonian Guar on't like to get up too early. They've usually runk a lot the night before."

"Mr Pumblechook!" said Dhikilo excitedly. "You don't have to talk like that any more! There's been a revolution in the city! The Gamp's been chased away and the Dynamo blew up and you can say any D-word you want!"

Pumblechook's forehead wrinkled as he processed the information.

"Truly?" he said.

"Definitely!" said Dhikilo, beaming.

Pumblechook nodded slowly, lost in thought. "Well, that has serious...administrative implications," he mused. "No doubt there will be all sorts of new procedures. I shall probably need extra staff..."

"But aren't you pleased?"

Pumblechook gave this enquiry earnest consideration for a few seconds. Then a shy smile broke out on his plump face, and the smile grew broader, exposing more and more big blunt teeth, until finally his grin was an impressive sight to behold.

"Yes!" he chirped. "Yes, I believe I am!" Then, immediately getting back to business, he added, "But seriously: was your passport ready?"

"My passport?" said Dhikilo.

"You didn't enquire at the White Hall?"

Dhikilo could tell that his feelings would be hurt if she didn't come up with a good excuse. "I was in jail for a bit," she said, "and then I was about to have my head chopped off, and then buildings started collapsing and exploding and we thought we'd better go."

Pumblechook nodded, evaluating the extenuating circumstances. "Well, you'll have to come back for it, then," he sighed. "Don't leave it too long, or they'll change the forms." He frowned for a moment, then grinned again. "Mind you, if you have any bother, just come to me, and I'll see what I can do."

He made a motion in the air with his thumb and forefinger, which Dhikilo thought at first was some sort of magic-spell gesture, but of course it was just a mime of a pen scribbling on paper.

"Now, I don't wish to be awkward, Miss Bentley," Pumblechook continued, turning his squinty gaze once more to Mrs Robinson, "but you really are going to need a licence for your dog."

Dhikilo looked at Nelly, tempted to tell her to change into a sphinx, so that the problem would be solved in a flash. But she didn't feel right about telling Nelly what to do. They had only just become friends.

Nelly yawned. In mid-yawn, her doggy teeth grew sharper, her size increased and luxurious hair sprouted out of her head. Within seconds, she was the exotic applicant Pumblechook had met before.

"My goodness!" said Pumblechook, impressed. "Now *that* is an admirable skill." He shook his head. "You really are an unusual pair. What a shame you're leaving Liminus; you might do the place some good if you stayed."

"We'll come back one day," said Dhikilo, hoping Mrs Robinson wouldn't mind being spoken for, and hoping it wasn't an empty promise.

HOMEWARDLY RE-ENCOUNTER 4: THE QUILPS

The next challenge for Dhikilo and Mrs Robinson was to decide what to do about the Quilps. It would still be broad daylight when they got to the village, and the Quilps were almost certainly the sorts of creatures who would appreciate a second chance to kill trespassers they'd failed to kill the first time round.

One option was not to pass through the village at all but to travel through a different part of the countryside. That was not so easy because the Quilps' village was in a valley, so in order not to be spotted from a long way off, they would have to veer a very great distance in another direction, and quite possibly they'd get lost. And what if they encountered something on this detour that was just as dangerous as the Quilps? Or a river they couldn't cross?

Another option was to wait until nightfall before approaching the village. The Quilps would be indoors then, maybe even asleep, and less likely to notice Dhikilo and Mrs Robinson sneaking through their village. But this would mean sitting around for many hours waiting for the day to pass and the sun to set, which felt all wrong. They should be moving. Their mission was accomplished and Dhikilo was at last able to consider some things she'd neglected to think about until now—like that she'd been away from home for five days without telling Malcolm and Ruth. Waiting till night-time would make it six.

Another option was to approach the Quilp village as discreetly as possible and then race through it at top speed—top speed for a sphinx—hoping that nobody would kill them before they got to the other side. This was too reckless a plan to even be called a plan, really. Any responsible grown-up would advise them against it.

"Yessss," said Mrs Robinson, nodding emphatically as soon as the idea was mentioned. "Yessss."

So that was what they did.

And it worked.

Homewardly Re-Encounter 5: The Bleak House

By the time they'd passed through the forest and reached the Bleak House hotel, they were tired and footsore and it was late afternoon.

The house looked much more cheerful in summery sunshine than it had looked in snowy twilight. The fountain was full of fresh water, the stone horse posed proud and calm, and the departure of the snow had revealed neat pebble paths and ornamental paving stones. Dhikilo gazed at the house, trying to detect some smell of evil, but sensing only an inviting air of hospitality. The lights were on upstairs, and she knew that inside those ancient cinnamon-coloured walls were comfy beds with soft pillows.

"Celebrate Spring" Special, said a placard in the dining-room window. Free Scone with Every Tea.

She took a step towards the house, and another step, and was about to take a third step when a heavy weight butted against her hip and knocked her sideways, almost off her feet.

Mrs Robinson had changed back into dog form, and her big bony face and soulful eyes were full of worry and warning.

Dhikilo blinked and looked at the house one last time. The placard in the window was exactly the same, except now it said, Two Free Scones with Every Tea.

With a deep breath of effort, Dhikilo turned her body around, and together she and Nelly walked away.

The house hissed as it watched them go.

Homewardly Non-Encounter: The Magwitches

The remainder of the journey was uneventful. Mrs Robinson stayed in dog form, padding steadily by Dhikilo's side, panting softly. A Labrador's legs are shorter than a sphinx's, permitting only a doggy trot instead of a feline stride, and there was a long distance to travel yet. Was Mrs Robinson making the journey harder on herself than she needed to? Was she just being considerate, avoiding the alien outward appearance that humans found so frightening? Dhikilo hoped not, because she didn't find the sphinx frightening any more. She liked the sphinx face just as much as the Labrador face. They were both beautiful in their different ways, and they both had the mind and soul of Nelly behind them.

"Which do you like being best?" she asked. "A sphinx or a dog?"

Mrs Robinson looked up at her for just a moment, wrinkling her brow, as if considering making the effort to change into sphinx form to give an answer.

"*Boaff*," she barked softly, and kept on walking.

* * *

Every now and then, Nelly paused and sniffed the ground, then proceeded with confidence. Dhikilo marvelled at this Labrador ability to retrace a path through a landscape that, to her, looked unrecognizably different. Every last vestige of snow had evaporated, the muddy fields had settled down and were speckled with soft green. A few dragonflies hovered around, not flying anywhere in particular, not carrying anything, just enjoying being dragonflies.

When Dhikilo and Nelly got hungry and thirsty, they stopped for a while and treated themselves to the supplies that the Drood had put into the backpack for them. Despite the long months of famine that the Drood had endured, they'd managed to rustle up some yummy and nutritious snacks, much better than the sugary rubbish the Professor had provided on the outward journey. Professor Dodderfield might be the best History teacher ever and a superhuman genius, but his standards in the food department had slipped.

The Drood's water bottles weren't disposable plastic ones, but made of a sort of hardened sap that was like glass but lighter. They were very pretty and must have taken some time and effort to make.

Well, I'd better return them some day, Dhikilo thought.

"Shall we get going?" she asked Nelly.

Nelly's snout and chest were dripping with water, and even her paws were wet. She nodded.

The last of their homewardly encounters with people they'd met earlier should've been with the Magwitches. Dhikilo was sort of expecting that the same four who'd chased them at the beginning of the journey—the chilly ones with the chains on their ankles—would ambush them again. But they didn't. No Magwitches popped up at all.

Four raggedy old ladies, slowed down by chains, shuffling

around in freezing conditions—might they have died of cold just before the weather changed? Their demands for warmer clothing had seemed rather desperate, after all.

On the other hand, maybe they were like those birds that only come out in winter, and you feel sorry for them because they're hopping about on bare trees and in the snow, but really they're special winter birds and you're not meant to see them in summer.

"Do you think those old Magwitches will be all right?" she asked Mrs Robinson.

Mrs Robinson's eyes flashed momentarily purple, as if she was going to change into sphinx form to reply. But instead, she just bared her teeth and snarled. Sympathy was not something she was capable of feeling for the Magwitches: that was plain. And Dhikilo understood that even though Nelly was wonderful and brave and loyal and even lovable, she was still a sphinx at heart, and would never truly be tame.

To End With: Dhikilo's Story

On the long journey back, Dhikilo had plenty of time to think about what might be in store for her at home. Ruth and Malcolm would've waited a few hours for her to return from the post office. Maybe they waited the whole day. But when night fell they would certainly have called the police. The police would've searched in all the places in Cawber that a runaway girl was most likely to be, and then, as more days passed, they would've started searching in the woods around the town, and along the seashore. A search like that cost thousands of pounds, and lots of people who didn't know her would buy the next edition of the *Cawber Gazette* to find out if she was dead.

When she walked through the door, Malcolm and Ruth would be relieved to see her safe, and then they would be angry and hurt. Causing them hurt was awful; she wished she'd had a chance to send them a message during her mission, to reassure them that she would be home soon—unless of course she got killed, in which case she wouldn't. But making them angry was more of a problem now, because they would demand to know where she'd been. *I've been on an adventure*, she could say, but that wouldn't be enough. They would want the whole story. Or at least a story that they could believe.

Dhikilo wasn't good at lying, but she knew that the most convincing lies were the ones that contained some truth. However, when she thought of all the true things that she might weave into a tale about where she'd been, she realized there wasn't much she could use. Almost being publicly executed on the guillotine...the last-minute rescue by the ectoplasmic helpers...almost being eaten by the Quilps...the snows of Liminus, the Tower of Light in Gampalonia...even the visit to the Professor that began it all...none of it would help. She'd be better off claiming she ran away to London to take drugs.

The sun was setting by the time she figured out her story. She would tell everyone she'd run away to find her real dad. She would say that she'd hitch-hiked, or even walked, to Dover, in the hope of smuggling herself onto a ship that was going to Calais. She had an atlas at home in which she'd often traced, with her finger, the journey that the baby Dhikilo must have made to get from Somaliland to Cawber-on-Sands. It was a long way. You started off in Laascaanood and then maybe went to Sudan, Chad, Algeria—or no, Egypt would be quicker—then you had to cross the Mediterranean Sea and maybe go to Crete or Italy, and then right through France, which was bigger than most people thought, and finally to Calais.

It was doable: loads of people had done it, even thirteen-year-olds. She would simply claim to have done it going the opposite way. Or as much of it as the police and her parents might believe she could do in five days.

Or maybe, to keep the story simple, she should just say she'd been in Dover all this time, waiting for a stowaway opportunity that never came? That sounded realistic, but also a bit sad. She was a proper adventurer now and didn't want to downgrade herself as some clueless kid who would sit shivering on the docks for several days and nights before admitting defeat. If she really *had* tried to go to Africa, she would've got further than that, surely!

She had half a mind to try it, just to prove she could!

"Yes, I think that's my story," she murmured to herself.

"*Fwuff*," said Mrs Robinson.

After Such a Grand Assortment of Words

Night had fallen by the time they reached the portal back to England. Dhikilo would never have found it by herself: the landscape had been completely transformed and, besides, it was too dark to see much. But Nelly ran straight up to a nondescript tree and barked.

At once, the door-sized rectangle materialized in the air. It shivered for a moment or two and then was solid. The oversized cover of a hardback book, hovering in space.

The door was shut, however. Nelly barked again. No response. Dhikilo walked up and felt around the edges of the rectangle with her fingers. The door swung open, and a musty dusty mothbally smell wafted out.

The attic room of 58 Gas Hill Garens had no lights on. Dhikilo and Nelly climbed up, up into the dark, up into another world—a Victorian house full of mouldering old paper and neglect, in a slightly crumbly English seaside town called Cawber-on-Sands.

Dhikilo turned to take a last look at the Land of Liminus, the place where her headless body might have been buried if Mrs Robinson hadn't rescued her, the place where she might have grown up if she'd accepted the Drood's invitation. Then she closed the door.

She fumbled around for a light switch, but Nelly nudged her to follow, and led her to the stairs. Together they descended, and at each storey down there was a little more light, filtering upwards from the ground floor. Nelly panted excitedly, and when they reached the living room, she scooted in ahead of Dhikilo.

When Dhikilo walked in, she was almost hit by a shoe, or actually a tartan slipper, which flew off the Professor's foot as he jolted awake. He'd been deeply asleep in his plump purple armchair, swaddled in pyjamas and a dressing gown and a knitted blanket. His hair and beard were a mess and he looked about two hundred years old.

"No!" he groaned, still trapped in his dream. "I'll not go back there! Can't you see I am a child of singular abilities!?"

"*Charlesss!*" cautioned the sphinx, for it was she, leaning her face close to the old man's ear.

The Professor lurched forward in his chair, and his blind eyes seemed to peer into the gloom. (The fire was out, and only a couple of the bulbs in the chandelier were on.) "Nelly?" he said.

"Yesss," said Mrs Robinson.

"Nelly!" he exclaimed, in sheer delight.

"Yesss."

"And the girl? Miss Bentley?"

"I'm here," said Dhikilo.

"Both alive!" crowed the Professor, as if this was an amazing stroke of luck that he hadn't been expecting at all. "That's *good*! Have you got all your bits? Toes, limbs and so forth?"

"Yes," said Dhikilo.

"Even better! And the Gamp?"

"He's gone," said Dhikilo. "Run away. There was a huge dynamo that was using all the Ds to make fuel. It blew up. And there was a tower that was using up all the fuel. It fell down. I think the Gamp's whole empire fell down. The city's got a new name already."

"All excellent developments! Did you have a hand in them?"

Dhikilo was suddenly exhausted and wished she was at home in the bath or even in bed. "I think I may have done some weather magic," she said. "I'm not sure. Maybe it was time for the winter to end anyway."

"I like a modest girl!" said the Professor, rubbing his hands. "Especially one who can save the world. Or at least rescue the D."

"I don't know if we've done that," sighed Dhikilo.

"Easy enough to find out," said the Professor, wholly awake by now. "What do you think, Nelly? Have a look out the window."

Mrs Robinson padded over to the window and swept the heavy curtain aside with a clawed paw. The lamplit street was revealed outside, with a few parked cars but no people because of the lateness of the hour. The street lamp stood right next to the sign that said "Gas Hill Garens," so the letters were well illuminated.

"All isss asss it ssshould be," said Mrs Robinson. Dhikilo looked more carefully at the street sign, and noticed that it didn't actually say "Gas Hill Garens" any more, but "Gad's Hill Gardens."

The Professor clapped his hands together in triumph, squashing his beard between them.

"Superb! Miss Bentley, I think you will find that where one D returns, others will follow. All manner of words will be restored, and you'll be Dhikilo again, I almost guarantee it!"

"Charles," interrupted Mrs Robinson. "I'm thirsssty. For milk."

"Of course! Of course!" said the Professor. "All too small a reward for a brave creature like you. Ahh…" He attempted to raise himself from the armchair, but was rather stiff, and still swaddled in the blanket. "Miss Bentley, I wonder if you could go to the kitchen and fetch Nelly a glass of milk? In a big glass, with two straws? Just through there, first on the left, you'll find everything in plain view."

Dhikilo followed the directions. The kitchen was indeed first on the left and everything was indeed in plain view, but the room was filthy. Professor Dodderfield and Mrs Robinson might be awesome in all sorts of ways, but they were also a blind old man and his four-legged companion, which was not a practical combination for keeping a kitchen clean.

She fetched the milk from the refrigerator, sniffed it and decided it was still OK. There were four loaves of soft-grain bread stacked up on a bench, in various stages of decomposition (including one that was entirely green); a clump of bananas that had gone black and shrivelled; quite a few used, mummified tea bags; and several jars of marmalade, all open and without lids. The floor was littered with little white things which Dhikilo at first thought might be spilled rice but were actually trampled coconut macaroons.

It was clear that the Professor would benefit from some extra help around the house.

Dhikilo brought the glass of milk into the sitting room and set it carefully on the little table near the fireplace. Mrs Robinson nodded her thanks, got into position and slurped the white liquid through the straws.

"I must go home now," said Dhikilo. "I'm tired and I want to go to bed."

"Quite sensible," said the Professor. "You'll have some explaining to do, though, before they'll let you rest."

"Yes," said Dhikilo.

"You'll need a story," said the Professor. "A believable

one. May I make a suggestion? Tell them you decided to go to Somaliland, to find your—"

Dhikilo burst out laughing. "That's the same story I thought of!"

The Professor beamed. "Great minds think alike," he said.

"I'll still get in trouble," said Dhikilo.

"So you will, so you will," said the Professor, as Mrs Robinson loudly slurped at the dregs of the milk. "A great stir will be made, and you will receive a reprimand from frowning authorities. No one will thank you for your brave achievement. That is the fate of many a courageous champion. The good that we do sinks into history like rainfall into the earth. The earth, being earth, cannot feel gratitude or award us with medals, but it can grow flowers, and that is our reward."

It was a nice speech, as good as some of the ones he used to make when he taught History at Cawber School for Girls. Dhikilo didn't know what to say after such a grand assortment of words.

"Erm…well…goodbye," she said.

As she began to walk away, the Professor spoke once more, this time with a quavery tremor in his voice.

"So, are you and Nelly friends?"

"Yes," said Dhikilo. "We're friends." And the way Mrs Robinson half closed her eyes and cocked her head to one side seemed to verify that she thought so, too.

"So…might you come and visit again?"

Dhikilo pictured the mouldy bread in the kitchen and the open marmalade jars and the crunchy macaroons underfoot. "I could come and"—she took note of his proud old face—"and read to you sometimes."

This pleased Professor Dodderfield very much indeed.

"Oh, I *do* like a happy ending," he said.

★ ★ ★ ★ ★

AUTHOR NOTE

I started this novel thirty-five years ago and finished it just in time for the 150th anniversary of Charles Dickens's death. As well as tipping its hat to Dickens, it acknowledges its debt to James Thurber's *The Wonderful O*. Oh, and of course to C. S. Lewis's Narnia series and Charles Lutwige Ogson's Tales of Wonerlan.

I am also grateful for advice from Sagal Farah, Yurub Farah, Mohamed Warsame Boss, Sue Hunt, Nadifa Mohamed and Louisa Young.